LEAGUE OF INDEPENDENT OPERATIVES
BOOK 4

NEMESIS

KATE SHEERAN SWED

Sign up for my VIP reader list at katesheeranswed.com to get *Power Struggle*, an exclusive LIO prequel novella!

DOLLY REYNA HAD ENDURED MORE than her fair share of dubious accommodations over the years. The early days of her tenure as the Pearl Knife had involved hiding from the authorities as much as helping them. And the best of times as LIO's leader had often required stakeouts that extended from hours into days, making tight quarters of even the roomiest vehicles. Dimly lit safe houses, dehydrated noodles, and trying companions had once been the norm on a fairly regular basis.

This was not the first time independent operatives had been reviled by the government, or chased into hiding.

It was, however, the first time Dolly had endured such indignities for three months running, huddled in a dump of a studio apartment in the middle of nowhere, with no power to alleviate the situation.

And with allies who, despite their best intentions, lacked a certain... style.

Take Ranger, for example. The man had somehow heaved his stocky frame up onto the kitchen counter—Dolly had missed the process by which he'd managed this—and was straining to reach the upper corner of the room, where a speck of a spider sat watching his efforts. Other animals came rushing to Ranger as soon as he called, but he'd always had trouble with bugs. Not that it stopped him from making a fool of himself.

No doubt Ranger could hear the arachnid laughing at him, or some such nonsense.

"Better to call the mice," Carlisle said. The weather worker sat staring out of the window, his cheek mashed against his hand. His dark eyes were so wide, Dolly could see the clouds—which the man controlled with ease—reflected in them. "Maybe I could make it warmer. Just a touch."

He said it without any real hope. He knew what the response would be, even before Dolly shook her head. "They'll be watching for strange weather patterns," she said. It was an effort to keep her tone patient. These were her only two allies. "We need to stay hidden."

Carlisle dipped his chin, brown curls quivering as he moved. Had his eyes not been sprayed along the edges with wrinkles, Dolly would have thought he resembled a forlorn child.

Giving up on the spider, Ranger dropped to sit on the counter with surprising grace for a man of his bulk. "Can't stay here forever," he said.

Dolly half expected the man to follow his friend's advice and call the mice to play—it wouldn't be the first time—but he simply banged his mud-crusted heels against the cabinets and looked at her expectantly. As if she could magically conjure a solution to a political environment that hunted enhanced humans, or remove an ungrateful daughter—two, really—at the head of the League of Independent Operatives. Though beset with difficulties themselves, Eloise and Mary were ever watchful. Were they to catch a hint of Dolly's location, they'd come after her without a thought.

If only Diana were here. If Diana were here, they'd be able

to put their heads together. Over a bottle of Aperol, they'd come up with a plan to rule all plans.

If Diana were here, Dolly might even risk opening a portal back to LIO HQ. But she suspected it was the Knife's proximity that had tamped down the powers it had transferred to her body during their decades of partnership. Why else would she now be capable of opening portals without it?

More than that, she suspected the Knife had intentionally made her sick. For years. Here and now, in this dingy apartment, she felt better, younger, than she had since her darling husband had ripped the blade out of her consciousness and transferred it to Eloise. Dolly's hair was still white, yes, and more lines scored her face than most people would have expected for her fifty-six years, but her muscles no longer ached constantly. She could walk. She could *see.*

And the *powers.* Now that she was away from HQ, she could feel the powers that had rubbed off on her like a thick sheen of dust. Portals, she suspected, were the very least of what she could do.

Should she try to go back to HQ, though, and attempt to claim what was rightfully hers? The Knife would stop her before she could get close.

If she did get her hands on it, however. That would change everything. Without Diana at her side—without Rocker and Goldi and the twins—Dolly couldn't see how it was possible. She'd need to rescue them from HQ before she could storm HQ to rescue them, and that was a tangle without a solution.

A drop of rain exploded against the window, and Carlisle sighed as if to say he could have prevented that. As Dolly watched it trickle down the pane, something... quaked.

That was the only word for it. The ground loosened beneath her feet, an intense shuddering that made her stumble, and she placed a hand against the wall for support. She breathed hard as the shaking tapered off, though it did not disappear entirely; everything around her vibrated, blurring the edges of the room.

The world rocked and shuddered, yet when she looked at her companions, their positions were unchanged. They looked entirely stable. As if they hadn't felt it at all.

Diana would already have been at Dolly's elbow to offer assistance. These two simply stared.

"Should sleep more," Ranger observed, banging his heels as though trying to break through the cheap wood of the cabinet. A clump of dried mud dropped off his shoe and broke apart, scattering across the linoleum.

No. No, this was more than fatigue-driven vertigo. This was... "A resonance," Dolly said, ignoring the way her stomach roiled as she forced herself to straighten away from the wall. Yes, a resonance. One that was very, very familiar.

Dolly lifted her hands, ignoring Ranger's gasp and the way Carlisle leapt to his feet as she allowed the trembling vibrations to course through her body. Focusing hard, as she'd done only a handful of times since her rescue from LIO HQ, she plunged her index finger into the void between physical spaces, dragging open a doorway. Her body was an extension of the Pearl Knife now, if a muted one, full of untapped power.

She'd only ever opened a door to a place she could picture in reality. This time, when she parted the air, she followed the resonance that hummed through her organs, allowing it to determine her destination. She didn't know what she was looking for; she only knew that something had arrived, and that she needed to be there.

Beckoning for her companions to follow, Dolly stepped through the portal and into the unknown.

Her first sensations were of dusty air and a bleached landscape.

It was all she had time to take in before hands closed around her throat, lifting her skyward. Behind her, Ranger or Carlisle—she couldn't turn to see which—gave a strangled cry.

Dolly clawed at her throat, blinking water out of her eyes to try and catch a glimpse of the one who'd seized her. She could feel each finger pressing into her neck, even the bite of finger-nails, but no captor stood before her. In fact, no human should have been able to lift her so far off the ground.

A full yard separated her dangling feet from the earth, if not more, yet her thoughts trudged on with maddening calm, as though something in her still trusted whatever resonance had brought her here, even with her airway half restricted.

Idiocy, to follow a resonance as if it were an old friend. Desperation had made her a fool.

She kicked, trying to loosen the invisible grip, but her efforts were useless. The air might have been made of chains.

"Speak your purpose quickly."

The voice came from below, and Dolly strained her eyes, trying to see its source. The person sounded calm, almost bored, as if they had better things to do. As if she were an annoyance.

Dolly gasped, and the grip around her throat loosened enough to let her choke out an answer. "I felt your arrival," she said. "I followed your resonance."

The hold around her throat vanished, and Dolly fell to her knees in the dirt, coughing. She heard Ranger and Carlisle thump down behind her. She sputtered, aware that she needed to lift herself to her feet, aware that there was a foe before her. From above, the sun scorched. Where had they landed?

A second voice said, "Is this wise?"

But the owner of the first must have decided it was. As Dolly lurched to her feet, he circled around from behind and into her line of sight.

He was a slight man, perhaps an inch shorter than she was, and he wore a long robe that should have trailed in the dust yet somehow seemed to hover above it. Thick, jet black curls spilled over his forehead, giving him almost a boyish look, but only at first glance. His eyes sparked with danger. Dolly thought, though she wasn't sure—the sun was very bright here —that she saw points of orange flaring in his pupils.

"You are familiar with the Blade of Starlight." He did not pose it as a question, and really, he could only mean one thing. The Pearl Knife. She didn't know why he called it that, but she intended to learn. She nodded.

The man studied her, unblinking. "I recognize your resonance as well. You have it with you?"

Dolly shook her head, pressing her hands to her thighs to hide their trembling. "I used to wield it. I now carry its powers. Some of them."

Whoever he was, he did not look surprised. "You no longer need the Blade to make use of its energies. As it was intended."

Dolly breathed, her brain struggling to keep up. Her portal had landed them in the desert somewhere. A broken strip of road extended beyond the strange man, a derelict airplane languishing in the distance. An old airport, then.

"In fact," she said slowly, taking a chance, "the... Blade... prevented me from using the powers it gave me. I escaped its proximity. Now I'm free."

At this, the stranger's lips parted, his dark eyebrows lifting a touch. Surprise, or so she thought. "You see, Morik," he said. "The Blade exerts its own will."

Dolly did her best not to react, not to show what she knew through her expressions. She knew about the portal that had spilled armored soldiers onto a convention floor back in March, and she knew the rumors of Wave's involvement were nothing but folly. Here, perhaps, there were answers to be had.

So she said nothing, while the stranger pressed a finger to his bottom lip, studying her. "You have seen the Blade of Starlight? Recently?"

Dolly hesitated, but there wasn't much time to survey her options. Might as well find out where this path led. "I have."

The man nodded, as though he'd expected nothing less. "As you've said, the Blade has a mind of its own. It needs to be destroyed."

As if she would ever let that happen. Who would want to destroy such a powerful tool? Either this man was lying, or he was a fool.

Dolly kept her expression still, calm. She knew better than to underestimate this person. She could still feel the phantom fingers closing in around her throat.

"What is your name?" Dolly asked, allowing the bare hint of a tremble into her tone. If it was a little real, well, there was no shame in nervousness before power. She'd learned long ago to respect her fear, to listen to it, and to engage it when necessary.

The man's companion, still out of Dolly's range of vision, drew in a breath. As though she'd made a breach in etiquette, or offended him somehow. But other man—the one who mattered —simply held up a hand, quieting his servant before he could speak. "They call me Sever."

The name meant nothing to Dolly. "And what do you know of... the Blade?"

The points of fire in his eyes flashed. Definitely not her imagination. "I forged it."

Dolly's throat went dry. No one knew where the Knife had originated. If her mother was to be believed, Dolly's grandmother had merely presented it to her one day. Like an heirloom. Grandma had kept it hidden behind a stone in the basement, gifting it to her daughter shortly before her death.

She'd claimed it was merely a souvenir from adventures long past.

But as Mother had always said: if that were the case, why had she kept it out of sight? For decades?

Dolly's mother had tapped into some of its powers. Dolly had uncovered many more.

Now, its maker stood before her. Perhaps she would uncover the rest of its secrets as well. Sever waited, watching her. "Do you know where to find the Blade of Starlight?" he asked.

Behind her, Ranger cleared his throat. Dolly gave her head a small shake, willing him to stay silent. "I do. We can help you."

After that... well, all Dolly needed was to get her hands on the Pearl Knife. Between its innate powers and the ones it had bestowed upon her, she'd be in control then.

"Good," the man said. "But the Blade is not our only mission here. I've got a job for you."

Mary's apartment at LIO HQ had long been a place for sleeping as little as she could manage before rushing off to something else. Compared with missions, sparring, or time in the labs, her rooms had always been little more than an afterthought. More space than she needed, by far, and she'd certainly never shared them with anyone else.

Not that the suite had the same sparse, scrubbed nature of her home in Malibu; here, there were always clothes on the floor, gadgets discarded on side tables, and abandoned designs scattered in corners. But still, she'd never thought of the rooms as anything more than a convenience.

Now, though, there was a pile of books on the nightstand. And there was Nathan, stretched out on the bed as he read one of them. He wore black-framed reading glasses, which she hadn't known he needed before three months ago, and a loose gray T-shirt.

He was getting ready for bed, while she was preparing for night patrols. Because thanks to Travis Bertram, the Enhanced Abilities Enforcement Association, and the U.S. President's horrific executive order, they needed night patrols. Humans with enhanced abilities had to register now, to put their names on a list of citizens for the government to keep tabs on.

And they all knew it was about more than keeping tabs.

Officially, LIO also answered directly to the federal government, too. Unofficially, they'd gone dark. At this point, they were probably considered enemies of the state.

"You know you can keep your books on the shelf," Mary said, pointing to the half-empty bookshelf in the corner. The full part of it contained her toolbox, a pile of batteries, and a pair of socks she'd forgotten to put away. "You live here, too."

Nathan kept his eyes on the page. "But I'm reading them."

Mary shoved her hands into her gloves. Coral's outfit was still the best for stealth, and she had to admit that it was good to be wearing it again. Even if it was for night patrols, of all things. How did the saying go, about being cursed to live in interesting times?

She finished with the gloves and started pulling on her boots. "You're reading all of them? At the same time?"

He placed a finger on the page to keep his place and looked up, quirking a smile at her that made her want to show up late to those patrols. "In rotation, but yes."

"How do you not mix them up?"

"They're too different. One is Arthurian legends. The second is about everyday physics, so I can at least try to keep up with you." He counted them off on his fingers as he spoke, still smiling at her. "This one is a straight-up sci-fi novel, though I'll admit the arrival of actual aliens is somewhat off-putting."

"Too realistic?"

"Precisely."

She finished with her boots and stood, heading for the door. When she got there, she paused. "Wait. You think you might be able to keep up with me?"

"Let a man dream, will you?"

Mary returned to the bedside, bending to kiss him. She'd meant it to be a quick goodbye, but he abandoned his book to plunge a hand into her hair, drawing her into the kind of embrace that made her seriously contemplate that longer stay. He tasted of mint tea, and his warmth enveloped her until she wanted to sink into it. Maybe for good.

With an effort, she pulled back. "I have to go."

He leaned toward her, catching her fingers between his. "Be late."

"The recruits are so gossipy, you have no idea."

"Let them gossip."

Mary picked up his book and shoved it back into his hands. "I'll see you in a few hours."

She left him quickly, so as not to be tempted. She'd been granted a slice of happiness in the midst of trying times, a home when so many were being driven out of theirs. To help those people, she had to keep LIO HQ safe. And that meant patrols.

The corridors were buzzing with night-shift team members scurrying to their stations as Mary headed over to meet her crew. Eloise had instituted round-the-clock staffing immediately after President Caldwell's executive order, though only a handful of people knew she'd also been thinking of the alien threat that still loomed beyond Earth's atmosphere.

Three months since Sloane and her friends had disappeared into the black of another galaxy, and LIO hadn't heard a word from her. Three months, too, since the president had declared LIO a threat. Somehow, in his mind—or someone's— that also meant all enhanced humans had to register or flee.

Between the aliens and the list-making psychos on Earth, Mary thought she might choose the aliens. But with Sever a no-show, Travis and his government goons were the more dangerous threat. Mary knew better than to assume Sever had lost interest in Earth, but still. A girl could hope.

LIO, though, had chosen their headquarters well. Canada wouldn't allow the U.S. to infiltrate the falls from their side, stating they'd enacted no anti-league laws—or, worse, anti-enhanced laws—and that the U.S. had no right to stage an operation from within their borders. With the underwater entrance still a secret—Mary didn't know which country it fell in, technically—the U.S. had no entry point. Though it didn't stop them from looking.

And Eloise reasoned that no diplomatic awkwardness would stop them from trying to find the Canadian entrances. Spies existed for a reason.

Mary's patrol team waited for her by the elevator that led to the league's casino entrance. They rotated exit points randomly, but Mary often wished she could hack out a fourth one. Just because they'd avoided notice so far—or appeared to have—didn't mean their luck would continue forever.

Quin nodded to Mary as she arrived, their dark hair tied low at the nape of their neck. Tally, the third member of the patrol team, grinned enthusiastically, pink-streaked ponytail quivering as she bounced on the balls of her feet. Mary did her best not to be annoyed by the woman's excitement.

"Tally and I will leave through the window tonight," Mary said, beckoning them onto the elevator. "Quin, I need you to do a random corridor sweep on the way out and then meet us outside. We'll make it a counterclockwise circle of the area. Might as well mix it up."

Quin's x-ray vision meant Mary's crew could clear half the town in the time that Nathan's—made up of ice-maker Elle and sticky-fingered climber Len—could make it through a couple of streets. But it also meant they took extra spots on the rotation. If anyone could zero-in on a suspicious hotel room—say, one filled with surveillance equipment or spies ready to pounce—it was Quin.

Tally didn't need the grapple that Mary secured to the hotel-room windowsill as soon as they entered the room. Instead, the recruit leapt out ahead, sticking her signature crouched landing in the middle of the quiet side street with a wide smile. Like a gymnast who knew she'd just won the top score at the Olympics. Although, Mary didn't actually think the woman had dropped the smile once since they'd started at HQ tonight.

Mary's feet hit the sidewalk, and she retracted her grapple, thankful for the noise that spilled out of bars along the next street over. The music and laughter covered all kinds of zipping wires and landing feet.

Not to mention over-enthusiastic recruits. "Your profile needs to be about four notches lower," she whispered.

Tally joined Mary on the sidewalk, moving into the shadows behind her. At least she remembered something about her training. "Why? We're in Canada. Nothing ever happens on this side. Patrol for hours, see nothing, go home. If they'd let us patrol on the U.S. side, then maybe we'd need to be more careful. Although I don't really see why we should have to sneak around like mice."

Mary drew in a deep breath, let it out. Not everyone had been raised in LIO. "First of all, being in Canada doesn't assure our safety. Second, you know why we can't patrol on the U.S. side."

"You could."

What, because she didn't have powers? Sure, she merely aided and abetted those who did. "My face is a little too famous for that. Let's leave it to Pete and surveillance. If they need us, they'll let us know."

They rounded the corner, and Quin fell into step next to Mary, their face much more appropriately sober. "Hotel's clear."

"Figure eights," Mary said, and they split off, Tally sweeping to the left and Quin to right. They were both in street clothes, and could blend in with the bar crowds. They'd each circle a main block, then crisscross in opposite directions. Quin's x-ray vision, Tally's roof-clearing abilities, and the job would be done in no time.

Mary did what she did best: she stuck to the shadows. With the recruits covering the major roads, she paced through alleys and squeezed through narrow gaps between buildings. She swept parking lots. She checked the corners. She listened in doorways.

And maybe, just maybe, Tally wasn't entirely wrong. Three months of this, and they'd never found so much as a hint of a spy. She knew who was cheating at cards, and who they worked for; she knew who was cheating in more salacious areas, too.

She wasn't sure that Travis Bertram, the EAEA, or the United States government would ever come looking for them here.

As soon as the thought crossed her mind, the back of her neck prickled with a sense of eyes on her, tracking her. She paused, scanning the narrow alley for signs of a pursuer. Might be paranoia, but there was no reason to chance it.

The street, if it could be called that, was too small to drive a car through. A couple of garbage bags languished outside of back doors, but otherwise the place was clean and pretty much useless. Just a gap.

An empty gap. There was no one behind her.

The almost-alley opened into a public parking lot, and Mary stepped out cautiously. People walked to and from their cars in groups and pairs, huddled together and laughing in the cool spring evening.

It wasn't a rendezvous point, but Quin joined her, stepping into the shadows like they'd been born to this life.

"Someone's tailing you," they said. "They're enhanced."

Mary blinked, surprised. "You can tell?"

"In this case, yes."

Mary would have to ask, later, how long the person had been following her. Why hadn't she heard them? Seen them? Maybe she was tired. Or getting overconfident.

"Do you think they're EAEA?" Mary asked. Nathan's sister and her band of Travis-approved cronies could give themselves temporary powers. Because why shouldn't an anti-enhanced-human hate group use enhanced abilities whenever they wanted?

Quin shrugged a thin shoulder, but Mary could tell they had an opinion. After a moment, they said, "They seem to be alone, and they're moving tentatively. Not the way I'd expect the EAEA to stalk someone."

Mary touched a finger to her lower lip, thinking. Quin waited, scanning the parking lot in silent patience. Protocol was to observe, withholding action unless absolutely necessary. If they confronted someone who happened to be a member of the Enhanced Abilities Enforcement Association, Eloise wouldn't be happy.

"OK," Mary said quietly. "Let's split. I'll start moving, you watch from out of sight."

"Follow your follower," Quin said. "Got it."

Hoping her follower's enhanced abilities didn't include super hearing, Mary started walking. She hugged the sidewalk, steering close to the row of restaurants and bars whose entrances faced the other street. People still moved in and out of the parking lot, but they tended to cut across it, heading straight for the cut-through that would lead them to the main street and avoiding the strip of shadows that navigated beneath fire escapes and around trash bins.

Even though she knew about her tail, Mary still couldn't

hear the person. She felt their attention on her, the tingle along her spine, but she didn't catch even a whisper of footsteps. She slowed her pace, noting an earthy, grassy smell cutting through the beer and fried foods, as though she'd stepped into a park without noticing. But she still stood in on the sidewalk, surrounded by brick and pavement.

Someone behind her shouted, and Mary whirled around in time to see three figures leaping out of the shadows, heading directly for a fourth. The liquid-yellow glow of the streetlights made it clear why Mary hadn't been able to hear her follower; the sidewalk behind her was coated in a thin layer of moss that hadn't been there when she'd passed mere moments ago. As she watched, weedy bunches of grass sprang up eagerly from between the cracks.

It was like watching a time-lapse video, but in real life.

The trio of figures moved with precision, pulling Mary's follower roughly off the sidewalk and into the street. Green vegetation trailed after them, cropping up between cracks and crawling along the top of the pavement.

The figures weren't LIO, and though they wore no badges or signature armbands—they wouldn't dare, on this side of the border—Mary knew they had to be EAEA. Swooping in to capture some poor person just because they had abilities. It was pretty much their regular M.O.

She swung up onto the lowest level of a fire escape, a plan whirling in her mind. She wouldn't let the EAEA take this person, whoever they were, but she needed to be strategic.

Mary opened coms to instruct her patrol team, but before she could speak, Tally dropped onto the street from above, using her momentum to knock Mary's follower from the EAEA operatives' grasp. Taking hold of the person's shoulders, she leapt, sweeping them to the top of the building.

Great. Just great. Cursing, Mary dropped from the fire

escape, tugging her grapple out of her tool belt. Seemingly unconcerned by the abduction of their quarry, the three EAEA agents reached into their own tool belts, withdrawing vials from leather pouches. They moved as one, their training stream-lining their actions, as they swallowed the contents and tossed the vials away.

As one, they bent their knees, then leapt after Tally.

Mary ran, shooting her grapple as she called for Quin to follow, requesting backup from HQ at the same time. At least she was partnered with someone who knew their tools; x-ray vision abilities were all well and good until you had to follow physically enhanced assholes to the top of a building. And Mary counted Tally in that assessment.

Quin's grapple caught the building a second behind Mary's, and together they vaulted up the old-fashioned way.

The EAEA agents were half a minute ahead of them, maybe less. But by the time Mary and Quin landed on the roof, the trio had Tally and the enhanced stranger on their knees, weapons trained on their heads. They moved like robots, these people. And Mary had seen—and fought—*actual* robots.

Grass ebbed around the new enhanced person, whose hood had been pulled aside. She was young. A teenager, Mary thought. Her ponytail was messy, askew, and tears tracked down her cheeks. A trickle of blood at the corner of Tally's mouth said she'd tried to resist, and the sneer on her lips said she wasn't done.

Good. Mary surged forward, surprising one of the EAEA agents enough to knock his weapon from his grasp. Guns. They made people so... lazy. The weapon skittered across the roof toward Quin, who kicked it away as they ran. The agent lunged, but Mary caught him by the arm, wrenching it behind his back and dropping him to his knees.

Tally was already on her feet, using the distraction to

disarm a second agent. The agent leapt away, but Tally followed. On the edge of Mary's peripheral vision, Quin took on the third. The teenager was still kneeling on the roof, though Mary thought she'd stopped crying.

Trusting her team, Mary leaned over her capture's shoulder, still holding him in a firm grip. "What are you doing in Canada?"

The guy laughed, an ugly bark that showed his teeth. "What's it look like? We're finding you."

"Oh, good job then. Was this what you'd pictured?"

"That girl was following you," the agent spat.

"I'm confused. Were you looking for me, or tailing her?"

The agent struggled, but Mary held on. She didn't need to hurt him to keep him still. "She's enhanced, and she's unregistered," he said. As if that explained it. As if Mary's response should be all gratitude, all understanding. The EAEA knew otherwise, of course. They knew LIO wasn't on their side. But maybe some of them still hoped an un-enhanced LIO member like Mary would agree with their bigotry, their hatred. Their warped view of the world.

Mary checked her anger, tucking it away. For now. "We're in *Canada*. Where she doesn't need to register."

The rooftop door slammed open, and Mary looked up as Ire and Eloise joined them. Quin had their agent in cuffs, while Tally had cornered hers. Either the temporary abilities had worn off, or Mary's team had been able to administer the power-dampening serum. The EAEA clearly relied as heavily on temp abilities as they did on guns.

Lazy, lazy, lazy.

Eloise surveyed the scene, eyes coming to rest on the teenager, who still knelt in the center of the roof. The place had been a bare, concrete patio just a few minutes ago. Now, it was a garden, with grass and vines sprouting out from the girl's knees and toes, wherever her body touched the ground. The smell of spring permeated the air, fresh grass and pepper-sweet flowers.

Eloise beckoned to Ire. "Drop our EAEA guests at the precinct. I imagine the Canadian government will want to know they were here. Quin can help."

As Ire and Quin ushered the defeated agents away, Mary headed for the girl, but Tally intercepted her.

"We saved her," Tally said, that smile back on her face. It had to hurt, given the cut on her lip, but her expression was pure triumph.

"And exposed ourselves in the process," Mary said. "*You* exposed us."

Tally's expression sobered. "I exposed us? I *saved* her. You were just going to sit there."

Mary let her anger bubble to the surface, and she raised a shaking hand in Tally's direction. "I was about to give orders. You acted out of turn."

Tally took a half step toward her, and Mary silently dared her to try throwing a punch. "And you didn't act at all."

Before Mary could respond, Eloise stepped between them. "We have a victim to care for," she said, quiet but firm. It was El's warning tone. Her boss tone.

Mary was too angry to be ashamed of herself, though it was a near miss when Eloise moved away to help the girl to her feet. "You're OK," Eloise said. "We're here to help. What's your name?"

The girl licked her lips. Her hair was stringy with grease, and dirt crusted under her nails. "I'm Rose," she said, her voice trembling. "I came to find you. It's my family. They're in trouble."

Eloise recognized the expression on Mary's face as they all settled into her office; she'd felt it on her own, frequently. And until recently, she'd felt it most often after dealing with Mary.

Tight-lipped, narrow-eyed, and probably ready to explode.

Only Mary was directing the look straight at Tally, glowering from where she leaned beside the door. Nathan's usual place, but Nathan wasn't here, and the difference was stark. He tended to prop himself against the frame, assessing. Guarding.

Mary stood there with her fists and her jaw clenched, like she was ready to wage war.

Tally must have felt Mary's gaze—Eloise didn't see how she could have done otherwise—because she stood in the center of the room with a ramrod-straight back, occasionally wiping her palms on her pants. Quin had gone with Ire to wake up some important Canadian officials and let them know about the operation they'd interrupted tonight.

Eloise would have thought it was funny, Mary glaring at a recruit over a breach in protocol—oh, how the tables turned— except for the sobering reality of the girl who cowered in a chair in front of Eloise's desk.

The chair had been plain before Rose had collapsed into it,

just an ordinary wooden seat with a pleather-coated cushion. Now, greenery sprang out of the grain, winding around the decorative backing and spiraling down the legs. Searching vines crept along the armrests where the girl's elbows touched them.

Rose herself sat with her shoulders hunched, staring down at the mug of tea in her hands. Her bottom lip trembled.

Eloise took a seat in the chair beside Rose, leaning forward and trying to make her posture open. Relaxed. "Tell us what happened," she said, keeping her tone soft. Comforting. "You're safe here. No one can hurt you."

Rose licked her lip, which didn't stop trembling. The plants on the chair's arms grew buds and bloomed in a matter of seconds, a parade of hopeful white blossoms. "I came to find you." Her voice was a whisper, a note away from tears. "My family needs help. They're hiding from the registry, but they're trapped."

The registry. It was Travis Bertram's making—she'd seen the photos of the president signing the order, with Travis beaming beside him like a spoiled child who'd just gotten his way.

"Can they do what you can?" Eloise asked.

"They can do more," Rose said. "That's why I had to be the one to come. I'm young, so it's mostly grass and stuff."

Eloise pictured brand new forests breaking through suburban concrete, moss stampeding out of the family's door to cover the neighbor's home. Yes, she could see how it might be hard for them to hide.

She wondered if Rose's family had sent her, or if the girl had set out on her own.

"They do control it better," Rose said. "We owned a greenhouse, before... before."

Before the president had criminalized enhanced abilities?

Well, not quite. But declaring that enhanced humans required 'oversight' and requiring them to register so they could be watched? Not much different.

In her mind, the Pearl Knife echoed a sad melody. During its tenure on Earth, she knew it had seen secret heroism, endured suspicion, enjoyed celebrity. Now suspicion had returned. No, it was more than suspicion. This was outright hostility.

Eloise ignored the Knife's plaintive song, its hopeless attempt to reach out. She hadn't touched it since she'd placed it in its case three months ago, and she wasn't going to change that now. It hadn't faded from her mind, either, but that was a conundrum for another day. If she could have erected a wall through the middle of her mind to bar it from her thoughts, she would have done it without hesitation.

When Sloane's box had cut the Pearl Knife off from Eloise back in March, she'd been sick for a few days. And then she'd started to get better—unlike her mother, whose illness had persisted, deepened. Dolly had gone blind, had been scarcely able to move.

Eloise realized now that the Knife had done that. The Knife had acted on its own to keep Dolly from using the abilities it had transferred to her—it must have, since she could make portals now; there was no other explanation.

The Knife could control people's powers. It had, under Dolly's firm hand, controlled Dad's abilities for years. The knowledge of its origin, forged among the stars, made Eloise hesitate even more. What else could it do? What were its limits? And how could she stop it if it decided it wanted something she didn't? Oh, she knew it meant well—unless it was an incredible liar—but she didn't understand enough about what it could do.

She couldn't risk picking it back up. It was too dangerous.

Eloise pulled herself back to the present situation, to the girl who sat trembling before her, staring off into space. If Rose noticed the pause, though, she didn't let on.

"Where is your family living?" Eloise asked.

"They're in Philadelphia."

"Pennsylvania?" The word seemed to fall out of Tally's lips without her permission, even as Mary dropped the glare to raise her eyebrows. "You walked here from Pennsylvania?"

Clearly she had. Her jeans were muddy, the hems frayed, and her dark blonde hair was stringy with grease. Philadelphia. So much closer to D.C., to EAEA headquarters and Travis's domain. No wonder her family was trapped.

Dread crawled through Eloise's chest, and she tamped it down as best she could. They'd help Rose's family. They'd get them out. But how many others were hiding like this? How many had abilities like Rose's, impossible to ignore? The girl had done a brave thing, coming out in the open like this, but she should never have had to risk herself.

The league needed a way to reach people in similar circumstances.

"It's not like I can hitchhike," Rose said, bitterness tracing through her tone. "It took me almost two weeks. Google Maps said 118 hours, but I had to sleep and eat. I had to zigzag off the road. And I don't walk that fast. I'm not like Frodo or something."

She sounded defensive. If Steve were here, he'd make a joke about Frodo walking pretty slowly. Being a hobbit and all.

The thought of Steve Taylor brought with it a stab of regret. His name rose into Eloise's thoughts often, unbidden, a ghost that she couldn't vanquish. She still didn't think she'd done wrong, sending him away. She missed him, anyway.

Eloise didn't know how to pull off a joke about hobbits, so she patted Rose on the shoulder instead, though she didn't linger. She didn't know whether the plants would see her body as a good canvas, and she didn't intend to find out the hard way. "What you did was amazing," she said. "You need food and rest. I bet you'd like a shower, too."

"God yes," the girl said. "I must smell like death."

Eloise smiled. "The team can help get you settled. Then I want you in surveillance so you can point out your family's location. We'll get them to safety."

Rose set the mug on Eloise's desk. "I should come with you," she said, her eyes big and round. Her faced looked drawn and pale, and Eloise wondered how much weight she'd lost, walking nonstop for the last two weeks. What had the poor girl been eating?

"It's safest here," Eloise said, keeping her tone gentle. "You rest, and we'll bring your family to you."

The girl looked dubious, but she nodded. The Pearl Knife sighed into Eloise's thoughts, sad, and she pushed it away.

Once Rose was on her way to a room, Eloise motioned for Mary and Tally to stay behind. Tally was still avoiding Mary's gaze, which Eloise honestly couldn't blame her for. She half expected the recruit to catch fire from all the glaring.

"We should get ready to go," Tally said. She sounded confident, but she shifted her weight back and forth as if expecting to be scolded.

"You?" Mary said. "You're not coming. You're benched."

The irony of it made Eloise want to sink to the floor and laugh. If Steve were here, she might—but no. He wasn't.

A year ago, Eloise had benched Mary for breaking protocol. Sent her off to L.A., and helped to launch them into this situation. They'd argued about it right here. Angrily.

And to be honest, Eloise had broken the exact same protocol today by bringing Rose directly to HQ. But that breach couldn't have been avoided. Things had changed, and the girl had nowhere else to go. Eloise doubted she'd turn into another Jenna Carpenter.

"Benched," Tally repeated. "Like hell. I saved that girl."

Mary planted her hands on her hips. Ready for a fight. Practically aching for one, Eloise thought. "You almost got her caught, and yourself with her. You betrayed our position."

"They already know we're here!"

Eloise held up a hand, but the two women were so focused on one another that they didn't notice.

Mary sputtered, shaking her head wildly. "I was about to—"

Tally rolled her eyes. "About to, about to. You'd have let that girl get taken just to save your own hide."

Or, Eloise thought, her own home. But no, Mary wouldn't have let that happen. She might not jump into the fray with the same abandon she'd had a year ago, but she'd have mounted a successful operation. Tally *had* gotten in the way.

Mary looked like she was about three seconds from throwing a punch.

"You're not benched," Eloise said loudly.

Both women turned to look at her, as if suddenly remembering who was in charge. Not, Eloise thought, that it seemed to change anyone's behavior by much. Tally smiled, smug, while Mary's scowl deepened, but Eloise shook her head. "But you're not coming to Philadelphia, either."

Tally's smile slipped. "Why not?"

"I need you on call. Mary and I will go. We'll bring Quin, when they get back. We might need their x-ray vision to find the family."

Tally nodded, accepting. It was Mary whose cheeks still blazed red with anger, Mary who stormed out of the room, slamming the door behind her. It was almost a relief to see her temper again. If she didn't release the tension, it would boil over anyway. Might as well happen here, in the safety of HQ, rather than out on a mission. After a moment, Tally followed her, closing the door carefully. As if to prove she could do better than Mary.

Eloise hoped she wouldn't have to redistribute patrol squads because those two couldn't get along.

Suddenly tired, she moved back behind her desk and sank into her chair. Rose's greenery was fading slowly, the faint trail to the door still bright against the darker carpet. They had time to let the girl rest, to learn what they could. And then they'd be off. The Pearl Knife trilled low notes into her thoughts, a question, but it already knew the answer. It must.

Eloise shook her head. "No," she whispered. "You'll be staying right here."

Nathan had seen Mary angry before. No small part of him suspected, in fact, that if he added up his hours spent with her, he'd find she'd been angry in his presence as often as not. Until recently, anyway.

This morning, though? This morning she was livid.

"She thinks because she's got springs installed in her heels that she can take over the mission and risk us all," Mary said as she followed Nathan down the wide staircase that led to the prison level. She'd returned to their rooms as he'd been headed out of them, too angry for pre-mission rest. Which he suspected she sorely needed.

"She's unbelievable," Mary continued. "The recruits are too green to be out. I told El, and she didn't listen."

He wondered if she knew how far they'd descended, or if she was too angry to notice. She usually avoided this area; in fact, he hadn't seen her down here at all since Diana and the other retirees had taken up residence in LIO's prison. Not that he could blame her for that.

"Quin does all right," Nathan said mildly.

Mary twisted her hair back as she walked, securing it at her neck in a messy bun. "Quin is a gem, and Tally risked their life tonight, too. El still won't bench her."

"Maybe someone showed Eloise that benching willful operatives only leads to trouble," he said.

Nathan was still navigating the intricate process of understanding when Mary needed an ear, and when she wanted an opinion. When in doubt, a smart man might have kept his mouth shut.

But Mary's tempers weren't aimless storms that she directed at anyone and everyone. They were usually born out of fear, out of an ingrained desire to protect the people she loved. She didn't lash out indiscriminately. Most of the time.

Mary huffed out a breath, shaking her head. "She's a liability."

He'd heard that word applied to her, too, but he knew better than to say that part. He stopped one landing before the prison level and turned to face her. "Maybe she is. But we're shorthanded."

Mary leaned back against the wall, looking suddenly tired. Nathan wondered if rescuing such a young girl tonight was bringing her back to her own childhood, to her early years at LIO. "I know we are," she said. "You should have seen those EAEA assholes, Nathan. They move in sync. It's uncanny. And they've got these tool kits full of different serums. Who even knows how many powers they can mimic?"

It was all too easy to picture it. And all too easy to picture his sister leading the pack. At least Mary never held that against him.

Nathan moved toward her and placed his hands gently on her upper arms. "They've got nothing on you," he said.

"I don't have powers."

"Exactly."

She dropped her chin to her chest, briefly. In that one

motion, he could see all the fear he'd known was there, brimming to the surface.

"HQ is secure," Nathan said, and she nodded, though he wasn't sure she really believed it. For a while, she hadn't wanted to leave HQ at all because she hadn't trusted herself on a mission. Now, he thought she didn't like leaving because she wanted to be here to protect her home.

He gave her arms a squeeze and stepped back. "Coming with me?"

Mary glanced toward the final flight of stairs. "No way I'm adding the Trap to my day. I need to get ready to go, anyway. I should already be on my way to the garage."

"No time to sleep?"

"I'll rest on the plane." She kissed him, lingering with her body against his, giving him the chance to breathe her in. She smelled like lavender shampoo and evening air, the Niagara chill still clinging to her clothes. "I wish you were coming," she murmured.

He trailed his fingertips along her neck, then dropped his hand. "I'm on call. Now go, before El swaps you out for Tally."

She smacked him on the arm, then kissed him again before heading back up the stairs. At least she was smiling now, and some of the tension had gone out of her shoulders.

HQ really was safe. He believed that. But three months living here with Mary had made him wonder whether there might be something... more. He'd wanted to be an IO for as long as he could remember. He'd wanted to help people.

Now that he had that? He liked it. He did. But he also couldn't help wondering what came next. What might ease the dark circles out from under Mary's eyes, and let the bruises fade from her skin.

Nathan took the final flight alone, nodding to the guards as he scanned his palm to enter the prison level. Mary wasn't the only full operative who avoided this place; Nathan alone came here regularly, and that was because Eloise had assigned him to oversee the captured retirees and their care. Yes, Diana and the others had hurt Mary, and Nathan hated them for it. But there wasn't a person at HQ—minus the recruits, perhaps—who hadn't been hurt by them. When it came to conflicts of interest, at least Nathan's was one removed. And Eloise believed he'd be fair.

Well, he certainly intended to be. The team ran the day-to-day operations down here, anyway, though Nathan checked in regularly. The new U.S. policies against enhanced humans had made it difficult to follow up on the legal issues, given that LIO had been essentially driven back into the shadows. But that would blow over—or Eloise would solve it—and then these people would get trials. Every one of them.

Diana Morton inhabited the first cell on the block, the one that had formerly housed Wave's Dr. Gordon. She wasn't the same pleasant conversationalist, unfortunately. She certainly wasn't falsely imprisoned the way he'd been, either.

The wall that faced the corridor between her cell and Monster's went clear as Nathan stepped between them, allowing him to see inside. Monster stood inches from the treated glass, as though he'd anticipated Nathan's arrival and wanted to intimidate him. Diana merely lay on her bed, staring up at the ceiling. The doctor's desk was still in the corner of her cell, though he'd taken his books and papers with him.

"Come to taunt us again?" Her hair was splashed back over the pillowcase, ribbons of silver running through the dark strands. She was rubbing her fingers together, as if wishing she could access her noxious poison through the gloves they'd locked over her hands. Little good that it would do her in there. She couldn't poison the walls into crumbling.

"I'm not typically the one who does the taunting," Nathan

said, stepping over to the console to check the logs. Who'd been in, who'd been out, and when. Just guards this week, in pairs and at the specified times.

Diana swung her legs around the side of the bed, moving to face him. "There's a girl here no one knows. Says she can shoot fire. Or could, before. Is she new?"

Jenna Carpenter. Nathan shook his head. "She's been here longer than you have."

"I can't see through the side walls, and she's kept her silence."

That was rather unlike Jenna, but OK. "Until now, I presume?"

Diana tsked. "She's a bitter little thing, all tangled up between Wave and LIO. And the daddy issues, my god. If there's someone around here who doesn't have those, will you please introduce me? The man's dead, and still she whines."

Nathan finished checking the reports and came around to face her, crossing his arms over his chest. "Your compassion is overwhelming."

Diana sat back, propping her palms behind her on the mattress. "Compassion is overrated."

Exactly the response he expected from the woman who'd tortured Mary. Among many others. "Is there something you want, Diana?"

"Jenna says you had a fit of morals and let a bunch of Wave prisoners go free. Any chance you're feeling similar twinges now?"

Diana must be bored today. Nathan raised an eyebrow. "The Wave operatives were innocent, and given that they were in prison largely because of you and your friends, I think you're well suited to your current situation."

"And your morals?"

Nathan smiled. "My morals sleep perfectly well at night, thank you."

He could sense Monster pacing back and forth behind him, a prickle along the back of his neck as the hulking retiree watched his conversation with the Trap. He could practically feel the others on the level—Goldi the illusionist, Rocker the camouflager, the mind-reading twins, and yes, probably Jenna —listening in as well. Diana was testing him, feeling at the borders. He wanted to know what she was looking for. What she was trying to learn.

She shrugged, affecting a bored pout that he didn't believe for a moment. Not when it was paired with those glittering eyes of hers. "You're getting awfully comfortable here, don't you think? So assured of your safety in your underground hidey-hole. You're too new to know the truth. You all are."

Eloise and Mary had grown up here. They weren't exactly new. "And what truth is that?"

Diana smiled. "You're comfortable because you don't realize you're cornered. Like rabbits."

With multiple exits and a garage full of tech, plus a Knife that could draw doorways in the air? Doubtful. And if Diana thought Dolly could leap into HQ through one of her portals, she was sadly mistaken. With the help of the technology Alex had left behind after jumping back into her own galaxy, Mary had set up portal-jamming gadgets that blocked the resonance Dolly would need to sneak in here.

But Diana didn't need to know that. If she was searching for details, Nathan wouldn't be the one to provide them. He smiled back at her. "Well, I hope you're comfortable, too," he said. "Because you're going to be here for a while."

FROM THE OUTSIDE, the florist shop was little more than a narrow storefront in Philadelphia's City Center. Wedged between a chain hotel and a men's clothing store, the windows bloomed with its wares—cheerful daisy bouquets and serious looking roses, vases and ribbons and a tasteful selection of greeting cards propped on a revolving stand.

Mary watched from the drugstore across the street, thumbing through a gossip magazine which, if the store clerk's glare counted as a prediction, she'd be buying on her way out. She actually kind of wanted it, anyway. In the middle of the magazine, they'd devoted a sliver of an article to Jeff Hayes and his crusade against anti-enhancement sentiments in the country. Mary hadn't heard from him in months, but the guy did seem sincere about the cause.

Beside her, Eloise stood unconvincingly in front of a stand of romance books, her gaze laser-focused on the shop across the street.

"Just like old times," Mary whispered. "Me getting bored on a stakeout and learning way more about my former Hollywood colleagues than I ever knew in the first place, while you... stay on task."

Eloise glanced at the clerk, but he was focused on ringing up a real customer. "It's been much too long, if you're going to announce what we're doing to the whole store."

"Relax. I whispered." Mary closed the magazine. "It's almost closing time."

They'd arrived in the neighborhood this afternoon, with plenty of time to sweep the block. Mary had on her brunette wig and a baseball cap—it still itched, though she attached fonder memories to the thing now, since she'd been wearing it when she first met Nathan—and Eloise wore dark-framed glasses that wouldn't have fooled a soul who looked carefully.

People didn't tend to look carefully.

Mary paid for her magazine and stuffed it into the tool bag she'd slung over her shoulder. It had Coral's outfit in it, in case she got a chance to wear that, and easy access to her tools in case she didn't.

As they crossed the street, the florist's clerk was just stepping out to remove the sandwich board from the sidewalk. She was short and blonde, with a paisley apron and no plants growing from her fingers. At least as far as Mary could see. "Sorry, we're closing," she said, as Mary and Eloise approached the door. "Open at nine tomorrow."

"We're here with a message from Rose," Eloise said.

The clerk dropped the sign. Mary caught it, and the woman's eyes widened in recognition when they fell on her face. "You—"

"Inside," Eloise said, and the clerk swallowed whatever she was going to say, nodding instead. Mary followed her into the shop, still hefting the sign, and the clerk locked the door behind them while Eloise closed the shades.

The shop might be small, but the owners had made good use of the space they had. Tiered stands displayed a rainbow of blossoms, the surrounding tables stuffed with candles, figurines, and stuffed bears. Wooden signs graced the walls, all bearing scripted quotes and random words like 'bloom' and 'blessing.'

The place smelled like a dream, too. Fresh. Wild.

"Rose," the clerk said, tangling her fingers together in front of her. "Is she all right? She didn't tell us she was leaving. Nothing but a text the next day. Her mother's beside herself, and it was all we could do to keep her father from chasing after her."

"I'm glad he didn't," Eloise said. "You've been helping them hide?"

The clerk nodded. "Rose's parents can control their abilities, mostly. They might be able to stay under the radar, running the flower shop and all. But Rose and her younger brother, they have more trouble. We haven't been able to figure out how to sneak them away." She swallowed, still twisting her hands. "Or where to go once we do."

Philadelphia wasn't exactly Travis Bertram's backyard, but it was close enough for discomfort. Not that proximity to Washington mattered much anymore. The whole country was under orders.

Still, Mary had seen far more EAEA armbands here in Philadelphia than anywhere else they'd glimpsed on the trip down from Niagara. The city seemed to be some kind of hotspot.

"Are they here?" Eloise asked, and the clerk nodded again. She'd led them into a back room, where glass cases lined the walls, all of them filled with blossoms. Long-stemmed roses and cotton-budded baby's breath, pink carnations and laughing yellow sunflowers. The refrigerators made the room cool, raising goosebumps along Mary's arms.

The clerk led them around a work table and around a towering shelf piled with vases, twine, and colored ribbons.

Behind the shelf, there was a tent. The kind of tent that

families took camping, green and sturdy. Fun for a weekend, but certainly not large enough for a family of four to find comfortable for any length of time. Mary's heart twisted at the sight of it. Did they stay in there all day?

No one stirred.

"It's OK," the clerk said. "It's me."

A beat, and then someone unzipped the flap. A man's head poked out. "Who's with you?"

The clerk glanced at Mary and Eloise, like she still couldn't believe it. "Mary O'Sullivan," she said. "Eloise... the Pearl Knife. I'm not sure what I'm supposed to call either of you now."

"Whatever works," Mary said.

The man crawled out of the tent, getting to his feet slowly. He looked pale and worried, like he hadn't slept in days. "Rose," he said. "She found you?"

"She found us," Eloise said. "The girl's tenacious."

A woman with dark blonde hair, presumably Rose's mother, exited the tent behind her husband. A little boy immediately tumbled out, practically on top of her. Green sprouts popped out of the concrete floor where his hands touched it, faster and wilder than Rose's had.

The boy bounced at the sight of Mary and Eloise, but when Mary gave him a wave, he rocketed behind his mother and stayed there.

"I'm Grant," Rose's father said. He pushed his glasses up on his nose. "This is Gina, my wife. The hiding one is Ethan."

"She's OK?" Gina's eyes were shining with tears. "She's really OK?"

"She sent us to find you."

Gina nodded. Grant drew the back of his hand across his forehead, looking like he might faint in relief. Ethan stuck his head out to say, "She stole my flashlight. Does she still have it?"

"If not, we'll get you a new one," Mary said.

Still half hidden behind his mother, the boy grinned.

"It's my fault," Grant said. "Not all the clerks are as trustworthy as Sara. What we'd do without her..." He shook his head. "We told them all we'd gone on vacation. But a couple of weeks ago, Jim stuck his head back here at the wrong moment. I thought he might've seen me, and I told Gina..."

He trailed off. Let out a breath. Gina lay a hand on her husband's arm. "And the next morning, Rose had gone. We got a text saying she was heading out to find you, but her powers... She doesn't quite have control yet. We were sure she'd be caught."

Eloise was looking around the room, and Mary could see her forming a plan. "We need to get you over the border," she said. "You've been lucky so far, but your abilities are too obvious to hide forever."

She glanced at Ethan, who was engaged in trying to crawl under one of the smaller shelves. Vines twisted around the legs of the furniture, grass and moss leaping across the floor. When Gina wiped her hands on her pants, Mary noticed a sheen of dusty pollen left behind.

Even the adults couldn't control it fully.

Grant nodded, ready. "What do you propose?"

Ten minutes later, Eloise had blooming vases in the hands of all three of them—though Ethan's was plastic, and she had him wear a pair of too-big gardening gloves, just in case.

"If you feel your powers running out of control, touch the plants," Eloise said. "That should help hide it. We've got a van out front. With any luck, we can slip out of the city before anyone notices."

"We should have thought of this," Sara said.

Subterfuge was a skill, especially when applied to

enhanced abilities. Mary patted the woman's arm. "You still would have needed a place to go."

"The escort doesn't hurt, either," Grant said. "Thank you."

Ethan was watching Eloise, his head tilted to the side. "Where's the Pearl Knife?"

Observant kid. Eloise smiled at him, though it looked strained to Mary. "Don't thank us yet," she said. "Let's go."

As they headed for the back door, though, a chime sounded in the front of the shop.

"Doorbell?" Mary asked.

Sara nodded.

"Stay quiet," Gina said. "Pretend we're not here."

Mary shook her head. If this was the EAEA, she doubted they'd hesitate to enter without permission. Given the president's order and the treacherous employee's evidence, they might even have the clearance to do it.

Eloise must have reached a similar conclusion, because she said, "Sara, answer the door. Mary will cover you. I'll get these three out the back."

Mary didn't like it. Eloise didn't have the Knife, and she was a good fighter—and she'd been training nonstop for the last three months to get even better—but Mary was more used to facing down enemies without the help of powers.

"I should cover them," Mary said. She wished they could ask Quin to come help, but they had to stay with the getaway van.

Eloise actually rolled her eyes. "I've got it, Mary. Go."

El was already moving, and there wasn't time to argue, so Mary just nodded to Sara. The chime was growing more insistent; whoever it was, Mary was pretty sure they knew there was someone home.

"I'll be right behind the door," Mary said.

Sara walked out, and Mary left the door ajar so she could

see what was happening. Sara unlocked the front, opening it a crack, and Mary could see two silhouettes looming on the other side of the glass.

"We're closed," Sara said, but the shapes elbowed their way inside without bothering to answer.

EAEA agents, no doubt; they even had their pretty crimson armbands on. Mary's stomach turned. If she had to be sick, she hoped it would be on the agents. Other than the armbands, all she could really make out in the dim light was that they were two white men, both wearing black caps. They looked identical in the darkness, though Mary was pretty sure the light wouldn't have helped much.

"We got a report of strange activity here," one of them said. His voice was deep, and Mary wondered if that was natural or if he was making an effort to seem more intimidating. Sara certainly seemed intimidated; she was twisting her hands together even harder now, licking her lips as the two men towered over her.

"A staff member called us," the other added. "Said there might be unregistered enhanced hiding here."

Already removing the 'humans' bit from 'enhanced humans,' were they? Sounded like Grant and Gina had been right to worry about this Jim character.

"We'll be having a look around," the first agent said.

"Now wait a second," Sara said, standing up taller. "You'll need a warrant for that. You need a warrant to be in here at all. I didn't let you in."

The deep-voiced agent shoved her aside, heading for the back door. Sara grabbed his sleeve, and he shook her off, hard enough to send her falling back to the floor.

Oh, this was going to be fun. Mary jumped, grabbing the top of the door frame and swinging her body back right as the guy pulled the door open.

As he started into the back, she swung her feet right into his face. With a little help from gravity.

Together, they crashed back into the shop, the agent sprawling across a table and knocking a display of vases to the floor with a crash. He grabbed at his face, yelling, but Mary's momentum sent her sliding over him and straight to the floor. She leapt to her feet in time to meet the second agent as he aimed a surprised punch at her head. Clumsy. Slow. Compared with the agents who'd attacked in Niagara, these guys were amateurs. She batted him away.

"Serum, serum!" the bruised-face agent was yelling, but Mary was keeping his partner too busy to reach for his belt. She knew how these guys operated now, and she didn't intend to give them an opening.

Still, the agents didn't rely entirely on their ability to take on temporary powers. As his surprise waned, Mary's opponent grew more controlled. He slashed for her throat with the side of her hand, and she avoided the hit by a slightly narrower margin. Worse, she had to step back, which was forcing her closer to the corner.

Corners were bad. Mary ducked under the guy's next punch and rolled. It gave him a beat to reach for his belt pouch, but she knocked whatever serum he'd chosen out of his hands. It shattered against the wall, leaving a blood-red smear behind.

Just like his partner, who was still gasping for breath on the table where she'd left him, this guy let emotions lose him a fight. He lunged for her, arms spread a little too wide, and Mary took superior pleasure in using that opening to swing a knee into his groin. He went down, and she plunged into her own tool bag for a fast-acting sedative.

As she turned, the bruised-face agent was finally staggering to his feet, fumbling for his serum pouch. Mary dove for him, but before she could reach him, a porcelain vase decorated with pink cherubs crashed onto his head, and he crumpled to the floor, revealing Sara standing behind him.

"Nice," Mary said. "You could be an independent operative, you know?"

Sara's hands were shaking, and she rubbed them on her apron. "I'll think it over."

"Let's head out the back. Come on."

They hurried through the storage room, past the tent and out through the back door.

If the fight in the shop had been a battle, the scene in the alley behind it was a full-on war.

Eloise was fighting two more armbanded EAEA agents, while Rose's family cowered out of the way against the wall. Eloise had always been a good fighter—she'd started her league career without any powers, just like Mary—but in the past three months, she'd really committed to the whole fighting-without-the-Knife thing.

Mary threw herself into the fray, kicking one of El's attackers straight in the stomach. The hit should have sent him stumbling at least a few steps, but he simply grinned and knocked her leg out of the way, sending her sprawling.

This guy had apparently managed to reach one of his serum vials. Fantastic.

How long had El been holding these two off on her own? Mary pulled herself to her feet as another pair of agents careened around the corner, shouting for additional backup. The EAEA really had staffed Philadelphia to the max. Why?

Didn't matter. They had to get the family out of here. Now. But as Mary staggered to her feet to launch herself back into the fight, she didn't see *how*.

In front of Rose's family, the air twisted, and a figure exploded into the alley with a loud crack. The family disappeared into a second twist in the air, and Mary ran for them, but the air twisted again—a milky spiral, here and then gone—and then there was pressure, squeezing the air out of her lungs, and Mary felt herself falling.

A second. That was all it took. She felt the sensation of landing, and she staggered, but she held onto her balance, ready to keep up the fight. It was dark, the air musty, and Mary staggered, trying to orient herself.

She might have been anywhere. This EAEA operative might have brought her straight to Travis Bertram. Or straight to the inside of a prison; it certainly felt like it could be one. But how?

A yellow light snapped on above her head, and Mary found herself staring into a familiar face with a fringe of bleached bangs around it, dark roots showing several inches. "Dawn Kimble," Mary said, exhaling in relief. The reporter who'd helped her beat Diana and the others a few months back. She'd looked for Dawn, tried to track her down after the executive order. She hadn't found a trace. "I thought you didn't want to be an independent operative."

Dawn gave her a wry smile, but it didn't reach her eyes. "I don't."

She winced, and when she touched her forearm, her fingers came away wet.

"Are you OK?" Mary asked.

"Yeah." She grimaced. "They cut a slice out of me, though."

The second figure twisted back out of nothing, bringing Eloise along. As soon as they appeared, Dawn turned toward a door that was built into the wall so seamlessly that Mary hadn't noticed it. The walls were made of stone, a tunnel bricked up at their backs. It smelled damp, with an undercurrent of burned rubber, or maybe exhaust.

In the corner, Gina and Grant hovered over Ethan, their eyes wide with fear. The boy had lost his gloves, and Mary could make out a tiny web of sprouts springing out of the fabric of Gina's pants as he clung to her legs.

"It's OK," Mary said. "This is Dawn. We know her."

Eloise raised her eyebrows—she didn't know Dawn, not personally—but she didn't contradict the statement.

Dawn nodded, apparently satisfied that they'd all teleported safely. That had to be what it was, teleporting, though Mary had never actually met anyone with that ability herself. The reporter—ex-reporter, probably—headed for the door, beckoning them to follow. She looked tired, with dark bruises stamped beneath her eyes.

"I don't want to be an independent operative," Dawn said. "But I'm an unregistered enhanced human."

She opened the door.

On the other side was a wide room, with the same stone walls mixed with bricked-up portions. Beyond that, Mary couldn't take in any of the details. She could barely compute what she was seeing.

People. A hundred of them, maybe more, staring back at her as she stepped into the room. Kids, teenagers, elderly grandparents. To the right, a young woman with glowing green skin. Just in front of her, a man with hands that curled into claws. She saw them in patches, shock and guilt clamping around her throat like a vise. She should have known, should have suspected... But there were so *many* of them. How were there so many?

As she stepped further inside, the teleporter collapsed against the wall to her right, sliding down to rest with his head against the wall. Just a kid. He looked about twelve. Maybe thirteen.

Dawn sighed, the breath a note away from sounding like a sob. "And unregistered enhanced humans go into hiding."

6 / ELOISE

STEEL BEAMS FORMED a supportive grid along the ceiling of the enhanced humans' hiding place, and matching doors dotted the walls at occasional intervals. The place smelled damp and rubbery, but someone was cooking, adding a pleasant smell of onions to the musty odors of the manmade underground. Teenagers played card games, kids played with dolls, while adults ladled soup and rocked babies. In the far corner an old man was engrossed in a game of solitaire, levitating the cards into place without touching them.

The only thing they had in common, besides their accommodations—and the fact that they all appeared to be enhanced—was that, when they noticed who'd arrived, they all stopped what they were doing to stare. Like Eloise might be their savior. Like she could do something to help them.

She could. She would. As soon as she found her voice.

"So many," Mary whispered. "There are so *many*."

Eloise's mouth felt dry, like it might crack in half. "Agnes always said..." She cleared her throat, breathed. Tried to look like a leader. "Agnes always said there were more people in the world with enhanced abilities."

"*This* many more?"

Eloise didn't know, because she'd always shut the conversation down. Agnes had wanted to recruit, to build a scientific investigation and give enhanced humans choices that went beyond 'independent operative or nothing.'

Eloise had refused to OK the project. Not so much because she'd disliked the idea, but because they'd been stretched so thin. Even more, back then.

Eloise glanced at the teleporter, who was asleep against the wall. A kid. These people, this community, had sent a *kid* in to help with Rose's family. They'd had to, maybe. As she watched, a woman approached him, hefted him into her arms, and carried him to a pile of blankets across the room.

"He does that," Dawn said. "In case you're wondering why we're all still here. He'll sleep for a day now. He did eight jumps tonight. About double the usual."

That explained why they couldn't simply zip everyone out of here. Eloise glanced back at Grant and Gina, but they were deep in conversation with an older Black man. A second, younger man crouched before a now half-hidden Ethan and pulled a quarter out of the boy's ear. Ethan giggled.

"Come on," Dawn said, "I'll give you the tour."

With her first shock-tinted reaction ebbing, Eloise could see that the community they'd built here was well organized. Efficient, even. They'd set up curtains for privacy, and Eloise could see sleeping bags and mats lined up neatly where the curtains drifted open. Laundry hung on lines across the back of the room. There was a generator for electricity, and several of the doors along the walls had bathroom signs. Eloise wasn't sure how that worked, exactly, but she supposed she'd be finding out.

"It was pleasant enough, when we first set it up," Dawn said. "Enough that the kids felt like it was camping. And anything was better than looking over our shoulders every other minute. But it was meant to be temporary."

Eloise swallowed. Pleasant enough. Sure, if you didn't care about seeing the sun. "How long?"

The ex-reporter slipped an elastic off her wrist, tying back her hair as she spoke. "I came down here two weeks after the president signed his executive order. A guy in my apartment building, he agreed to the registry. Said he might as well. He had healing abilities. Thought maybe he could help. Not sure what he thought they'd ask him to help *with*, but he had good intentions. Trusted them, I guess."

Dawn paused. Around them, most of the community had gone back to whatever they'd been doing before. Chores. Games. Conversations. But Eloise could still feel their sidelong glances. Their hope. Behind her, Mary listened to Dawn's story in silence.

Dawn shook her head. Took a breath. "Two days after my neighbor registered, he got arrested. Suspected murder. They claimed he'd used his abilities to stop a person's heart or something. These guys, they go big or they don't go at all. They hauled him off, and we didn't see him again."

She told the story calmly, like she'd said the words before. Repeated them to some of the people here, or maybe to herself. Planning for this moment. Hoping for it. With the league in hiding, there'd been no real way to contact them. No way to reach out.

"So that sealed it, as far as registering," Dawn continued. "But I figured once people stopped registering, they'd come after those of us who refused. I remembered a friend of mine from college, he'd done a story about Philadelphia. How there were all these tunnels and things underground. Old canals, repurposed sewers and pedestrian walkways. Lots of them filled up with rocks, but pockets. Wave used them as hideouts, a long time ago, until the Pearl Knife came and cleaned them out."

That would have been Dolly, of course. Eloise didn't recall the specific mission, but there'd been so many of them back then. And she'd been a kid. Preoccupied with helping Mary recover from the crash, among other things.

Eloise realized she'd pegged Dawn as someone who'd come along after the fact, someone who'd discovered this community, though maybe early on, and become a leader. A face of the organization—if it could be called that.

But Dawn was clearly one of the founders. She'd found a place for them to hide.

"I can track people I've met before," Dawn said, nodding to Mary. Whom she'd tracked earlier this year, in search of a good news story. "That's my ability. So any enhanced person I'd met in the area over the years, I tracked. That got us started. Some of them, like my neighbor, had disappeared. I can't feel them anymore."

A whining tone buzzed in Eloise's ear. Dawn couldn't find them anymore? What did that mean? That they'd been put somewhere like the holding facility where Travis had stashed her a few months back? Eloise didn't know how even a horrible place like that could hide enhanced humans from a power like Dawn's.

She swallowed, not wanting to follow the other, more obvious line of thought. That the government had taken the opportunity to rid the world of Dawn's neighbor.

They needed to get these people out of here.

"Like I said, this place was supposed to be temporary," Dawn said. "It's been too long. But we're trapped in the city, and as much as we've explored the tunnels, there's nothing that connects to a good escape. And there's nowhere to go."

"You need to get across the border," Eloise said. Her voice

felt far away. She hoped it sounded confident; she couldn't tell. "You need to get out of the country, at least for now."

"How did you know Grant and Gina would be in trouble tonight?" Mary asked. She, at least, seemed capable of keeping her wits about her.

"We listen to the scanners. The EAEA uses a pretty simple code." Dawn smiled, but it didn't reach her eyes. How could it? "Didn't expect to find you there, though."

Yes. That had been a stroke of luck.

Dawn squeezed Mary's shoulder. "It'll be OK. Now that you're here, it'll be OK."

She walked away, heading over to a corner to speak to a man who withdrew a bandage from a metal box and began wrapping it around Dawn's injured arm.

In the opposite corner, the two men who'd greeted Rose's family were helping them to get settled in an unoccupied area. Blankets, bowls, even a dinosaur toy for Ethan—who, Eloise realized, must have left his own toys back in the shop. For some reason, that detail was the one that made her heart feel like it was going to split in two.

Mary stepped in close, leaning into Eloise's ear. "El. We need the Knife." Her words were so quiet, her tone so low, that Eloise barely heard them. And no wonder. These people didn't need to wonder why she didn't have it with her. Didn't need to doubt.

The Knife. Colors surged in her brain, and she tried to siphon them away, tried to block them as she did the blade. But they continued, arching down her spine and sending tingles out to her fingertips. She squeezed her fists and let them go, trying to increase the circulation, but the feeling only intensified.

That was... new.

Feeling unsteady, Eloise took care to keep her voice as low

as Mary's as she said, "The Knife will cause more harm than help."

Mary leaned in closer. "It can create *portals*."

"And control people's abilities, and make independent decisions." Like draining Dolly's life force to punish her. "It could hurt everyone in this room. It's too dangerous."

Mary leaned in, her green eyes solemn. "El, it's worth the risk. A single portal, and everyone steps through to safety. We need it."

The tingling in Eloise's fingers crawled up her knuckles, as though her refusal to release the energy outward had forced it to go searching in the other direction. It was a strange sensation, half as though her hands had fallen asleep and were regaining their circulation, and half as if... Like they might try to set something on fire.

Eloise let out a long breath, grasping for reason. Logic. Mary was right. New sensations or not, Eloise had used the Knife for years, and it would be foolish to deny these people the possibility of escape. She could handle the balance between control and surrender, one more time. She'd have to.

"All right," she said. "I'll go get it. But while I'm gone, you need to find a Plan B. And test it. We're getting these people to safety, with or without the Knife."

THE STREETS of Berlin turned to blurry streaks as Steve ran, cutting around cars, bicycles, and pedestrians, all of them a wash of color. He moved with precision, his senses as elevated as the inherited *thing* in his cells—whatever it was—let him dance through the world as if everything else were spinning in slow motion.

Running was a pleasure. Especially when he didn't have to dash headlong into danger, or swipe someone out of it, or escape from enhanced-human-hating radicals. No, nighttime in Berlin was all light and kitchen noises, soft bass resonating in the ribcage, the smell of recent rain.

Steve raced the canary-yellow street trams to his last delivery, speeding upstairs—no doorman—to Mrs. Becker's second-floor apartment. The elderly woman had been working her way through the restaurant's entire menu, informing him every evening of how she'd enjoyed the previous night's selection.

He wouldn't have been surprised to learn she'd taped a pad of paper to the inside of her door, just so she could give him her notes.

Mrs. Becker opened the door now, grinning when she saw him. She had on a bright, flowery blouse with neon pink buttons, green hoop earrings looped into her earlobes. "Tell Ben I liked the baba ganoush well enough, but maybe he should think about mixing it up. Adding a kick. Chilis. Hot peppers."

She spoke in heavily accented English, and Steve thought she might enjoy the opportunity to practice the language when he came by. He laughed and handed her tonight's bag. "I'm not sure how well that would suit the German palate."

She scowled at him. "I've got a German palate, young man."

He winked. "An adventurous one, Mrs. Becker. Enjoy your meal."

Steve turned to go, but Mrs. Becker cleared her throat. When he turned back, she was watching him carefully. Almost tentatively, though that didn't fit with the little he knew about Mrs. Becker. The woman was a walking art exhibit, loud and brimming with confidence.

"You're enhanced, yes?" she said.

Steve felt his shoulders go tense, brief flashes of his rushed escape from Boston echoing through his mind as he tried to hold his smile. He'd tried to go back home after leaving LIO HQ, had tried to claim back a semblance of his old life.

The EAEA had been waiting.

But Germany was not America. No one here had signed any anti-enhanced human bullshit, and based on the outcry—not to mention the complaints Europe had filed against America in the U.N.—they didn't plan to.

He'd taken too long to respond, and now Mrs. Becker was pressing her brows together in a concerned expression he'd never seen her wear. "Don't worry," she said. "This is Berlin. City of freedom."

Steve force himself to smile. "Right. Of course. Yes, ma'am, I do have enhanced abilities."

She scoffed. "Ma'am? Please. I only wanted to tell you it's

wrong what they're doing. I gave a donation to Jeff Hayes's cause. The actor. He's working against them, yes?"

Steve swallowed back a lump in his throat, moved by her thoughtfulness. "I believe so. Thank you."

Mrs. Becker gave him a curt nod. "See you tomorrow."

By the time Steve got back to the restaurant, his friend Ben was already prepping the kitchen for tomorrow. A big guy with shoulders that sloped into enormous arms, Ben chopped vegetables with a precision that looked like its own kind of dance in his large hands.

"How many deliveries did you fit in on that run?" Ben spoke in crisply accented English, keeping his focus on the cutting board in front of him. As soon as the U.S. had said 'list,' Germany had been among the first to denounce the move. When he'd run into trouble in Boston, Steve had called his old college buddy for an assist.

A week later, Ben's Berlin-based Mediterranean restaurant had been able to boast the fastest delivery service in the city. It was, Steve thought, the least he could do to thank Ben for getting him out. Registration for enhanced humans? No thanks. The U.S. still hadn't closed the borders to them, but Steve figured that was a 'yet' kind of a statement.

"Thirteen." Steve opened the employee fridge and swiped a Beck's off the top rack, popping it open against the counter before leaning back to watch his friend work. Any attempt to assist in the chopping would end with him getting shoved out the door. Likely with a mop in his hand.

Ben sneaked a pointed look at his watch. "In eight and a half minutes? Losing your touch, Taylor."

Steve didn't feel like recounting his conversation with Mrs. Becker. "Three people tipped in cash, and one lady typoed her address. What do you want from me?"

"Perfection." Ben took a break from chopping to point his

kitchen knife in Steve's direction, using it as an extension of his finger. "This is why I hired you."

Steve tipped back the beer. "You didn't hire me. I had to beg you to let me work."

Ben sniffed. "And a good thing I did. In fact, you're so useful that I'm reluctant to tell you there's someone else here seeking your services."

Steve put down the beer. "Is it Eloise?"

He could no more have stopped himself from saying her name than he could have stopped the Enhanced Abilities Enforcement Association all on his own. He didn't *want* to say her name, didn't want to hope that she'd decided to come for him after all. Or at least, he didn't want to make his hope obvious to the world.

Ben shrugged. It was like watching a mountain shiver. "Is Eloise a little old lady with a cane?

Steve let out a breath. Relief? Disappointment? Well. Why not a bit of both? "No."

"Then no."

Steve sidled to the kitchen door, which featured a stereotypically round window meant to make sure you didn't crash into another server while coming and going, but equally helpful for spying on the dining room.

There was, in fact, an elderly woman seated in the center of the restaurant. She had her silver hair tied into a severe looking bun, as if she'd read what little old ladies ought to look like and committed fully to the part. She sat with her back straight, hands in her lap, lips pressed into a thin line.

On second thought, this woman had probably *defined* what little old ladies ought to look like. She looked vaguely familiar, like he ought to know her, but he couldn't shake the memory loose. Maybe it was just her general 'severe old lady' look.

"You let her in after hours?" Steve asked, still trying to place her.

"Go talk to her," Ben grumbled. "See if you think I had a choice. And bring her that cup of tea."

"You let her in after hours *and* you made her tea?"

Ben scowled at him, and Steve held up his hands in surrender. "I'm going, I'm going."

Steve swiped the teacup off the counter and headed into the dining room, delivering the cup to the woman's table with a smile, the kind that usually melted old ladies. And young ones. Pretty much everyone, actually. Not Ben, though. Come to think of it, not El either.

Maybe it wasn't as good a smile as he thought it was.

"Putting your talents to good use, I see," the woman said.

Steve dropped into the chair across from her without letting his smile falter. "Nothing wrong with food service."

Her expression didn't change. "I didn't say there was, and I'm too old to be teased into defensiveness, Mr. Taylor. You know what I mean."

Steve watched her, taking his time in responding so he could assess her. She looked back at him with a frank expression, as if she could see past whatever role he might try to play.

"Nothing wrong with hiding, either," he said.

The woman folded her hands on the table in front of her, shrewd gaze locked on his face. "Mr. Taylor. You are putting words into my mouth in an effort to disconcert me. It won't work."

Steve wished he had his hat with him so he could play with the brim. Flip it around in his hands, if nothing else. "You know me, but I'm afraid you've got the advantage. Who are you?"

The woman stirred a dollop of honey into her tea, taking her time. When she was satisfied, she took a sip, then placed the cup neatly back on the table and looked up, meeting his gaze with steely blue eyes. "You may call me Fran. I represent an organization you're familiar with."

Steve raised his eyebrows. "It's not LIO, so it's gotta be W—"

"Yes." She sipped her tea. Watched him.

Right. He did recognize her, then, from the abandoned airport in the desert. From the day Mary and her alien friend had returned the Pearl Knife and tried to convince the two organizations to work together, citing a larger threat. One that hadn't yet materialized, as far as Steve could tell from his view outside the loop.

It was also the day El had sent him packing.

He remembered this woman, her blue gaze leveled at Eloise rather than at him, her clear leadership. One of Wave's higher ranking operatives, definitely.

"You were at the meeting on the airfield," he said.

"Yes."

"You've been spying on me."

"Of course." She sipped her tea. Set it down. "We're aware you left the league."

Steve stifled the urge to sweep through the room at a blur to comb for bugs or hidden cameras. Though Wave could just as easily use human spies. Regular customers, vendors, bus boys. The artist who lived across the street. Maybe even Mrs. Becker. Who knew which of them could have been watching him this whole time? "Three months ago," he said. "And I wasn't *with* them."

Fran lifted a penciled eyebrow. "No? You were standing behind Eloise Reyna when we met those charming alien people, were you not?"

He couldn't deny it. In his mind's eye, he could see Eloise looking at the Pearl Knife, trepidation in her eyes. Trepidation, and no small amount of fear. He wasn't arrogant enough to think she needed him, but he liked to think... At least, he'd hoped that he'd become something of a confidant. An ally.

But she was stubborn. He was, too.

Steve wrenched himself back to the moment, and the shrewd lady sitting across from him. "What don't you know?"

She inclined her head, as if he'd finally asked the right question. "We don't know why you left the league. And we're not asking."

"Why are you here?"

Fran set her forearms on the table and laced her fingers together. "We want to help you. And we were thinking you could help us, too."

Steve expected her to expand on this. When she didn't, he dropped his lounging posture and sat up in his chair. "You didn't ask, but I'll tell you. I left the league because I couldn't make peace with all the secrets." And because El had kicked him out the door, but Wave hardly needed to know about that part. "You want my help with something? Cut the cryptic rhetoric, and we'll talk."

The corners of her mouth lifted, ever so slightly. The ghost of a ghost of a smile. She slipped a pearl-white business card out of her cuff—the corners unnaturally crisp, considering where she'd been storing the thing—and slid it across the table. "We want to recruit you, Mr. Taylor. That's all it's about. We want to recruit you."

Fran stood, leaving her card behind and picking up the cane that had been resting against the table. "You don't have to decide now. But think on it. Think on the type of work you'd like to be doing." She paused, gripping the head of the cane as she leaned her weight on it. "The world needs you more than ever."

Without waiting for a response, she turned and headed for the door.

THE RANCH WAS SITUATED MORE than twenty miles from the nearest town, if one grocery store and a post office even merited that title. Patches of clouds streaked across the cornflower sky, as if someone had stretched them near to dissolving. The horizon looked as far off as it might at sea.

The ranch's owner was kneeling in her vegetable garden, casting occasional wary glances at Dolly and Sever as they walked together along the perimeter of the chicken yard. Though she might have been watching Ranger, who'd accumulated three coyotes from the distant hills and was now leading them *through* the chicken yard. Tongues dangling like house pets, the coyotes ignored the hens as Ranger scattered food, laughing when the chickens darted beneath the wild dogs—or whatever they were—to peck at corn.

"Do predators here not eat domesticated livestock?" Sever asked, watching Ranger dance around a pair of especially fat hens. He nearly lost his balance, but one of the coyotes flashed into motion, rushing to his side to steady him. Its reddish-brown fur was thick and streaked with white, its ears perked like a pet's.

The owner was still watching from her garden, hardly

keeping up the pretense of weeding now. She'd had rooms to let, a loft in the barn. Where *she* was currently spending her nights, while Dolly and the others took up residence in the house.

"Oh, they do," Dolly said. "Usually."

Sever kept walking. He might have been strolling through the halls of a palace, the way he propped his hands behind his back. He certainly held himself like a prince. Or a king. "Tell me about your powers. About how the Blade of Starlight affected them."

Dolly knew her way around a good manipulation, and this scenario called for a little bit of feigned fear. A little bit of weakness. In the little time she'd spent with Sever so far, he'd not changed his tune about wanting to destroy the Knife. She'd do well to play its victim, at least for the time being.

She had no problem feigning weakness if it served her purpose. Besides, she was starting to think this Sever character wasn't nearly as frightening as he thought he was. Yes, he'd demonstrated incredible abilities at their first meeting. But what had he done since then? She was less than impressed.

Still, Dolly affected distress, keeping her voice quiet as she laid out of the facts. As if it caused her pain to discuss it. "There's not much more to say," she told him. "My mother bequeathed the Knife—apologies, the Blade—to me when she died. I carried it for more than two decades. But my husband betrayed me. The night he died, he leeched its power away from me and bestowed it on my daughter."

Sever's dark brows drew together, but he didn't speak. Dolly didn't want to describe that night, the awful burning of the Pearl Knife tearing away from her consciousness. She cleared her throat. "After that, I aged practically overnight. My hair went white. My vision abandoned me. I could hardly move. It left me with some of its powers, but I didn't know that until it was far away from me. It kept me from using them."

Sever stopped walking, sympathy burning in his strange, orange-sparked eyes. "I am sorry," he said. "I never intended that. I owe you my sincerest apologies."

Dolly squinted at him, but the man—god, alien, whatever he was—looked as if he really meant it.

He hadn't yet given her whatever job he had in mind, and she certainly hadn't told him what she wanted. What she thought they ought to do. Now, when she had his ear and his sympathy, she squared her shoulders and took a deep breath. "I know where to find the Blade. We should invade the league's headquarters. We should take it."

Sever began walking again, hands still clasped behind his back. He had on a tunic-like getup, something out of a Greek mythology play. Only it was royal purple and embroidered with silvery thread that seemed to slip into different positions as she watched. At her insistence, he'd agreed to put the tunic on over a pair of dark-wash jeans, though they didn't help him to blend in as much as she might have hoped.

They passed Carlisle, who was sunning himself happily against a fence post, before Sever spoke. "It is my fault that your world worships the Blade as it does, and my fault that you rely so heavily upon it. I forged it, and it carries a drop of my essence. Unfortunately, it also appears to have inherited some of my will."

"Why did you make it in the first place?" Dolly asked.

Sever's lips curled in a sort-of smile, though no mirth reached his eyes. "Like the most foolish of men, I fell in love."

Dolly wasn't sure Sever was a man at all, but she held her tongue.

"Unfortunately," he said, "she was a mortal woman, and

she didn't fit well in my court. She didn't belong there. It was a place of beauty, of art and heavenly enlightenment."

Dolly refrained from making a wry comment about mortals and their stubborn, un-heavenly ways. "So you made the Knife for her. To bridge the distance."

Sever inclined his head. "I forged it out of starlight and metal and bone. My blood, my tears, my love for her."

Dolly resisted rolling her eyes. Narrowly.

Sever's gaze was far away, and Dolly wondered how often he'd told this story. Was she the first to hear it? The fifth? Or the five hundredth?

Men, in her experience, did not hesitate to whine about their misfortunes. Often. And loudly.

Sever ran one hand along the fence as he spoke. Immune to splinters, perhaps, or uncaring. "When I finally presented it to her, I explained that its powers would eventually become a part of her. That she would not always need the Blade." He shook his head, eyes locked on the distance. This had to have happened over a century ago, but he told it as if it were fresh. "She was... offended. In a fit of anger, she used the Blade to strip my court of all its powers. She drained its life force, every-thing that made it what it was. And then, like a coward, she fled."

Or, Dolly thought, he'd let her go. Love. It was foolish. She'd succumbed to it, too, and Will had betrayed her. She actually sympathized with Sever's story, though she'd made peace with Will's actions. He was dead; there was no point in dwelling on it. Sever, though, spoke as if he could benefit from a nice dose of closure. Though presumably Sever's girl was long dead, too.

Perhaps he'd done the job himself. "Did you look for her?" Dolly asked.

"I scoured the galaxy. When she could not be found on her

planet, I reduced it to ash." He told it in such a clinical tone, as if he were discussing math equations rather than the ending of entire worlds. "I would hear whispers of her presence elsewhere, and when I could not locate her, I assumed she'd run again and that the people had helped her. Quite a few planets found their last moments this way, yet I never found her."

Perhaps his ability to search entire planets had failed him. His beloved had probably died screaming along with everyone else, somewhere or another. Dolly suppressed a shiver, trying to imagine whole worlds blown away by this man's hand. This *god's* hand, unless he was somehow delusional about what he had done. He told it all so plainly. No ice or revenge in his voice. Simple reporting.

She waited for him to continue. When he didn't, she said, "But how did the Knife get to Earth?"

"That, I don't know. I locked it away. Foolish of me, I know, but my heart was sore from Adina's rejection. I still loved her." He shook his head, that boyish look returning for a flash as he basically admitted that he'd failed to destroy the Knife because it had sentimental value. An odd sort of tyrant, this one. "My vault ought to have been secure. But a century ago, I found it had been stolen. I punished more planets, desperate to find such a dangerous weapon. It was gone."

Dolly decided to refrain from pointing out the problem in demolishing planets in order to save them from the Knife's powers. "I don't know how it came here, either. Only that it's been in my family for generations."

She didn't want to find out what Sever would do if he decided she had stolen the Knife, or her family had.

To be honest, he'd just *told* her what he'd do. She simply didn't want to picture it.

A dangerous game, this alliance. But a crucial one. If she wanted the Knife back, if she wanted to free her friends and control LIO again—or some new version of it—she would need to play it. Once the Knife belonged to her again, she'd have the power to extricate herself.

Sever finally looked away from the horizon, meeting her gaze once again. "You are afraid for your own planet, perhaps."

Dolly licked her lips, hoping he hadn't been reading her mind. Could he do that? There was nothing to lose by playing into the fear, though. "The thought had crossed my mind."

Sever shook his head. "I may have been... hasty. With the other planets." He frowned. "In some cases. But this time, the fault is mine. I forged the Blade of Starlight, and I was foolish enough to lose it. I must be the one to save your planet from it."

So he was a genocidal, megalomaniac demigod with a sense of responsibility. Great. "OK," Dolly said. "But the people who protect it, and consider themselves to be Earth's heroes? They have... powers. Most of them."

"Powers like mine?"

Dolly pointed to Ranger, who sent a coyote trotting across the chicken yard to greet them. To her surprise, Sever crouched and reached a hand through the fence to pet the wild dog on its head. The animal actually dropped and rolled onto its back, and the planet-destroying demigod proceeded to administer a tummy rub.

"Like his," Dolly said. "Consider how Ranger could turn these animals into soldiers, instead of cuddly toys. Consider people with overblown muscles, people who can throw fire, teleport, fly. That sort of thing. A few of them, you could face. Together? They're a problem."

Sever gave the coyote one last pat and rose as the animal loped back to Ranger's side. "Then we need to solve it."

She had to convince him, somehow, that the Knife was worth retrieving. That he wouldn't win without it. "The Knife can control powers. Can you?"

"I've never attempted it. Aside from my courtiers, I never knew anyone in the Parse Galaxy with powers woven into their bodies. And my betrothed used my creation to drain those."

Dolly nodded toward Ranger. "Try it."

She wasn't sure she ought to be giving him instructions. And maybe she should add a 'my liege' to the end of it, or something.

But Sever was apparently not the sort of demigod who needed that sort of assurance from his people. He turned to face Ranger, gaze leveled at the animal-wrangler in concentration. It might have been her imagination, but she thought the sparks in his eyes grew larger.

She held her breath, half expecting the coyotes to turn toward Sever. Or start tearing up the chickens. But they continued to trot along at Ranger's feet. A second passed, then ten. Nothing.

Finally, Sever shook his head. "I cannot. It must be an anomaly of the Blade. I told you I was foolish to create such a thing."

Dolly stepped closer, swallowing back a wad of nerves. She didn't want to admit it could be actual fear—no feigning required—but, well, so what if it was? Surely a bit of healthy fear was to be expected. Sever had destroyed planets, had admitted it with a mere sliver of possible regret.

But Dolly needed to get the Pearl Knife back, and she couldn't do that without help. Not when its mere presence made her sick and drained her powers.

Once she had it, she would force it to realign with her. And then she'd deal with getting rid of Sever. She'd be Earth's hero once again. "That's why we need to go and get it."

"No. That's why we need to let it go." He placed a hand on her shoulder, a fatherly gesture that she nearly flinched away from. "We will secure the Knife, Dolly. I promise you, it will soon cease from causing harm to anyone. But it's too dangerous to use. We need to find another way to neutralize its guardians."

Dolly sighed. Nodded. She had a part to play, and she'd play it well. "In that case, I know about a serum we could use."

WHENEVER MARY LOOKED around the underground community of enhanced humans, she felt as if her heart might rip itself out of her chest in its grief. They'd spent nearly three months underground, with only old train tunnels to exercise in. Three months underground without fresh air, without sunlight. It was too much to bear.

Yes, the room was big, but there were also more than a hundred people in here. A hundred people who'd gracefully made a corner for the flower shop family to call home, shuffling their belongings aside as if they'd done it many times before. They'd set up a pallet for Mary to rest on while Eloise headed back to HQ for the Knife, shared canned soup and crackers, and watched her every move with hopeful eyes.

This was why she'd become an IO. Things got so tangled, but it all came back to this. To helping people. She wanted to get them all out of here, immediately. Back to safety. Back to *life*.

Thankfully, Eloise agreed. Not that Mary would have expected otherwise. They'd called in Nathan, Ire, and Tally to join her and Quin here. If Sloane and her friends had left the magical Knife box behind, could have brought it with them, but they were left to wait and plot alternate escape routes while Eloise made her way north to retrieve the Knife.

But El was so worried about the Pearl Knife that she'd told Mary to test a Plan B, not just make one. So test it, she would. As dusk came around again, Nathan finished plotting out an escape route with Pete, who'd been combing security feeds ever since they'd arrived here to try and find them a way out of the city.

Dawn chewed on her nail as Nathan called them together. She'd selected a trio of college-aged women to test the route tonight, and Mary could almost see her worrying about whether they'd be OK. Dawn had spent the day assembling packets of food for them.

"Pete's charted the best path for us," Nathan said, as Tally and Ire joined the circle. "The tunnels can get us there."

Dawn frowned. "Are you sure? We've done some exploring, and we've never found a route out using just the tunnels."

Nathan hesitated. "That's the hitch. We'll have to take three blocks above ground. It will get us from this section of the underground to an old train tunnel that leads out of the city. Eloise wants Mary and me to escort. Quin and Tally will stay here."

Sure, seeing through walls was helpful for a lookout. And she supposed Tally's powers were useful in a fight, if the woman could control her urge to show off.

"We have powers," Tally said. "We should be the escort."

Mary rolled her eyes. "Please. You'd go looking for a fight, or expose your abilities."

"I wouldn't."

Mary felt like she was lecturing a child, even though Tally couldn't possibly be that much younger than she was. A few years, maybe. "You don't even take this seriously." She pointed to Tally's lapel. "You've got pastel horses pinned to your outfit. What independent operative pins horses to their outfit? That one has fruit on its butt, what even is that?"

Ire cleared his throat. "It's Apple Jack." Everyone looked at him, and he shrugged. "She's a My Little Pony."

Nathan grinned. "Ire was a kid once. Who knew?"

Tally was still glaring at Mary. "LIO doesn't have standard uniforms. I don't see why I can't add some flare to mine."

"At least make it Velcro so no one can impale you on it."

Dawn was looking back and forth between them, like she was composing a story in her mind. Or like she was wondering if she might have to step between them because of a My Little Pony. "I think it makes the most sense for the people without powers to go," she said. "In this case."

Tally crossed her arms, clearly disagreeing, but at least she backed off. She stalked over to where the kids were still playing games and dropped down to sit cross-legged beside them.

Mary wanted to wait for El to get back here. She didn't see the point of this, if the Knife could just cut a hole to Canada. But Eloise wanted them to find a route. So, a route they would find. Might as well liberate a few enhanced humans in the process.

"We don't have abilities," Mary said, "but we do have famous faces."

"You've been handling that little problem for years," Dawn said. "I'm sure you can make it work."

The tunnels were old, brick-walled passages that, in some cases, Mary didn't think had ever been used. At least, not for their original purposes. Her flashlight beam bounced along the walls, illuminating faded bricks that looked like they'd once been meant to make this a pleasant passage. It was wide enough for a train, and smelled musty enough that she was pretty sure a few dozen varieties of mold must be invading her sinuses.

The high ceilings made their footsteps echo, the place surprisingly alive with sound. Small pebbles dropping from god knew where, water splashing cryptically into random corners.

The women they were escorting had gotten stuck here after the EAEA raided one of the schools in town. They'd been friends already, drawn together by their powers—one could camouflage, the second walked on water, and the third had an uncanny ability to melt into a puddle of silvery water whenever she wanted to—and now, Mary suspected, they'd be inseparable for life. They walked quietly a few steps behind Mary and Nathan, Dawn's snack bags tucked into backpacks, their feet scuffling on the stone floor as they moved.

Phil walked with them, occasionally sweeping his hair out of his face to cast a glance at the girls, as if he'd like to speak to them but wasn't sure what he could possibly say that might interest them.

"So," Nathan said as they walked, eyes scanning their dark surroundings, "do you really think I have a famous face?"

Mary raised an eyebrow at him. "Excuse me?"

"Back there, you didn't say *you* had a famous face. You said *we* have famous faces. Do you think I'm as famous as you yet?"

"Those are two different questions," Mary said. "Yes, you have a famous face. The comic con fight made sure it was plastered all over the internet, if it wasn't before."

"True." Nathan tapped a fingertip on his lip. "Our foes do enjoy broadcasting our misfortunes."

Mary kept half an eye on her feet, the stones slightly uneven beneath her boots. "As to whether you're as famous as me, that's obviously a no. I've been working on it my whole life, so good luck catching up."

She glanced back at their charges, who were following quietly, helping each other along. These girls—these young women—were family now.

Nathan looked around at the walls, tipping his head back for a second to survey the ceiling. Mary half expected him to trip, but he managed to keep his footing as he walked. "Do you think there are personality quizzes out there? Like 'which LIO member are you?'"

"Why, worried you wouldn't get yourself?"

"I'd probably get Ire."

"Ire is too mysterious. My Little Pony? Really?"

Nathan avoided something in his path, though it was too dark to make out what it was. "Please don't hurt me for pointing this out, but you were the only one standing in the circle who *didn't* know My Little Pony."

Mary shrugged. What was so fascinating about sherbet-colored horses, anyway? So her life hadn't been typical. Typical was boring, anyway.

"What do you think comes after this?" Nathan said.

"We finish this mission and get everyone out. Are you having a memory blip?"

Nathan hesitated, and for a moment Mary actually worried that he *had*. It wasn't like head injuries were uncommon in this business. "No," he said finally, "I mean in a larger sense. What comes after LIO? Independent Operative-ing?"

After LIO? She'd never really thought about it, not seriously. When LIO hadn't been in her life, she'd still been an independent operative. She wasn't sure she knew how to be anything else.

"When I met you a year ago, the only thing you wanted

was to be an IO," she said. "You hounded me until I gave you a shot at it."

"Technically, it was Eloise who gave me a shot."

"Yes, well, even she has her pushover moments."

Nathan rubbed the back of his neck. "I mean, at one point or another, one ceases to engage in full-on operations."

Mary wanted to make a crack about Will being so inactive these days, or Diana. But Nathan looked so sincere, like he was bringing something up that had been on his mind. So she bit back the defense mechanism and made herself listen.

"Maybe one day the world won't need the league," he said. "If the president suddenly retracts his order, and the league gets the freedom come back to the light again... should we?"

Mary wasn't sure if he meant the league as a whole, or the two of them, or both. Or, maybe, if he simply meant himself.

Maybe he didn't know, either. He said, "I wanted to be an IO because I thought the Pearl Knife had saved Chloe and me. And even after I learned the truth, that it was all a frame job against Wave, I still wanted to do it. To help people."

"But now you want to retire and write your memoir or something?"

Nathan shrugged. "Maybe."

What would the world look like if LIO simply dropped off the map? He was setting up a scenario that didn't exist. They couldn't disappear, not with the EAEA tormenting enhanced humans and mysterious extraterrestrial threats out there somewhere. He wasn't suggesting they leave the world to flounder.

But hypothetically? If the league won and saved the enhanced humans, convinced the country to reverse its hateful policies... and if Sloane's alien enemy never appeared... what did Mary want out of LIO? Out of life?

She'd once pictured living her life in the mountains, at

Aries. But in reality, she wasn't sure she knew how to be anything but this.

They reached a service ladder, a set of rusty rungs jammed into the stone wall. Their exit point. She waited for Pete to confirm it, wondering what he thought of this whole conversation. She'd actually forgotten he was in her ear, that half the surveillance team was listening in.

"I don't know what comes next," she said finally. "But we can... talk about it?"

Nathan grinned, then leaned in for a brief kiss. "Thank you for not kicking me or punching me in the face."

"I mean honestly, your timing could be better with a conversation like this."

He just shrugged. He didn't even look sorry.

Pete confirmed the ladder as their exit point, and Mary had to stifle the urge to leap onto it simply to escape in case Nathan decided to continue this conversation. She pointed her flashlight at the ladder. "I'll go first. Then Phil, in case we need to get the girls out fast. The girls next, and Nathan last. We've got three open-air blocks to cross, then we'll be back in the tunnels."

She could make out the girls' nodding, nervous twitches in the darkness.

The ladder was old, rough with rust, but serviceable. It didn't wobble as she started to climb, and in a few minutes she'd reached the top. She shoved the access portal aside—not a manhole cover, but the rectangular metal thing that weighed a ton—and slipped above ground.

She'd only been underground for a day, and yet the smell of fresh air might have been the sweetest thing she'd ever breathed.

They'd emerged into the Center City, not too far from where they'd rescued Rose's family. Taller buildings here, though, a brick-fronted convention center, a Hardrock Cafe sign glowing red on the corner.

Phil was already climbing out behind her, and Mary stooped to give the girls a hand as they followed. Nathan replaced the grate, and Mary followed Pete's whispered instructions.

"Link arms," she said. "Look like you're out for a stroll. Coming back from a bar or something."

Mary preferred shadows, but most people weren't adept with those, couldn't navigate them the way she did. When EAEA eyes were watching, it was better to look normal. As unsuspicious as people could, when escorted by famous faces.

She'd never *not* had a famous face. She never would, even if she did retire one day. Sometimes the best thing to do was disguise the color of your hair and try to blend in.

In fact, she'd have preferred a crowd. They'd nixed the idea of leaving during the day; crowded streets were unpredictable, always with a chance that someone would recognize her, or Nathan, or El, and shout it out.

Now, though, the sidewalks were *too* quiet. A few people out and about would have hidden their trek.

Mary beckoned Phil to her side, and Nathan fell to the rear. Together, they walked. She tried to look like she was taking in the sights of the historical city at night, like she wanted nothing more than to stroll along slowly. She tried to imagine Phil as her nephew or something. Now he was casting glances at *her* from beneath that swoop of hair.

All she could think was that she wanted to take the person who'd forced these kids into hiding and kick them straight into a jail cell.

One block down. Then two.

She heard them a second before they landed in front of her, the clank of a fire escape ladder shuddering as someone let go.

Several someones, their ugly armbands clear in the wash of the streetlights.

And at the head of the pack—that was what they were like, a pack of souped-up rats—Chloe Pearce stood with her hands on her hips. "Mary O'Sullivan," she said. "How lovely to meet you at last."

NATHAN HADN'T SEEN his sister in months. She looked the same, mostly. Her red hair had been pulled back into a low ponytail, and she wore a uniform now. Black, sleek. Ugly crimson armband proclaiming her hatred. Someone had given the EAEA a tailor's budget, clearly.

The way she'd landed, dropping out of the sky from nowhere, he had a feeling she was hopped up on serum. Great. Despite her direct involvement in Eloise's capture a few months ago, Nathan still had trouble picturing his tidy sister as an on-the-ground kind of operative. And yet here she was.

Before Nathan could register much else, Phil had grabbed one of the girls and twisted away into the void, carrying her back to the safety of the hidden community. Nathan wouldn't have expected the boy to move so quickly, but then, he hadn't stayed hidden for all these months by accident.

Mary stood in front of the remaining two girls, and Nathan kept his position at the rear of the group. No doubt there were more EAEA operatives waiting in the wings. No doubt at all.

Chloe was smiling, smug as anything. As if she'd already won, not only the forthcoming battle—they were standing on the edge of it, the air practically shimmering in expectation—but the war itself.

Not long ago, Chloe had tried to recruit him. He doubted she'd be renewing those overtures.

"Get the serum," Mary said, but Nathan couldn't get anything. He couldn't move. Not when he stood between the two remaining enhanced women and the EAEA operatives; when the operatives attacked, he'd be leaving the women wide open.

Chloe smiled, as if she knew all of that, knew they couldn't retrieve any serum she wore at her belt. And then she and Mary were running toward each other, as if a silent bell had rung in their brains to signal the start of the fight. Instead of landing a punch, Chloe leapt over Mary—confirming his suspicion that she'd already taken a serum, maybe one that gave her jumping powers like Tally's, or super strength—and caught her from behind, pulling her off her feet.

Phil zapped back into the scene, touched a second girl on the shoulder, and was gone.

Mary shifted in midair as Chloe carried her skyward, and Nathan—still protecting their third charge, trying to keep her between him and the shop wall as the other EAEA operatives considered their options—could see in an instant the benefit of training against enhanced humans for so long. Mary swung, using Chloe's shoulders as leverage to push back, separating just long enough to let gravity slam her well-positioned feet into Chloe's stomach.

It all happened in a blink, and then they were falling. Chloe landed on her feet, pavement caving in around her heels, but she dropped to her knees, clutching her gut.

Without the assistance of a serum, Mary tumbled more forcefully to the sidewalk, spine curled, hands lifted to protect her head. Fear lanced between his ribs, but before he could shout, she was already back on her feet and aiming for his sister.

Maybe it was foolishness to think they could one day lead a quieter life. Nathan wasn't even sure what that meant, exactly.

And there certainly wasn't time to contemplate it. As if responding to a second bell, or some kind of silent command, the trio of non-Chloe EAEA agents stalked toward Nathan. The woman looked angry, while her partners projected grim solemnity on one hand and gleefulness on the other.

The gleeful one, Nathan thought, was the one to watch. With his eyebrows raised and his head bobbing, the guy was practically aching for a fight.

"Hey friends," Nathan said, hoping to stall, the last woman still at his back. "Can't we talk this out?"

The angry agent scowled, the solemn one shook his head, and the gleeful one looked a beat away from bouncing on his toes.

Phil returned, and not a moment too soon. He dove for the last girl, zapping her away to safety. And helpfully releasing Nathan from his charge so he could start punching people.

As predicted, Gleeful led the charge toward Nathan, with the others close behind. Nathan made a grab for Gleeful's forearm, hoping to pull him off balance and upset at least one of the other two. But Gleeful wrenched Nathan forward, much stronger than he ought to have been, and slammed his skull into Nathan's.

Fireworks exploded in Nathan's vision, and he stumbled, falling to the pavement as he let go of Gleeful's arm. OK, so these ones were hopped up on serum, too. He probably should've expected that.

Still seeing stars, Nathan rolled to his knees, vertigo threatening to pull him back down again. He could feel Mary and

Chloe still battling it out in the middle of the street, but there wasn't much he could do. About anything.

Strong hands locked around his arms as Solemn and Gleeful flanked him, pulling him to his feet. Angry was pacing toward him, a grimace on her face, and Nathan could see her intention written there, plain as day.

Before she could hit him, he took a page out of Mary's book, using his captors' grip as leverage to swing his legs into her stomach. The operative didn't even stumble, though she did pause.

"I realize this has been pointed out to you in the past," Nathan said, "but for people who claim to hate enhanced abilities, you're incredibly... enhanced."

Phil cracked back onto the sidewalk, and Nathan stifled a groan. The kid was supposed to stay behind after saving the girls, not return to help. And there was a solid reason for that. Phil wavered on his feet, a trickle of blood leaking out of his nose.

On the street, Mary landed an uppercut to Chloe's jaw, jarring her teeth together and knocking her backward. "Phil," she called, breathing hard, "get out of here."

But Nathan could see the truth written across the kid's paper-pale features: he could hardly walk, let alone teleport. He'd carried twice as many people the other day. They hadn't given him enough time to recover.

However, his presence had split the attention of Nathan's captors. The wheels were clearly turning in Angry's mind, but Nathan didn't wait around to see what she was contemplating. Ignoring the spinning in his head as best he could, he let his body go limp. Gleeful had loosened his grip, no doubt considering his options for attacking Phil, and Nathan was able to wrench his arm from the man's grip as he turned his fall into a dive.

The Solemn agent, though, held on tight, leaving Nathan off-balance as he hit the pavement, dragging the agent with him.

Unfortunately, the agent landed on top of him. He was the biggest of the three, and Nathan struggled, anticipating a plate-sized fist slamming into his face in punishment.

But Solemn merely produced handcuffs from his belt. "You've caused enough trouble," he said, his voice gruff. At least someone around here had the presence of mind to keep things professional.

Mary slammed into Solemn from the side, knocking him to the pavement. She was on her feet before he could twitch, running to Nathan. Gleeful came at her with his teeth bared—not so Gleeful now, Nathan supposed—and Mary punched him in the face before turning to help Nathan to his feet. "You really need to stop getting cornered like that."

"Excuse me," Nathan said, "there were three of them. Where's your *one* opponent?"

Mary lifted her chin in the direction of the street, where Chloe was attempting to lift herself to her feet. So far, she'd only managed to crawl. Well, Mary had always wanted to kick Chloe's ass. Now she had.

Mary ran to Phil, who looked like he might empty his stomach at any moment. "Can you walk?"

Phil nodded. And then, with a grimace, he fainted.

Nathan caught the kid and hefted him over a shoulder. "There'll be more. Where do we go?"

Mary pressed her lips into a grim line. "To the tunnels," she said.

"We can't lead them—"

"No," Mary interrupted, casting a significant glance upward. The EAEA could be listening, even now, and they couldn't give away the community's existence. "We head away from the city center until we lose them. But we have to hurry."

Mary led the way along the remainder of the block, looking over her shoulder every few seconds, and Nathan realized that Pete's voice had vanished from his ear. His com unit was still there, but he couldn't hear any of the chatter from HQ. He indicated as much to Mary, who nodded. She stopped at the corner, scanned the area for spying eyes—though surely someone could have been watching from a nearby building, and they'd never have known—then knelt to heft another rectangular manhole cover from the sidewalk.

They'd nearly made it the whole way. That was almost more difficult to stomach than if they'd missed their mark by a mile.

It was a precarious thing, carrying Phil down the service ladder and into the darkness of a new set of tunnels. In this kind of exercise, at least, Nathan had trained for years. Well, he'd trained carrying dummies over a shoulder and running with them. The ladder and the ancient tunnel were a bit beyond the scope of his cadet academy, but his time with LIO was helping to close that gap.

He had to take his time, but finally he made it down the ladder. Mary followed, after closing the lid behind them. She flicked on her flashlight, waited a beat—listening, he assumed, to Pete's instructions—then beckoned him on down the passage.

This tunnel was narrower than the last, and more modern looking, as if someone had once expected it to be used in large numbers. Tiles on the floor, though stained with rust, and a grid of iron beams above gave the place a solid, utilitarian kind of feel.

"How did they know," Mary said, her low voice whispering into the darkness. "How did they know where we'd be?"

Nathan adjusted Phil on his shoulder, double checking that

the kid's chest still rose and fell. "What, the EAEA? I assume they've got patrols all over the place."

"They caught us on our *exact* route, just a block before we reached safety. And it was Chloe who met us. As if she knew you'd be there."

"Chloe's been involved in this for a long time. Longer than we knew the EAEA was even a thing. We were bound to run into her eventually."

Mary was shaking her head, unconvinced. "They've got hundreds of operatives, Nathan. They must. And *she* was the one who met us? Who showed up on the mission where you just happen to be? Something isn't right."

Nathan gripped Phil's legs, his head throbbing. Was Mary suggesting there was a mole among them? If the EAEA had a fake enhanced human hiding with the community, their location would have been raided months ago.

"You can't think it's one of us," Nathan said.

Mary opened her mouth to answer. Before she could speak, an armbanded figure rocketed out of the shadows, slamming her into the wall and sending the flashlight spinning out of her grasp.

The EAEA had followed them into the tunnels.

Two ambushes. It was all Mary could think, as the new batch of EAEA agents did their best to pound her into the walls of the tunnel. The street ambush might have been a coincidence. But this? Hiding in the tunnels? Unless there were far more of them than she realized, they had to have known where the group had been headed.

Had possibly even herded them here.

One of the agents barreled into her in the darkness, slamming her into the wall hard enough to squeeze the air out of her lungs. She narrowly prevented her head from whipping back against the tile as she swung a desperate punch at an attacker she couldn't even see. Her fist sailed through air seconds before the agent crashed back into her, using his whole body to crush her into the wall.

"Which one did you take?" she coughed. "Super strength? I know someone who uses it with a lot more finesse than that."

Based on the shouts and intense shuffling she could hear, Nathan was still battling his opponent. Or opponents. She couldn't see a goddamn thing. She could only hope he was OK, hope she could fight her way to him. And poor Phil.

Instead of answering the question, her attacker simply

growled.

"Now *that* reminds me of Monster," Mary said. "But I don't know how you could be using his powers since he's safely locked away."

Unless HQ was hosting a spy. Of course, who knew what the EAEA labs were cooking up? Lab baked powers were all the rage with them. Maybe someone had figured out the secret to Monster's abilities.

Mary's com crackled in her ear, someone shouting instructions, but she couldn't make out a word through the static. Sabotage hammered in her mind as the EAEA agent hammered her against the wall. Could they see in the dark or something?

Nathan shouted, and she tried to twist out of her captor's grip. Instead, she felt cold metal close around her wrist. Handcuffs.

If she ended up in some unmarked prison, she'd never see daylight again. Not after Eloise and the others had escaped last winter. Travis Bertram's embarrassment over that incident might not have been public, but Mary could imagine it well enough. And she could imagine the security measures he'd have added, the sedatives, torture sessions, and impenetrable doors.

He definitely wouldn't allow any attorneys this time, no matter who'd sent them.

The souped-up agent tried to grab her other hand, but she twisted her arm to dig her nails into his wrist. The agent grunted, but they only pressed harder.

"Get Phil out of here," Mary shouted.

And then the manhole cover above the tunnel shifted with a grinding clank, revealing a sliver of daylight. An orange stick plummeted into the darkness, and Mary squeezed her eyes shut just in time to avoid being blinded by the flare.

Her captor, however, must not have been familiar with the blind-em-and-bind-em technique. Mary cracked her eyes open to a tunnel bathed in neon-orange light. The guy who hulked over her was nearly as tall as Ire, his muscles bulging. No scales, though. Growl aside, he probably wasn't a Monster copy.

And then Ire himself dropped through the manhole, not bothering with the ladder. Mary's strongman was still rubbing his eyes, but he turned his head at the sound of Ire landing on all fours in the tunnel.

A perfect opening. Mary shoved her attacker's shoulders as hard as she could, and the surprise of it allowed her to shift him backward. A minuscule shuffle, but was all the opening she needed. He whipped his head to face her, but it was too late; her knee connected with his groin, and a quick follow-up elbow to the back of the head made him crumple to the ground.

Down but not out, he attempted to roll, but Mary had time now. She withdrew a syringe from her belt and stuck it into his arm.

"I carry serums, too," she said. "Nighty night."

The EAEA strongman passed out.

Mary stood, ready to leap into the rest of the fight even though her head was throbbing from having been tossed back against the wall. But Nathan was helping Ire to cuff three EAEA agents who lay in heaps at his feet. Mary couldn't help picturing him using one of them to knock the other four down, like dominos.

Maybe that wasn't how it had happened, but she figured she might as well picture it that way, anyway.

"Three guys attacked Nathan?" Mary said, stepping over her conquest to help Ire with the zip ties. "I'm a little insulted."

"There were four." Nathan rose, and when he turned, his eyes were dark with fear. "The last one took Phil."

WHEN THE ELEVATOR doors opened back at HQ, Gail was waiting for Eloise in the hall. Her former assistant was still officially the public liaison for LIO, even though the league had mostly gone back underground since the U.S. president's executive order. In truth, Gail had always been... Honestly, she was the person who kept this place running behind the scenes. She tended to coordinate the other team departments, stepping in where she found gaps.

Gail matched Eloise's steps as she headed toward her office, and Eloise didn't mind slowing on her way to pick up the Pearl Knife. If she could have put it off forever, she would have.

"How's the mission going?" Eloise asked. She knew Mary was going to test her escape route tonight, but she hadn't received an update since she'd left the airport.

"There's a problem with the coms," Gail said. "There's some kind of interference. When we can hear them at all, it's choppy. Staticky."

Eloise rounded the corner, forcing herself to keep up a quick pace as she headed for the Knife. Staticky coms? That wasn't the norm. "Well, we are operating in a lot of tunnels," she said. "Maybe it's that."

Or maybe luck just refused to side with them. Gail's phone buzzed, and she punched the speaker so Eloise could listen in as Pete said, "The EAEA followed them into the tunnels. They took the teleporting kid."

Eloise cursed and broke into a run. "Take the portal jammers offline," she said, not waiting for confirmation. She didn't know how Mary's invention worked, but hopefully they could pause it by pressing a button or something.

She flung her office door open and tore across the room, forcing herself not to hesitate when she reached the Pearl Knife's case. The blade vibrated in greeting as she snatched it off the shelf, sending flashes of green countryside and distant hills swirling into her mind. And, even more mysteriously, a yard full of chickens. She shoved the images away, impatient. She didn't have time for cryptic clues today.

"Can you see where they're taking him?" she asked.

Pete hesitated, and she could hear keyboards clacking frantically on the other end of the call. She'd been in there often enough to know he was accessing every traffic and security camera in the vicinity. "Back above ground. They came out a block north from where Mary went in, right outside a bank."

"Handy," Eloise said. Banks tended to have good cameras.

"They're in a white van. Unmarked. No license plates."

Sloppy. Eloise waved Gail toward the door, switched on the com in her ear, and thrust the Knife into the ether, letting go of her control—it had to be done—as she pictured the spot where the escape tunnels connected. She'd helped Pete plot the course herself. She knew the corner.

The Knife cut through the miles that separated Niagara from Philadelphia, and Eloise stepped out of her office and into the middle of the street. A couple on the sidewalk stopped walking to stare at her, but she ignored them and ran north, following Pete's directions. Her com seemed to be working fine, at least for now. Maybe the EAEA had been using some a jammer of some kind. Maybe it was temporary.

They did like temporary solutions.

With the Knife humming in her brain, part of her felt complete again. Had she been overreacting to its complicated history these last few months? Maybe she should have worked harder to understand it, to communicate. But the Knife never made it easy.

After this, she'd try. She'd have to.

The van was parked on the corner. Eloise didn't know how many average people could spot a stakeout position, but this hulking vehicle certainly had to be drawing some eyes. Even now, with the streets quiet, someone would surely notice its presence. The EAEA hadn't even bothered to put fake plumbing logos on the sides or anything. Sure, the group was sanctioned, but there was such a thing as subtlety.

Apparently, they didn't care. Eloise approached the van slowly, keeping an eye out for guards. Either the EAEA was spread thin tonight, or they hadn't bothered—or, she supposed, they'd set another trap—because no one stopped her as she slipped behind the vehicle.

The Pearl Knife made short work of the handle, and Eloise threw the doors open. Yellow-orange light streamed onto the darkened street, and Eloise leapt into the van as a pair of black-clad figures scrambled deeper inside. They both had on black knit caps and dark jackets. It was all she had time to register before her eyes found Phil.

The teleporter lay curled in a ball at their feet, his black hair splashed over his cheek. Eloise couldn't tell if the kid was even conscious.

One of the figures pounded on the front of the cargo area, and the van lurched as the driver stepped on the gas, taking them away from the corner. She braced herself, all too aware of the open doors at her back, the pavement racing beneath her feet.

When the pounding figure turned, Eloise gasped. She couldn't help it. White-blond hair peeked out from under his hat, his blue eyes sharp as icebergs as he stared her down. "Travis Bertram," she said. "I didn't think you'd get your hands dirty like this."

The van turned a corner, and Eloise grabbed the back of the van for purchase, the doors swinging wildly behind her as the driver roared through the streets.

"I'm pretty sure you're driving above the city speed limit," she said.

Travis's face was red, and he knelt in front of Phil as if to shield the kid from Eloise. The movement was almost a protective one, except for the way Travis's eyes gleamed when he looked at the kid. Like he meant to protect a bag of stolen gold, rather than a person.

Travis nodded to his EAEA friend, and the guy charged her, teeth bared. Eloise gripped the top edge of the door and swung her feet inside, kicking her attacker in the chest. "Where do they even find you people?" she asked.

The EAEA agent fell back, and Eloise used her momentum to drop into the van. The driver pulled around a corner, knocking her sideways into the wall. As she pulled herself back up, Travis knelt beside Phil, bracing himself with one hand and shaking the kid as though trying to wake him.

"I need answers," Travis said, teeth gritted. When Phil didn't stir, Travis kicked the kid in the stomach. Eyes still clenched shut, Phil curled in even tighter.

Eloise knew how much damage someone could do working in an office, sending others out to do their dirty work. Creating policies designed to hurt other people, placing their own greed above human decency.

After their experience in the secret prison facility in California, she should have realized that Travis would be willing to throw a punch himself. Or a kick, as the case may be. It was one thing to see him face down a group of enhanced humans; she and her friends, at least, threatened him.

It was another thing entirely to watch him strike an unconscious teenager.

Eloise started forward, but a wave of dizziness sent her spinning back into the side of the van. Shoulder smarting, she forced herself back on her feet as the Knife stuttered in her mind, reaching out beyond her control. Beyond their partnership, such as it was. She grabbed for it, but it was like a balloon string slipping through her fingers as the Pearl Knife seized control.

One moment, Travis was kneeling beside Phil, a hand on his arm—the poor kid was cringing in his sleep—and a syringe gripped in his fist. Eloise's stomach jerked as both of them zipped out of sight.

A blink, and they whirled back into the van, reappearing in midair and rocketing toward the ceiling. Travis's head slammed against the roof of the van, his body cushioning Phil's from injury. Then the two of them fell toward the floor before zipping back up again, falling back and forth through space.

The Knife was controlling Phil's powers. Without Eloise's go-ahead. She could feel each lurching squeeze of the teleporting in her stomach, but she had no control whatsoever. She gripped the hilt of the blade, as though her fingers could squeeze it into submission. *Stop it*, she thought. *You're hurting both of them.*

The air hardened around the Knife, loosening her fingers and pushing her hand away from the hilt. Like it had formed some a shield around itself. Eloise fought back, not so much because physical contact had ever increased her control, but out of pure panic. How was it *doing* this?

Travis's EAEA partner watched the scene from the back of the van, eyes darting back and forth as if he had no idea how he was meant to intervene in something like this. Blood poured out of the Phil's nostrils as she begged the Knife to stop, blue veins showing through his increasingly papery skin. The amount of energy the Knife was stealing... it could kill him.

Eloise started forward, trying to get to Phil, to pull him away from Travis. The van swerved, and she fought the motion, reaching for the kid.

A shield of energy blasted her backwards, and her fingertips caught the end of the doors, feet nearly slipping out of the van.

What the hell was that?

The Knife didn't answer.

The van lurched to a stop, sending Eloise tumbling forward. The endless circle of throwing Phil and Travis around the van ceased, too, as Tally appeared at the back doors.

"Hey," she said. "Thought you could use an assist."

The Knife reached for Tally's abilities, sending tendrils of control out into the atmosphere, but Eloise gripped its power in her mind, locking it into a vise. This time, the blade yielded, allowing her to wrap her fingers around the hilt. It seemed almost... surprised. Like it had woken from a dream.

With muscles trembling and pain squeezing through her chest, Eloise knelt beside Travis to make sure he was breathing. He'd have a hell of a headache in the morning, and no small amount of bruises, but he should be all right.

She should have known this would happen. She *had* known, but she'd told herself a different story. Let herself believe the Knife would behave, would act like the partner she needed it to be.

With a heavy feeling in her stomach, she nodded to Tally, who must have incapacitated the driver before intervening with Travis. Thank goodness she had. "Get the kid out of here. I'll catch up."

Tally swept Phil out of the van and leapt away. Afraid to use the Knife to portal—afraid to use it for anything—Eloise fled on foot.

WITH HER COM still fizzling in her ear, Mary managed to get close enough to the surface to send Pete a regular old-fashioned text message, and to learn that El and Tally had been able to secure Phil. They were headed back to the hideout, and Mary, Nathan, and Ire were cleared to do the same.

And yet... and yet, Mary hesitated. There really was no way to know how many more EAEA operatives might be tracking them, and an uncomfortable itch at the back of her neck told her there was more going on here than just superior numbers of EAEA agents. Though, to be fair, there was that, too.

Mary hopped down from the ladder, feet scraping against the stone. She'd have to look up the origins of this tunnel system later. Or, more accurately, ask someone on the team who got excited about research to look it up.

She joined the men where they were hanging out against the far wall, patting Ire on the shoulder. "Thanks for the save, by the way," she said. "How'd you get here so fast?"

Ire grunted, but he smiled. A little. "I'm only slow compared to Steve Taylor. But don't tell him I said so."

Mary smiled back, even though her whole body hurt after

the marathon fight. Her neck twinged painfully from the multiple hits, like whiplash. She'd probably need to get that checked out. But smiles from Ire were rare enough to merit encouragement, under any circumstances. "I wouldn't dare."

"What do we do, leave these packages for the EAEA to find?" Nathan asked, tipping his chin toward the trussed-up agents who were still passed out against the wall.

Ire nodded. "That's the protocol."

Unless they were in Canada, in which case it was marginally more satisfying to drag them off for a lecture at the embassy. Either way, these people deserved a lot more than slapped wrists and instructions to be quieter next time.

"We should be locking them up," Mary said.

She half expected Nathan to be the one to protest. Instead, it was Ire who said, "That's exactly what they're hoping we'll do. As far as nations like Canada are concerned, we haven't done anything wrong. Except fail to cooperate with a new, prejudiced policy. Handling our own retirees is one thing, but if we start capturing EAEA agents and throwing them in jail cells? The rest of the world will reevaluate. They'll have to."

He was right. Of course he was right. She didn't have to like it, but there it was.

Nathan motioned toward the ladder, clearly ready to ascend back to the surface world. "We should get out of here in case backup comes."

Mary swallowed. She wanted nothing more than to get to a place where she could lie down. Preferably for a good long while. "I don't think we should go to the hideout right now."

The men stared at her. She cleared her throat. "We're free to go, according to Pete. But I think there's a spy among us. We were ambushed twice tonight. How else could they have known where we were going to be?"

"If that's the case, then they already know where the hideout is," Nathan said.

Mary shook her head. "Phil teleported us out each time. I didn't know where we were in the city until we planned today's route. None of us did."

Nathan shifted his feet, glancing around as though the spy might suddenly leap out and announce their presence. "What should we do, then?"

"We find a machine room or something and hole up there for a while. Wait until Phil feels well enough to come get us."

Poor kid. Even without Travis Bertram's inhumane interview tactics, Phil had needed to sleep most of a day before he'd been well enough to go on today's mission. And Mary was pretty sure the kid hadn't been at full capacity when they'd started out of the tunnels tonight.

Still, maybe Phil could heal enough in a few hours to bring a couple of people back to the hideout.

Mary's flashlight was history after the fight down here, but Ire had brought a new one. They walked the tunnels in silence for half an hour, maybe more, taking several random turns that Ire noted on a pad, ignoring Mary's impatience while he carefully charted their turns. Apparently, he kept the pad in his pocket at all times; the paper was wavy, as though it had been waterlogged and dried out, and he wrote with a miniature pen that looked like a toy in his huge hands.

Mary couldn't help wondering if he always wrote mission-specific notes on his pads, or if he used them for something else. For some reason, she pictured him penning lines of poetry, which made her think about Nathan's question. What would Ire do, if he had the option to retire?

With her sore neck and her banged-up head, she should probably be thinking about her own answer to the question instead of distracting herself with musings about her colleagues. But the truth was, she'd never really thought about Ire might want. What he might do, if he could blend back into the world.

After a while, they reached an unlocked door in the wall. There was no indication of what the place might once have been—an office, maybe, or a machine room. It was empty now. Nothing but cobwebs.

Mary ducked inside, collapsing gratefully against the far wall, where Nathan joined her. "Doing OK?" he asked.

"Just got my head slammed a few times."

Nathan peered into her eyes, which might have been romantic except that he appeared to be checking for a concussion. "Should probably stay awake a while, just in case."

Mary groaned. "And they say playing football is dangerous."

Nathan draped an arm around her shoulder. "I don't think independent operative-ing counts as a sport. And that would be American football, sweetie. Real football players rarely feel the need to bash one another over the head."

"Call me sweetie again, and I'll wrench your arm out of its socket."

"So loving. So kind."

Ire, who'd settled against the wall in the far corner, cracked his eyes open. "Please don't forget I'm here."

"Wouldn't dream of it," Nathan said.

Either satisfied or accepting his fate, Ire closed his eyes again.

Mary let her head drop back against Nathan's arm, let herself sink into the comfort of his presence for a moment. He was still fresh air in the midst of stale tunnels, pine and cedar and mountain air. She didn't see how it was possible.

"What are we dealing with here?" she heard herself say, though she hadn't quite planned to speak. "How is the EAEA getting all these different powers, so quickly? You don't think Agnes could be helping them."

"With her moral center? I doubt it. And they'd certainly consider her to be a threat."

Mary didn't think the EAEA would hesitate to partner with a powerful enhanced human who saw things their way. Hypocrisy was practically a part of their mission statement. But Agnes was nothing if not ethical. Wherever she was, she'd be objecting to this treatment of enhanced humans, too.

Mary missed her friend. But she also hoped that Agnes was far, far away. That Wave was keeping her safe.

"If there really is a spy," Mary said, "then the EAEA will be inside HQ soon enough."

"But if there's a spy, why does the EAEA keep looking for entrances to HQ? They'd already know how to get in."

That was... a good point. "I don't know. But I don't know how to stop them, either. Not with the weight of the president behind them."

Nathan squeezed her shoulders. "We've got this. The league is strong."

She knew he wasn't attempting to comfort her with empty words, that his faith in LIO was unshakable. She didn't understand how it could be, after everything that had happened. Yes, they'd made strides. Thanks to his presence, and El's leadership. But their numbers were still fractured, the recruits largely untested. And now, it was possible that they'd been infiltrated.

"I'm not sure we're strong enough," Mary said softly. "I think we're hanging on by a thread."

And so were the enhanced humans in this country. She'd never imagined there to be so many, though it was true that Agnes had always said there had to be more than anyone realized. Over a hundred people were packed together here in Philadelphia, hiding. Frightened.

How many across the country had put their names on Travis's horrible registry? How many more were huddling in pockets like this one, scared and alone? Maybe hoping that LIO would swoop in and save them? How many of them faced far worse circumstances?

Muscles screaming at her to sleep, Mary forced herself out of Nathan's embrace and onto her feet. "I need to go back to HQ."

He gazed up at her, concern obvious in his gray eyes. "They *can* protect themselves. They really can."

For a second, Mary thought he meant the enhanced humans. But he had to be talking about HQ, about the team and everyone there. And she did want to keep them safe, to do everything she could to protect them. But they knew how to stay hidden.

Mary ran a quick inventory on her tools, making sure everything was back in its proper slot on her belt. "It's not that. I need to talk to Pete. See if he can help me figure out a way to find more communities like this. People who are in hiding."

Nathan nodded. And then he stood. "All right. I'll come with you."

She loved him for not telling her she needed to rest—though surely he'd have been right—or for questioning the idea. She loved that he trusted her.

She placed her hands on his shoulders. "They need you here. El needs an unenhanced operative to help. If there's a way to get these people out, they need everyone on it."

Nathan pulled her into a kiss, enveloping her in pine and cedar, with a hint of mint. She tugged him in closer, hating to leave him, hating the constant goodbyes. But she couldn't protect everyone at once, and he had El and Ire to look out for him.

"Still here," Ire grumbled from the corner.

Mary drew back reluctantly, and Nathan cleared his throat before saying, "And the EAEA perimeter?"

Mary patted him on the arm before bending to pick up her tool belt. "If they think a few sad checkpoints can stop me from going wherever the hell I want to go, they're sorely mistaken."

It took over two hours to reach D.C. from Philadelphia, and that was with Travis urging the driver to ignore the speed limits. If they got pulled over, he'd deal with it. In fact, if they got pulled over, the cop would be pretty damn sorry.

Travis's whole head was throbbing from the way the Eloise Reyna had bashed him against the inside of the van, throwing him around like a doll. He'd been completely helpless, unable to resist the woman's power.

It was insulting, a woman like that controlling him. Making him out to be a fool.

Dead of night or not, Travis burst into his office building and ignored the questions from the slow-moving guard. He pushed past the metal detectors—they knew who he was, the idiots—and staggered up to his office.

No more basement hovels for Travis Bertram. He was upstairs now, mere steps away from Senator Jones and anyone else who might need his expertise at a moment's notice. His new situation included relatively new carpeting—not brand new for him, though perhaps to the previous occupant—plus fresh paint, an upgraded computer, and, best of all, an assistant. Who spent a lot of his day on social media, supposedly scanning for LIO sightings, though Travis knew he also used the time to post about his side job. Vic made colorable postcards, or something like that.

But incompetent or not, an assistant was a 'thank you.' It was an indication that Senator Jones valued Travis's work.

Travis didn't have a first aid kit in his own office, so he started ripping Vic's drawers open, hands shaking as he rifled through stacks of papers. Vic definitely seemed like the kind of person who would keep a first aid kit. Maybe a deluxe one.

Finally, he found it in the bottom drawer. It was purple and coated in glitter, because *that* was a refined choice for a job in Washington. Travis ripped the box open, grabbing a packet of ibuprofen and swallowing it dry before taking a fistful of bandages into his office.

He dropped into his desk chair and pulled up his web cam to use as a mirror.

And to wait. Because Chloe Pearce owed him a call, and she'd better have something good to tell him.

Bandages applied to the scrapes on his neck—no worse than cat scratches, he'd been lucky—Travis sat back, trying to calm himself. He needed to be calm. It would help if he had a nice landscape on the wall, something soothing to look at, but his request for artwork hadn't been fulfilled yet. He'd need to yell at someone about that; he'd asked them to choose pieces out of the library weeks ago, and he was tired of staring at blank walls. It wasn't right. It wasn't *fair*.

When Chloe's call came through on the computer without video, Travis grimaced. That could only mean one thing.

"How badly did they beat you?" he asked.

Chloe, who was surely hiding cuts and bruises—not to mention the absence of LIO operatives in cuffs—took a beat before answering. "We made progress."

"But LIO slipped away," Travis said.

Chloe pressed her lips together. "Did *you* get the teleporter's blood?"

Travis gripped the desk, taking a deep breath to calm himself before replying. Sometimes the silence spoke volumes. He liked to keep the yelling to a minimum. For one thing, it ensured that people listened when he did yell. For another, his face tended to turn an awful red when he raised his voice, which rather undermined the action. So even though Chloe couldn't see him, he gave himself a moment.

"No," he said finally. "The Pearl Knife intercepted me."

Chloe should have enough sense not to rub it in. Travis wasn't a trained fighter. He shouldn't have even been there today, except that these people were so slow, so incompetent, that they needed onsite supervision.

But they also needed the teleporter's blood, if they wanted to replicate his powers. It was that simple.

Travis opened his mouth to speak, but Chloe beat him to it. "There were others with them," she said.

"What, that reporter? She's a nuisance."

"No." She never said sir, which was annoying, though Travis supposed he couldn't require it since he wasn't technically a military commander. "Three young women. We think the league was trying to move them out of hiding."

Travis's lip stung, the medicine taking its time in dulling the pain. He wondered if he should go to the hospital. But that would mean filing a report. Explaining why he'd gone to Philadelphia in person. "Hiding. Like the flower shop family. I thought they were an anomaly."

They'd been getting plenty of registrations, after all. And with no sense of how many enhanced humans might be in the country, Travis had felt relatively secure about the percentages of people who were signing up. You couldn't usually look at a person and tell they had abilities. Plant freaks aside.

"So did we," Chloe said.

"Can you track them back to the hiding spot?"

A beat. "No. Mary O'Sullivan didn't return there. We tried to find her in the tunnels, but the abilities wore off and we haven't had time to make more serum. We only just obtained the reporter's blood, and her abilities are... more finicky than the others. They require the same person to take the serum again."

"Let me guess. You didn't consider giving it to more than one person."

"We can't double up the serums like that. We might kill our own guys that way."

Travis rubbed a hand over his face. Patience. He needed to show patience. And feel it, too. If he'd learned anything, it was that patience brewed rewards. It just took time.

He stared at the blank wall before him. Never mind the landscapes. A portrait would be good there, a large one. Yes, a portrait of a powerful man, someone whose name might not be common knowledge, but whose actions had reverberated through history. Yes. He'd write to the archives tomorrow and amend his request.

"Make more serum," he said. "Find where they went. And get that teleporter's blood."

THE RESTAURANT DIDN'T DELIVER breakfast—Ben discussed half-cooled eggs with the kind of horror that others might use to describe a car accident—so Steve often found himself helping in the kitchen at opening time. He stood beside the stove, chopping and sautéing onions, which was about all Ben would agree to trust him with.

"I don't want you rushing through that," Ben said, catching Steve in an attempt to match his friend's speed with the chef's knife. Apparently he didn't even quite trust Steve with this task. "There's some things you can't hurry."

"Like chopping onions. Sure."

Ben waved a spoon at him, sending bits of yellow sauce splattering across the wall. "Like making the perfect quiche." He grabbed a kitchen towel out of his apron pocket and wiped up the mess. "So tell me again why you're still here instead of going to work for that hawk lady?"

Hawk lady. That was a good description of the Wave woman who'd come around trying to recruit him.

Steve gave Ben a sidelong glance. "How'd you know what she wanted?"

"A mysterious woman showed up asking for my friend, who just happens to have kickass enhanced abilities and hasn't been doing anything to hide them. I guessed. And you just confirmed."

Steve rolled his eyes. He'd have told his friend about Fran's visit, eventually. He was just still trying to figure it out himself. Wave, an organization his father had battled for years, which Steve himself had been raised to consider as a mortal enemy, now wanted to hire him.

The abilities game was always strange. But for some reason, this one really had him stumped.

"I'm not sure I want to be in that world at all," Steve said. "That's the whole problem."

"Do not stop stirring those onions. If they burn, you're doing this again." Ben stared at him until he complied, then nodded and returned to his own bowl. "What is it that you want, then?"

The image of beautiful brown eyes crowded into his head, completely uninvited, along with the smell of lavender. The cadence of a voice, low and musical. The glow of a blade that shone like the moon.

Steve stirred the onions too hard, sending half of them spilling out of the pan and all over the stove. And all over the hand that had been keeping the pan steady. He cursed, wiping his stinging hand on his apron.

"Ah," Ben said. "Love. Got it."

"Because only love could make someone spill onions?"

"For everyone? Obviously not. For you? It's surely on the list." He sprinkled some cheese into the bowl. "Also, you were pretty hopeful the other night when you thought your visitor might've been someone called Eloise."

"It's not like you've never heard of her. She's the Pearl Knife."

Ben shrugged. "I don't like to assume. So, what's the problem? You can't go get her?"

He could not. She'd rejected him. After returning his kiss, yes, but there couldn't be more between them than mutual attraction, or she wouldn't have sent him away.

Steve gave his hand a shake, though the pain was fading quickly enough. That was obviously clouded-mind thinking, and not at all fair to El. He hadn't given her a lot of choice, really. Not when he couldn't decide whether to stick with the league. She had a job to do, and a big one at that.

Still. It felt like rejection.

"Onions," Ben said, and Steve dutifully presented his frying pan so Ben could scrape the onions into his bowl.

"I'm tired of the secrets," Steve said.

Ben snorted. "Isn't that the whole deal with a superhero league, friend?"

Maybe it was. "Why does it have to be secrets or nothing? Wave is even more covert than LIO."

"Out of necessity though, yeah? You say they're all right, that LIO framed them as villains a long way back, and I believe you. But the world doesn't know that. And if their people've got powers, the U.S. is chasing after them, too."

True. That was all true. Maybe Steve could talk with Fran again. Maybe, if America could get its act together about enhanced humans—and keep from dragging the rest of the world into the pit—then Wave would be willing to go public one day.

But LIO and Wave would never see eye to eye. The meeting on that crumbling airfield, when they'd been facing nothing less than an alien invasion, had proven that.

If Steve chose Wave, Eloise would never forgive him. He'd been there for her blowup with Agnes—multiple blowups, if you counted the airfield meeting and the Vegas altercation last winter. Wave and LIO would never work together. He didn't know if she'd ever forgive him, anyway, but if he chose Wave, then he'd definitely be closing that door. Possibly forever.

Steve returned to his cutting board and selected a fresh onion. "I just want to serve food," he said.

The big decisions? Those could wait for another day.

For Mary by herself, sneaking out of Philadelphia was child's play. Without untrained civilians to protect, it felt like a puzzle. It would've been a treat, even, had the stakes been less sobering. The shadows had always been her allies.

She'd made it back to HQ without incident, and she'd even tried to sleep. But Eloise had called with her mind-churning update about the Knife's rogue behavior—not that Mary objected to knocking Travis Bertram around a bit; it was the principle of the thing—and Mary couldn't even begin to unpick what it might mean. El had come and gone via helicopter while Mary was still on the road. She'd deposited the Knife in some secret spot at HQ, only to take off again.

Mary couldn't help worrying about El. All the back and forth with that Knife. It was enough to give Mary a headache, and she wasn't telepathically linked to the damn thing. At least Nathan and Ire had made their way back to the main hideout. They'd help Eloise out.

Mary had work to do.

But even HQ felt... uneasy. Like everyone she passed could be a spy. Maybe it was the lack of sleep making her suspect everyone. Or the whack on the head.

Or maybe there really was a mole on the inside.

At Mary's request, Pete had once again set up a satellite surveillance station in Eloise's office. He and Gail had done something similar when the Pearl Knife had been missing, and she hadn't wanted the entire team to know what they were doing. So Pete arranged a couple of workstations on the guest-side of Eloise's desk, while Mary turned the wall-sized video screen into a map of the United States.

Contrary to her request, however, Pete had also let one of the recruits tag along. According to Pete, Rajni—whose abilities let her control water—showed a strong interest in the surveillance aspect of the job and could help them brainstorm ways to find hidden communities of enhanced people.

Rajni was currently sitting in one of El's guest chairs with a laptop, making a list of documented enhanced human arrests and representing them on the map with yellow pins. Rajni's family was Indian, though she'd been born here in Canada herself. She wore her black hair in a long braid down her back, small gold hoops shining in her ears.

Mary hadn't wanted anyone in the room who might inform the EAEA of hidden pockets of enhanced humans in the country. But Pete had insisted, and Mary hadn't wanted to reveal her suspicions of a spy in their midst.

Fine. If this information leaked, at least that would narrow the pool. She had to protect HQ, at all costs.

Mary stood behind Pete, barely keeping herself from pacing while he squinted at his own screen. Most of her interactions with the man were limited to information delivered via a crackling voice in her ear. He wore black-framed glasses, the light of the screen shining blue in the lenses, and his dark hair had been gelled into submission on top of his head.

"I'm looking for strange phenomena," he said, and Mary

startled, her body too primed to leap into action. She was low on sleep again. She didn't care.

Pete gave her a sidelong glance, eyebrows raised, and she dropped into a chair beside him, trying to relax. Or at least to look more casual. "Like unexplained plant growth?" she asked.

"Sure. Though that kind of thing doesn't tend to make the evening news."

"What does?"

He pointed to the screen. "Here. Holyoke, Massachusetts. A grocery store was robbed overnight, but no money was taken. Only food. The silent alarms summoned the cops, and the responding officer here claims that the thief escaped by flying away."

Mary leaned over his shoulder, the words of the police officer's report blurring together. Pete dropped a red pin on the video-screen map, the animation dropping out of the sky and bouncing once before sticking.

"OK," Mary said. "How did you come up with that?"

"Most of the police reports in the country copy to us. I'm just running keyword searches. This one was easy. This officer says it outright, that the intruder was clearly enhanced. We'll have to brainstorm more keywords."

"We can do that."

Pete swiveled his chair around, turning to face her directly. "It's a big job. Police reports are just a start. We might want to bring more people in."

He'd run last night's operations from behind the scenes, and spent Mary's travel time back setting up this workspace. It was getting toward noon, and she was pretty sure the guy hadn't slept. He had to be exhausted.

Still, the idea of more people made her stomach clench. "Gail?"

"Maybe, but I think she's on a project, and she's not on the surveillance team."

"She's always happy to help."

"She always *agrees* to help. Not the same thing."

Mary sat back in her chair and crossed her legs, tapping her fingers together in front of her. She knew everyone on the team, but she worked closest with the engineers. Luke might be willing to help out, if she asked, but he was busy keeping the portal jammer online so that Dolly couldn't sweep into HQ whenever she felt like it.

Pete had gone back to scanning and clicking, with occasional pauses to type.

"Who on the surveillance team do you know particularly well?" she asked.

"I know all of them. I hired them."

"I thought Eloise hired them."

Pete stopped typing and looked up from the screen. "I advised her."

"On her request?"

He narrowed his eyes. "Obviously. What's this about?"

Mary could practically hear the follow-up question in his tone. *Do you not trust us?* And here she'd thought she was being so subtle. She glanced at Rajni before replying. "I feel like maybe there's a reason Eloise didn't tell everyone when the Pearl Knife went missing. She just can't admit it to herself."

"That," Pete said, "was a tactical decision based on a desire to avoid causing a panic."

Mary caught a glitter from across the room, and her eyes were drawn to where the Pearl Knife usually sat in its case. Mary wasn't sure where Eloise might have stashed it, or what spot at HQ could be more secure than this office, but when it came to the Knife, El knew best. Mostly.

The Pearl Knife was a central representation of the

league's power. But it certainly wasn't the only one. Yes, Eloise had wanted to avoid what might have been a devastating blow to morale when the Knife had gone missing. But maybe she'd also been afraid of something else. Something more insidious.

Pete pushed his chair back from the desk, clearly interpreting her hesitation as an insult. "That was *leadership*. But you're trying to accuse the team of what, sabotage? We live here. We support your work. We work our asses off for you."

Mary held up her hands, trying to radiate a calm she didn't feel. Not her specialty. El was the one who excelled at conversations like this, at diplomacy. Why had Mary thought she could handle it? "I'm not accusing anyone of anything. I'm just trying to figure out what's going on. Why our missions keep getting compromised."

He held up a pair of shaking fingers. "Twice. You were intercepted twice, and it happened in an EAEA stronghold city."

"Three times." It was impossible to keep the heat out of her voice now. She only hoped it sounded like anger, rather than fear. "First the flower shop, then two ambushes last night."

"My point stands." His nostrils flared, cheeks flushing red. "Your missions went wrong, and your first thought was 'hey, maybe the team is reporting to the EAEA.'"

Not her first thought. Not exactly her first thought, anyway. "That's not what I'm—"

Pete stood up. "It's exactly what you're saying."

Was he seriously going to leave? Refuse to help her find people in danger? Well, fine. Mary had run plenty of surveillance on her own, from her basement apartment in Malibu. And from Aries, too. She'd avoided setting up an iteration of the System, still too hurt by its destruction to face a new version, but she could do it.

She stood to face Pete, ready to kick him out before he left on his own.

"Oh, look, there was an arrest two weeks ago in Niagara Falls." Rajni's voice was practically a quiver, and Mary whipped her head around to look at the recruit. She'd completely forgotten the woman was here. Rajni licked her lips, plainly trying to distract them from their argument. "On the U.S. side, of course. Not Canadian. The Canadians won't allow it. Because it was an enhanced person. Did I say that already?"

She was rambling, but she'd snapped Mary out of her rage. Mary shook her head, made herself unclench her fists and address Pete with a calm tone. Or calmer, anyway. "I don't think you're reporting to the EAEA."

Mary might be trying to breathe her anger away, but Rajni's interruption hadn't stopped Pete from glaring daggers at her. "Oh, really? Because it sounds like that's precisely what you think."

Rajni hit a button, presumably to drop another yellow pin on the map. "I'm from Niagara Falls," she said. "Canadian side, though. Born and raised. So much water to work with here."

That seemed to catch Pete's attention. He stared at Rajni for a moment, lips parted. His anger seemed to be draining away, and Mary practically held her breath hoping for it, but ready for him to round on her again.

If Nathan were here, he could have probed with more subtlety. Or even asked Pete directly for help in rooting out a traitor. Probably over a beer or something. El would have had a frank conversation with him. Even Ire would have handled the situation with more grace. Probably.

Mary had never been good at this sort of thing.

Pete sat back down at his own screen and dropped a green pin into Niagara Falls. "Might as well track the origins of the enhanced humans we know. Ire's deal was what, Nevada or something?"

He was obviously making an effort to get back to the task at hand. Mary nodded. "It'll be in his file. Maybe make him light green or something, though, since we know his powers came from a chemical weapons malfunction." She turned to look at Rajni, whose brown skin was flushed with apparent relief. "Do you know where your powers came from?"

Rajni gave her braid a brief tug before tossing it back over her shoulder. "No idea."

Pete nodded slowly. "Light green for human-caused abilities. Dark green for unknown. We can get years down, too, where we know them. Try to find a correlation. This feels like a separate project, though."

"Or maybe there are hotspots," Rajni said, talking fast now. Excited. "Places where more people get powers. Then we'd be able to check those spots for hidden enhanced communities."

Pete was already typing, pulling up files for all the enhanced humans they knew. He'd been right to include Rajni in this. She did have good ideas.

And it did seem like Mary could trust them to handle this. That Pete and Rajni—and some of the other team members, maybe—would help her find more enhanced humans in trouble. More people they could save.

The problem was, there wasn't enough data. She already knew that. The retiree files certainly had gaps, and while Nathan might be able to fill them in on some of the Wave operatives whose convictions Dolly had manufactured, Mary doubted that Dolly had made sure their files were accurate when she'd had them arrested. If they had files at all.

They needed more information. Someone who knew more about enhanced abilities and their origins. Mary's first thought was to reach out to Agnes, but after the disastrous meeting between Wave and LIO a few months back, she didn't know if her friend would respond.

Or whether they were still friends at all.

She had no idea what it would take for Wave and LIO to work together, but if it wasn't aliens, she doubted it would be this.

Mary headed for the door. Pete and Rajni had more than enough on their plates. If they needed more data, she'd have to get it. "Keep doing what you're doing. But first, get some rest."

"Where are you going?" Pete asked.

Mary turned back to face him. Maybe a show of trust would help patch things up between them. "There's someone else at HQ who spent her life in an enhanced abilities lab."

Pete actually took his glasses off. "Oh, no," he said. "This is not a good idea."

Rajni looked back and forth between them, like she was trying to watch a game of tennis but had lost track of the ball. "What?" she asked. "Who?"

Mary opened the door. "I need to talk to Jenna Carpenter."

Dolly had always felt that it was best to pursue a goal through the path of least resistance, when possible. So when aiming to find the power-erasing serum for Sever, the best place to start—according to her vast experience in such matters—would be with scientists.

Unarmed, unprepared scientists.

The California Laboratory for Enhanced Abilities Research was located in the center of Santa Monica, not far from the Boulevard. Her daughter had faced Wave operatives here, not so long ago. Eloise had lost Agnes Jenson here, too. And had yet to recover her.

That day, they'd all learned that Wave was still working behind the scenes. Dolly included. No one had been more surprised than she to find that her efforts of weeding out that chaff had been in vain.

Her life's work, in some ways. Though it had seemed much more tragic when she'd thought every breath might be her last, because of the Knife.

On to better things, now. She'd scanned through the last month of the lab's security footage, watching their comings and goings, their little routines. Monday bagels, Thursday staff meetings. The interns who showed up on Saturdays to do extra work. The bosses who snuck out early.

And the one scientist on the second floor who stayed late every single night. Even on Fridays, when the others cleaned up and cleared out, she remained. Sampling. Testing. Mixing. Whatever it was these people did.

There was no need to shoot out any cameras when they arrived at the box of a lab building after dusk, a few stars pecking their way through the blue-toned sky and L.A.'s light pollution as Ranger took care of the lab's outside eyes, calling in mice and squirrels to chew at the cords until they snapped.

But there were hundreds of cameras, and it was unlikely that even Ranger's minions would be able to fry them all. So now, as they stood inside the hallway—wide and blandly institutional, with glossy yellow walls and buzzing fluorescent lighting—Carlisle called in the fog.

He stood by the doors, eyes closed, breathing in through his nose. Some kind of meditation, and Dolly knew better than to try and hurry him along. That would only result in a pouty lecture about how controlling the weather took time, especially indoors, followed by an even longer delay.

They waited a beat, another. Ranger muttered under his breath.

When the fog rolled in, it was as if a cloud had descended on the lab in full force. It rushed in through the open door at their backs, through vents and windows, until it completely obscured the hallway. Dolly couldn't see three feet in front of her.

And neither could the cameras. When the authorities reviewed the tapes later, they'd know they were dealing with someone enhanced. They just wouldn't know who.

Even in the gloom, Dolly found the scientist's work station easily enough. The woman was clattering around, perhaps trying to put her things away, and whispering to herself that those clowns down in atmospheric affairs had really done it this time.

When Dolly stepped into her line of sight, she actually screamed.

Dolly held up a hand, placating, and the woman stopped. "You scared me," she said, accusing. "Who are you?"

"Tell me where to find the serum that erases enhanced abilities," Dolly said. "That's all we want."

The scientist was older than Dolly had expected her to be, with thick streaks of gray running through her brown hair. Her workstation was neat and tidy, with a couple of hot pink post-it notes lined up along the edge of the counter. Dolly couldn't help wondering what enhanced-ability projects the government was allowing them to work on at the moment. It was a wonder this place hadn't been shut down yet.

In the background, mice clattered against the sides of their cages. It sounded like they were throwing themselves against the bars.

The scientist shook her head, even as Dolly backed her up against her lab table. "We don't have that stuff." There was a panicked edge to her voice, a trill at the edges. "It's incredibly restricted."

"Can you make it?"

The scientist shook her head so hard that Dolly was sure she'd make herself dizzy. "Of course not. We'd be shut down if we tried. We've lost half our funding as is."

Ranger's silhouette appeared through the fog. "The mice are distressed."

"Of course they're distressed," Carlisle said, his voice eerily calm. Probably he was concentrating heavily to keep the fog in the room. "They're test subjects."

"They would like me to let them go," Ranger said.

Dolly waved him an acknowledgment, and the scientist actually bristled in protest. "We've been working with some of those animals for months! You can't just..."

"We can," Dolly said as Ranger unlocked the cages. She couldn't see him, or the mice; she could only hear them skittering away. And only that, she suspected, because they went in such large numbers.

Sever wasn't going to be pleased at their failure to obtain the power-erasing serum. But Sever also seemed like the kind of man—if she could call him a man at all—who understood that missions like this were often more complicated than they seemed at first.

At least, she hoped that was true.

Dolly stepped toward the scientist, who cowered back against the table, bracing her hands behind her. "Who does have the serum?" she asked. "Where can I find it?"

The scientist licked her lips. "Well, Wave has it. Wave developed it."

"Mange developed it, but all right."

"He developed it for Wave."

Dolly blinked at her. "For someone in such a precarious position, you're awfully eager to correct me."

The scientist licked her lips again. "LIO has it," she said. "And the EAEA. Probably the military, I guess. But as far as I know, that's it. Like I said. It's restricted."

So much for the path of least resistance. Anyone one of those organizations would be ready for an attack, and prepared to execute good defenses.

If Diana were here, things might be different. The Trap's powers, her tactical skills, would be invaluable. Her rage, too; Diana had always been able to channel her fury into action. Dolly would not have complained about Monster's bulk on her side, either.

"We need to go," she said. "Sever will be waiting."

The scientist blinked at her. "S-Sever?"

The woman really needed to learn to keep her thoughts to herself.

"We must take her." Carlisle spoke so little when he wasn't working weather. Then all of a sudden, he became the wise man on the hill, all musical tones. It was irritating, really. "Otherwise, she'll report this."

Ranger returned to the circle, smelling of sawdust. "They'll notice she's missing." He dropped a handful of mouse food into his mouth and crunched. "Probably."

Disgusting, but logical. "But they won't know who's behind it," Dolly said. "Do we need to knock you out, or will you come with us quietly?"

The scientist screamed.

Dolly sighed. They really never made it easy.

From behind, Ranger stuck a needle into the woman's arm, catching her as she slumped back against the table. He swung her over his shoulder without being asked. Probably still on a high from freeing those mice.

"Let's go," Dolly said. "Time to report back to Sever."

And hope his disappointment wouldn't turn deadly.

TRY AS SHE MIGHT, Eloise couldn't get much of a sense of how the tunnels around the hidden community fit together. Some of them seemed to have been originally meant for pedestrian traffic, with glazed tiles shining on the walls, while others were forged out of concrete. Frequently, she'd pass a bricked-up arch or a patch of roughly stacked stone.

It was as if the city's entire history were wrapped into this underground network, the years retiring one passageway to make room for others, the advent of motor vehicles making old canals and waterways obsolete.

But frayed as they were, the roots remained.

As she patrolled the area with Nathan and Ire, scoping out the usual perimeter—such as it was, when they had to patch a route together underground—while Quin and Tally watched over the community, Eloise couldn't help imagining being stuck down here for three months.

She didn't want to bear the thought of it.

"Maybe we can try moving a single person," she said, stepping around a half-exposed pipe in the floor. "Maybe we could test a route that way."

"Would be helpful if their abilities included invisibility," Nathan said.

Yes. Yes, it truly would. Unfortunately, she didn't think anyone in the community had that power.

Anyone who'd had it was probably long gone. They could cross a border as easily as Steve had. Oh, she knew he'd gone overseas, that he was safe in Germany. She couldn't help herself from finding out that much. As soon as she'd learned it, though, she'd left him alone.

She'd told him to leave. She couldn't justify tracking his location once she knew that decision hadn't cost him his freedom.

Voices echoed along the passageway ahead, and Eloise beckoned the men into one of the recessed arches to either side. Flashlight beams bounced along the walls, and then a pair of armband-wearing EAEA agents appeared.

Just the sight of them, in their black jackets and their serum-stocked tool belts, made Eloise want to scream. They moved slowly but with purpose, which was a good thing in this case, since they didn't shine the flashlight into any alcoves.

Ire gave Eloise a questioning tilt of his head, eyebrows raised, which she interpreted as a question—attack the agents, or no?—but she shook her head. It might not be likely, but they could be down here by accident. They needed to observe, at least for a few minutes. They couldn't risk giving the community away if the EAEA hadn't already located them.

As the thought crossed her mind, Nathan peered around the corner of the bricks that hid them, squinting toward the agents.

"It's Gleeful," Nathan whispered. "I thought it was him."

Ire gave him a sideways glance that perfectly mirrored Eloise's confusion. "What?"

"Gleeful," Nathan said. "Right, so he was one of the guys

that showed up when we tried to evacuate before. When Eloise was at HQ. I fought him."

"Let me guess," Ire said, "he was happy about it."

Nathan craned his neck to look after the EAEA agents. "You could say that. But how did they find us? You don't think Mary's right, about a spy?"

The agents had paused a few yards down to hold a whispered conversation, and Eloise frowned. No, she didn't think Mary's spy theory was right. One of the agents—he *was* grinning in a disconcerting way—pointed back down the passage toward their hiding spot, then in the opposite direction. Directly toward the community.

It was as if he could sense them down here.

"Dawn Kimble got hurt at the florist shop," she said softly. "Ire, could the EAEA be replicating her powers?"

Ire paused, still watching the arguing agents. "Probably. Complicated, though. The same guy would need to take the serum each time, I think. Otherwise they'd have to start all over with the head-tracking thing."

Eloise pressed her lips together, thinking. "Interesting. We may need to invite him to join us for a while."

Ire rubbed his chin. "And if it really is temporary... That would add another layer."

Nathan sighed. "Remember when there was just one serum to worry about?"

And they'd thought things had been complicated then.

The agents had started moving—they'd chosen the direction of the community—and it was time to get in their way.

"Nathan, circle around to the community the long way," Eloise said. "See if you can make some noise doing it, draw them off. Ire and I will go evacuate everyone."

"To where?" Nathan said.

Eloise didn't know. But Ire said, "I've got a few ideas."

Eloise nodded. "Go."

Nathan went, flicking his flashlight around as he moved and letting his footsteps echo across the corridor. A beat, and the agents took the bait, shouting as they tried to chase him down. But Nathan had scouted these tunnels, and they were down here for the first time. She didn't doubt he'd be able to avoid capture.

Trusting Ire to follow, Eloise ran for the community.

She didn't know what she'd been expecting to find—people hesitant to abandon their safe haven, maybe—but as soon as she burst through the doors shouting, the people started arranging themselves into groups, organizing, pairing up. Even before they knew what the crisis was, they were ready to fight it.

Dawn Kimble really had thought of everything.

"There's only the one exit," Eloise said.

Ire nodded to one of the bricked-up archways. "This one's got a tunnel behind it."

"How can you tell?"

He held his hand up to a crack in the mortar. "Breeze."

Before Eloise could ask how he planned to actually break through it, Ire reeled back and slammed a shoulder into the wall. Cracks spider-webbed across the barrier, and a second hit sent half the wall crumbling into a dark tunnel.

"Let's hope there's an outlet," she said.

"All we need is to hide," Ire replied, and then he was gone, leading a single-file group of enhanced humans into the darkness. Tally and Quin took up the rear, though Tally kept shooting glances at Eloise like she hoped to be drawn into whatever fight was coming.

Ire needed her help, though, so Eloise just gave her head a little shake. Next time.

As Eloise watched, four women broke out of the line to approach her. They were young, and she recognized three of them as the ones Mary and Nathan had tried and failed to evacuate on their own. They'd picked up a fourth friend, a Black woman, Liz, who could bend shadows to her will.

A blonde with a long braid was the first to speak. "I'm Kay. This is Mel and Cara and Liz. We don't want to hide. We want to help."

Eloise considered them, four women who'd been stuck in this place for three-plus months. She shouldn't bring civilians into the fray, but honestly, their talents could come in useful. They'd been present at Gleeful's original fight; the serumed-up EAEA agent could probably track them as well. If they stayed behind, they'd be able to set a believable trap.

And Ire truly did need more LIO operatives at his side in case the EAEA cut him off in the other direction, which left Eloise and Nathan on their own.

Besides, Kay's mouth was set in a firm line, and the others were meeting her gaze with matching determination. These women weren't going to take no for an answer.

"I have to admit, we could use the assist." She glanced at the line, catching Phil's eye and beckoning him over. "With your help, we can draw them off long enough to get everyone else to safety. Phil, I need you to go with Ire. Find the new spot, then come back to us so you can help if we need to escape quickly."

He nodded, brushing his hair out of his eyes and ducking his head as if he wanted to melt into the floor.

Though if Eloise recalled correctly, the ability to melt into a puddle was *actually* Kay's talent.

She led her new team out of the abandoned community, giving her heart a single beat to ache at the sight of abandoned clothing and food and toys. Somewhere in the tunnels, Nathan was leading the EAEA agents back her way.

And when he did, she'd be ready for them. She arranged

her new allies on either side of the tunnel, instructing them as quickly as she could. Dim light leaked out of the community's former safe haven, providing just enough light for her to see—and just enough shadows for her group to hide.

It felt good to be setting an ambush for the EAEA, instead of walking straight into one herself. "Use your powers," she said. "They'll come in handy."

"Not much water to walk on here," Mel said.

Eloise squeezed the girl's shoulder, all too aware of the hole at her waist where the Knife's sheath should be. "Enhanced abilities don't make an independent operative."

Running footsteps pounded along the passage, growing ever closer. Across the way, Cara flickered out of sight, allowing her body—and her clothing, impressive—to blend into the rock.

"Let Nathan pass," Eloise whispered. "Then we're all in. Your job is to obstruct and confuse."

Nathan darted through the passage, and Eloise barely had time to wonder if he realized they were there. The EAEA agents were right on his heels—they'd picked up more friends along the way, brilliant—and the first one went flying, their hands splayed as Cara used her hiding spot to trip them.

The agent went face-down on the floor, and before his colleagues could leap by him, Kay's silvery puddle ripped across the floor, and she materialized at Nathan's side, blocking the passage beyond while Liz threw up an army of shadows that made it look like they had twice as many fighters on their side.

Eloise grinned. Letting the women help? Definitely the right call.

The EAEA agents balked in confusion, stumbling backward and knocking into each other, one of them even stumbling over the one who'd tripped. Eloise couldn't make out any specific details about them—beyond the ridiculous armbands, anyway—but Nathan was concentrating his energy on a tall man at the edge of the group.

He didn't look all that Gleeful to Eloise, but fine.

Mel dodged away from Eloise's side, adding to the confusion by diving straight for the nearest agent's armband. She pulled, hard, and it ripped away from the agent's uniform. The agent whirled around, trying to hit her, but Eloise pushed away from the wall and intercepted the punch while Mel scurried beneath his arm.

With the crimson strip of cloth hanging loose, the agent whirled to go after Mel, but the fight was close, movement flurrying and brushing against them on every side, and Mel was already ducking into the action to grab at another armband.

Eloise used the first agent's distraction to punch him square in the jaw.

Satisfying, that. She could see the benefits of hand-to-hand combat, occasionally.

The agent staggered, wheeling back around to come after her, but she was already hooking her leg around to sweep them off their feet.

Nathan's voice cut through the scuffling fray, and Eloise looked up to see that he'd secured Gleeful's arms behind his back, though the man was snarling like something rabid.

Great. He had the tracker. But how were they supposed to extricate themselves from the fight?

Dark shapes rose along the walls, the shadows collecting into unnaturally swollen beasts. At least, that was how it seemed. Even Eloise's heart stammered in her chest as Liz's creations loomed, mouths gaping.

The EAEA agent she'd been fighting fled first. They scrambled up off the floor, limbs flailing, and threw their body back down the corridor.

Their companions followed. All except Gleeful, whom

Nathan had pinned against the wall. Though the man had quieted down as he stared at the shapes with dark eyes.

The young women cheered, pressing their palms together in a kind of a group high five, and Eloise couldn't help grinning along with them. But then Phil emerged from the shadows, ready to teleport them to the new spot—or some of them, anyway—and she sobered quickly.

"They'll be back soon," she said. "We need to move."

THE NEW HIDING spot was worse than the original one.

Nathan wanted to enjoy the energy of a fight well won. Truly, he did. But as he guided his no-longer-so-Gleeful prisoner into the corner, he couldn't rejoice at the new accommodations.

He never thought he'd have regretted moving the community out of their previous home. But this one was even tighter quarters, and it had none of the elements of home these people had built over the past few months. No cooking smells, no soft blankets. Only a hard floor and musty air.

And fear. The EAEA knew they were using the tunnels to hide; they'd be back, and soon.

From victory to despair. That felt about right, for LIO; it was always something.

He wished there were a way to get through to Chloe, to make her see the true horror of her crusade. At this point, he wasn't sure it would help; this went beyond Chloe now. And he doubted she'd see reason, in any case.

Still. He could wish.

Eloise was talking to the team at HQ, no doubt trying to form a new plan, while Ire stood next to Nathan by the wall, surveying the new place with his lips twisted in distaste. "I want to know how they make the powers temporary," he said.

That wasn't at all what Nathan had expected him to be focusing on right now. He sometimes forgot that before Agnes Jenson had left LIO, Ire had frequently assisted her in the labs.

"You'll never find out," the captive agent said. "You can torture me until I die, I'll never tell you."

Ire gave him a bland look. "You're the ones who do the torturing. Not us."

The prisoner spat. "Sure, but a bit of kidnapping never hurt anyone."

Ire just rolled his eyes and looked back out across the room. "I could test his blood, if I had access to a lab. Might take me a while to figure things out, though."

Not a bad idea. They'd captured this guy to keep him from giving away their location, but maybe they could learn something in the process.

"Could you give me powers?"

Nathan started as Ethan appeared at his side. The boy tended to appear as if from nowhere, though Nathan supposed that was a power unique to five-year-olds and not related to his plant-growing abilities. His cheeks were still stained with tears, but he was gazing at Ire in adoration as if he'd already forgotten his fear.

Ire squinted down at the boy. "You already have powers."

"I want different powers. Dinosaur powers."

Ire stared. "What are dinosaur powers?"

Ethan curled his gloved fingers into the shape of claws, let out an enormous roar, then skipped back over to his mother. She was sitting with some other people who were huddled over a tablet Eloise had given them. For a distraction, most likely. They were watching Jeff Hayes talk to yet another interviewer about enhanced abilities. Nathan wasn't sure what the movie star hoped to accomplish by talking himself hoarse over this, but he had to admit that it was giving these people some comfort.

And if anyone could drum up support, Jeff Hayes might be the one, with that too-charming smile of his. Most of the world didn't realize the smile was a front.

"I think you have a fan," Nathan said as the boy settled on his mother's lap, still roaring. Ire just grunted.

Eloise ended her call and beckoned them over to an unoccupied corner of the room. Nathan doubted it would keep anyone from overhearing; the people's eyes tracked them as they moved, and he'd have wagered a good amount that someone among them had enhanced hearing.

"Plan?" Nathan asked.

Eloise glanced around. "We don't have one."

Nathan followed her gaze, taking in all the hungry eyes. These people must be desperate to see the sky again. To be free.

"It's only a matter of time until they get in," Ire said.

Very little time. They'd be back soon, and they'd come with an army.

"We need to move them all at once," Nathan said. "No more hedging. No more experiments."

Eloise let out a breath, like a half laugh. "And how do you suggest we do that? They outnumber us. They out-power us."

At least until Ire could figure out their secrets, they did.

LIO could pull in all their allies, for a start. Nathan would have been pretty thrilled to get Steve back—his friend had taken off to Berlin, he knew that much—but he doubted Eloise would be willing to hear it.

But Steve couldn't get the whole community to safety all by himself, any more than Phil could.

In the background, the interview droned on, and Nathan

glanced over to see Jeff leaning toward the camera. Intense. Focused. Not the man Nathan had hated once upon a time, though he suspected he'd never love the guy.

Nathan had a feeling he was going to regret suggesting the other obvious course of action. A lot. But he couldn't think of anything else, unless the Knife wanted to decide to behave itself and create a portal without stealing everyone's powers, or slamming the good guys around by accident. Or hell, breaking the time-space continuum, for all he knew. There was no telling what more it could do.

There was no time to figure it out. He sighed. "We need a distraction," he said. "We need to call Jeff Hayes."

MARY WASN'T USUALLY MUCH for psyching herself up. When something needed to be done, the best course of action was to do it, not waste time in thinking about doing it or playing power music, or whatever.

But in this particular case, as she descended the stairs that led to LIO's prison level, she was all too aware of what—and who—waited in the cells below. Jenna didn't concern her, or not much. Mary could handle a little snark. To get to Jenna, though, she'd need to pass the Trap and Monster, and if there was one thing Diana Morton excelled at, it was making people feel like she had the upper hand in any situation. Even when she was trapped in a cube with nothing to keep her company but three bland meals a day and the company of her friends' voices through the walls.

She wasn't in control, however she might pretend. The Trap was behind bars, and even if the anti-power serum didn't work on her, the gloves locked around her wrists kept her poison at bay. Monster was contained, too, along with camouflaging Rocker, the mind-reading twins, and illusionist Goldi. They had no power over her, or anyone else.

But they did have words. Goldi might blame Mary for the

injuries she'd sustained. The twins might bait her. Mary could match wits with any of them, but she couldn't help feeling that these people—former family, in many respects—would fluster her no matter what she said.

She didn't like feeling off balance. But she had the upper hand here. She did.

By the time she reached the landing, her hands were damp with sweat. She patted them against her hips, hoping it wasn't too obvious, and nodded to the guards before swiping her way onto the prison floor.

Don't think. Act. Mary took a breath and plunged into the walkway that ran between two rows of box-like cells. The glass shifted clear as she passed, revealing a sleeping Diana. A sleeping Monster, too.

The relief was almost physical. A release. Mary could handle them—she could—but it was better if she didn't have to.

Jenna's cell was at the end of the block. As if by a silent agreement, all the retirees were stretched out on their beds, asleep. Mary half expected to find Jenna sleeping, too, but the girl sat on the edge of her bed with her legs crossed, examining her fingernails.

When Mary stopped in front of the glass and crossed her arms over her chest, Jenna looked up. "She must want something, if she wanders to my cage in the dead of night."

Mary frowned. "It's not the dead of night."

"It may as well be. Everyone else is asleep. They sleep a lot, you know. And who can blame them?"

Mary couldn't help the thread of pity that twisted in with her anger at Jenna, at what she'd done. Revealing Mary's secret identity, unveiling the league, and murdering her own father. But it was old anger, now. More remembered grief than anything else.

Mary made herself drop her arms to her sides. She'd read

somewhere that open posture invited open conversation. Couldn't hurt to try, at least. "I want to talk to you about your father."

"And I want a Reese's peanut butter cup, but we can't always get what we want in life."

Mary blinked. "I mean, that's a pretty minor request. I feel like I can get you a Reese's."

"Promise?"

Mary tried to find the trap in Jenna's request, but decided she was just being... herself. "Um, sure?"

Jenna gave a little bounce on the bed, making the springs creak. "All right, you can talk to me about Daddy Flambé. Maybe I'll even listen, who knows."

What had it been like for Jenna, growing up in Mange's lab? Mary knew she might be asking the girl to relive some amount of trauma, some bad memories. She didn't want to ask directly, but she couldn't help wondering how that life had corrupted this girl so deeply. Especially since Mange had had some sense of a moral compass. At least, he had at the end.

"You must have learned a lot about enhanced abilities," Mary said carefully. "With Mange as your father."

"I learned it burns when they go in." Jenna grinned. Like a cheerleader, ready to rev up a crowd. She winked. "At least it burns on the way out, too."

To the detriment of all involved. "Did Mange ever try to track down hotspots of enhanced humans? To learn about their powers?"

Jenna's grin widened. "Hotspots? Like an outbreak? 'Excuse me, sir, we need to quarantine this area as people have been taking flight without warning.'" She laughed at her own joke, clutching her stomach as she giggled.

From somewhere down the line of cells, someone said,

"You're crazy." Mary thought it was Rocker's voice, rumbling. She couldn't be sure.

Not that anyone here had much room to criticize on the crazy front. Mary just waited for Jenna to stop laughing, keeping her hands at her sides, her fists relaxed. Open posture. Open communication. No punching.

Finally, Jenna finished her laughing and wiped her eyes. "But seriously, no. My dad was obsessed with Agnes Jenson's work, that kind of thing. He was a lab abilities guy."

It was pretty much what Mary had expected. Still, a disappointment. She knew Mange and his dubious research methods had been turned away from every prominent lab in the country —and probably a bunch of not-so-prominent ones, too. She'd hoped he might have sought out alternative avenues for studying enhanced abilities even before Wave had come calling.

She was on the verge of leaving when Jenna spoke again. "Although." She stopped. Put a finger to her lips. "Once we were in like... I don't know, some forgettable city. The one with the arch, maybe."

"What, Paris?"

"No, U.S. Big ugly metal... St. Louis. Yeah. Dad was knocking on the university door there, his favorite waste of time. Figuratively knocking, obviously. He might have tried physical knocking, though, if he'd thought it would—"

"And?" Mary interrupted.

Jenna tipped her a sloppy salute. "Yes ma'am, sorry ma'am. So we were at the university. I remember there were snacks in the waiting room, but no toys. And Dad probably didn't have an appointment, because he never had an appointment. So we were waiting, and he got to talking with this guy outside the research office who'd also shown up without an appointment. What a coincidence, right?"

"What did they talk about?"

Jenna flipped her dark hair over her shoulder and rolled her eyes. "I was five, Coral. I don't know. But because I was five, I hadn't developed the elegant sense of propriety I have now, and I couldn't stop staring at the guy's veins. They *glowed*. I thought it was super pretty."

So Mange had met an enhanced human at a university research lab. Someone with glowing veins. That told Mary... next to nothing.

But Jenna wasn't finished. "Then the dean-boss-general guy showed up and kicked them both out. The glowing guy offered to buy Dad a coffee. He seemed kind of desperate about it, all twitchy and stuff, but Dad said no. Which sucked, because coffee places have sticky buns, so I pitched a fit about it and he dragged me off. And that was that."

Mary frowned, trying to sort through Jenna's nonsense to the meat of the story. "So maybe the guy needed help from Mange?"

Jenna shrugged. "When you put it that way, he must have been even more desperate than he looked."

True enough, if he'd known who Mange was. He might have been grasping at any thread of hope, no matter how thin. "What do you think he wanted?"

Jenna rolled her eyes. "I don't read minds, I incinerate them. Did I say enough? Do I get a treat? Do I?"

Yeah. Mary supposed she did. She headed back down the corridor, too distracted to be startled by the fact that Monster was now awake and pacing in his cell.

She supposed this information meant a pin on the map for St. Louis. Probably a new color, for... what, for 'we know an enhanced human was in this city at one point in time'? She wanted to bang her head against the wall in frustration, but she already had a headache, so that probably wouldn't be the best way to proceed.

On her way out, Mary instructed the confused guards to get Jenna a Reese's peanut butter cup. It couldn't be the weirdest thing they'd ever been asked to do at LIO HQ, though they both stared at her like she'd lost her mind.

Nathan called just as Mary was leaving the stairwell. She picked up, wishing Nathan could have been with her while she questioned Jenna. He was better at that kind of thing. Probably didn't need to think about not punching people at all. At the very least, he could help her sort through Jenna's story. Pick out a detail she'd missed.

Phone to her ear, she started up the stairs. "Did you get the girl out?"

"We did. But we've got another problem."

"Wouldn't be LIO without another problem."

"Hey, that's what I said."

Mary exited the stairwell, marveling at the actual physical relief that came with leaving the prison level behind. "Great minds. So what's going on?"

Nathan hesitated. "I'll text the specifics. But the upshot of it is that I need you to call Jeff."

Mary stopped so abruptly that a team member walking behind her had to swerve to avoid a collision. She waved her apologies, and her thanks, too, since he was carrying a tray of test tubes. And who knew what those might contain. "Jeff Hayes?"

"Yeah. We need a favor."

Nathan sounded about as excited about calling Jeff as Mary would have expected. They weren't exactly friends. "I kind of owe *him* a favor," she said. "Give or take a hundred."

Jeff had helped her when she'd been hellbent on bringing the retirees to justice. She knew he'd helped El and the others get out of Travis Bertram's prison of horrors, and he'd certainly dedicated a fair amount of his influence—which wasn't insignificant—to fighting the country's anti-enhanced bullshit.

She wasn't sure how much more she could ask of the man.

"Well, we need one more." Nathan paused. "Actually, I think we need two. Do you think he'd be willing to pick someone up in Berlin?"

STEVE WAS NOT AT ALL CONVINCED that the building in front of him housed an art exhibit, though Ben seemed certain enough. Yes, there was a short line of people waiting outside. And yes, there was a poster outlined in neon colors that claimed the existence of an art gallery somewhere within these walls.

On the outside, though, the place looked like a sex shop.

"I know what you're thinking," Ben said.

Steve raised his eyebrows, trying to avoid looking directly at the window display. "I really doubt it."

Ben clapped a hand on his shoulder. "You need to get out. All you've done so far in Berlin is to work and sleep and brood."

"Don't forget the clandestine meetings."

Ben held up a finger. "One clandestine meeting. Only one, so far. This is not a city for brooding, it's a city for living. Which you would know if you took the time to experience it. You won't go clubbing, which is a true shame. So art it is. My friend just happens to have this gallery opening tonight. Lucky you."

Steve frowned at the windows, which displayed surprisingly realistic looking... toys. Well, they did say that all of Berlin was a canvas, every wall a place to paint, every pole a place to cover in posters. "And this is art?"

Ben pointed to where the line of people had begun descending a narrow staircase and into a door below the shop. "Perhaps so, in a certain light. But we're going elsewhere."

The basement gallery was as cramped inside as it looked from the outside. At least, so it seemed, from the little Steve could make out in the dimly lit space. A video played across the floor, the movements blurry and disorienting, while deep-toned techno pop churned in the background.

Ben steered him to a bar in the corner—the presence of which suggested that, despite the hole-in-the-wall nature of this place, events must be common enough—where the bartender presented them with beautifully foamed amber lager.

If nothing else, Steve could appreciate a good pour, and Germany was among the best places in the world for that.

Drinks in hand, they began a slow circuit of the room. Steve hadn't visited many art exhibits, though he'd brought a date or two through Boston's Museum of Fine Arts. This gallery was pretty much the opposite, no classical columns or stone sculptures or mile-high portraits of important rich people. The room was dark, with squiggles of light playing across the floor. He wasn't sure what he was supposed to be seeing.

As soon as they reached the first painting, though, the reason for the dark room became apparent: the artwork was all done in UV paint. Each piece had a blacklight aimed strategically at it, so that the piece was all but invisible until you stood right in front of it.

The first painting was about speed. The card taped to the wall beside it didn't say as much; the card translated to 'untitled 42.'

But Steve recognized speed when he saw it. A flurry, a blur of almost-images that shifted like an old-school hologram when you changed angles, a spiraling mess of neon color. Like getting lost in a Wonderland-bred tornado.

Steve licked his lips, leaning in closer. "Who did you say your friend was again?"

Ben just grinned. "My friend, he's a genius. You see your troubles in his work? I see mine."

Maybe. But as they continued around the gallery, it became apparent that the artist definitely had Steve's kind of troubles in mind. Threads of fuchsia musculature glistened in one painting, ragged cellular structures central in another. When Steve looked at these paintings, he saw LIO. No, more than that; he saw his friends.

By the time they reached the end of the row, Steve was not at all surprised to find a bird's-eye view of the Horseshoe Falls. Niagara at the center of it all. The strip of canvas stretched nearly the full height of the ceiling. Which, given the small space, gave the piece the heftiest chunk of real estate in the room.

A man stood in front of it with his arms crossed, frowning at the painting as though he could convince it to explain itself by staring it down. He wore a dark suit, and the handkerchief in his breast pocket glowed purple-white as he leaned in to examine the painting.

If anyone could convince a painting to explain itself, it was Holland Gold.

The lawyer stepped back from the painting as Steve approached, holding out a hand to shake. Which Steve did.

"It looks like it's moving, doesn't it?" Holland said. "The painting, that is."

Steve glanced at the orange and yellow streaks. Something about their arrangement did give a definite sense of motion. "This is a surprise."

"Artists can do incredible things," Holland said.

Steve folded his arms. "I meant—"

"I know what you meant, Mr. Taylor."

Ben looked back and forth between them in surprise. "OK, I take it back. Clandestine meetings, plural."

Steve half expected Holland to correct Ben by saying that even though the gallery audience was on the small side, they were technically in public at the moment. But Jeff Hayes's lawyer simply straightened his tie. He might as well have been an automaton, a thought that passed through Steve's mind with no small amount of guilt. Holland *had* helped him escape from a secret government facility, where he'd probably have been tortured if he'd stayed.

Still. The guy was... quirky.

If Holland was concerned about Ben's participation in their conversation, he didn't let on. "Eloise needs your help on a mission," he said.

No small talk with this guy. Got it. Steve tamped down the thrill of hope he felt at the sound of her name—she was OK, and she was asking for him, and he should go to her *now*—and made himself answer reasonably. "Eloise kicked me out of LIO. So you can tell her—"

Holland held up a hand. "Eloise doesn't know I'm here, of course. She'd never allow that."

Steve tried not to show his disappointment, though he was pretty sure he failed. Ben said, "Intrigue."

Holland indicated the painting. "There are people in the U.S. who wish to flee, as you did. But they're trapped."

"I'm aware of the issue," Steve said slowly. Not everyone could blur past borders whenever they wanted to. If anything, the theme of this exhibit addressed the same problem. Hidden abilities. Hidden beauty. Hidden danger. "Your boss talks about it a lot, right?"

"Jeff Hayes is not my boss, he is my client. But yes. He

excels at talking. And now he's taking action. The plan requires the league to divide forces, however, and we could use someone with your skills."

Steve wanted to laugh. Jeff and Holland—and probably Mary, who would have sent them here—must have no idea how adamantly Eloise had pushed him away. He'd kissed her. She'd rejected him. He still cared for her, yes, but he wasn't the kind of ass who pushed in where he wasn't wanted. It wasn't like she'd wounded his pride.

El hadn't sent him away because of the kiss, though. She'd sent him away because he hadn't been able to make up his mind, or commit to LIO. He wasn't thick enough to pretend otherwise.

OK, so maybe his pride was a *little* wounded.

Before Steve could form a response, Holland slipped a card out of his breast pocket and into Steve's hand. "I have to go back tomorrow. Please take some time to think about it, and meet me at this address in the morning." Not much time, then. "You'd be helping a great many people."

The lawyer didn't give Steve a chance to answer. He simply turned and moved smoothly back through the gallery, heading directly for the exit.

Automaton. Definitely.

"So you're going, right?" Ben said. "Please tell me you're going."

Steve couldn't turn away from the door. What did he think, that El was going to walk in next? Holland had made it clear that she hadn't been the one to call him. "I'm not wanted."

Ben rolled his eyes, tipping his head back toward the ceiling in exasperation. "Oh, please. Someone sent a movie star's lawyer to come get you, in person, from Berlin. Maybe it wasn't your girl. Or maybe it was. Either way, she needs you, and she's not the only one. You said you wanted to help people. So help people."

Steve gripped Holland's card, shaking his head. "I don't know. I need to think."

Ben took a gulp of his beer, draining half the stein in one go. "You know best, friend. But it sounds like time is of the essence. So you'd better think fast."

IT TOOK some digging for Dolly to find where the Enhanced Human Enforcement Agency was headquartering their operations. Dolly had assumed these people would be stuck in a basement office of Homeland Security, or something like that. Highly guarded, hidden, difficult to unearth.

That was how she'd handled her enhanced abilities, and the abilities of those around her.

Alternatively, given the high-profile nature of their mission to register all enhanced humans, Dolly half expected to find them living it up in a media-surrounded wonderland. Something with glass walls. Not dissimilar, perhaps, to the way Mary had lived her life in Malibu.

But the EAEA, and their friends in Congress, clearly had other ideas. They weren't listed anywhere, boasting anywhere, or hiding anywhere that she could find.

Dolly might have spent years digging through identically beige government buildings within the borders of Washington, D.C., if Carlisle hadn't thought of the Pentagon. Which led them to Arlington police radio chatter, which led to what should have been a private conversation between two officers.

These two clearly thought they were clever, gossiping

on a separate channel while on traffic duty or something—she couldn't see what they were doing, but Dolly liked picturing traffic duty or meter maiding or something like that.

"We were supposed to get offices," one of the cops said. "I was going to paint mine blue."

Too on-the-nose, Dolly thought. Not a creative thinker, this one.

"Now these new assholes move onto the second floor with their labs and shit, and we gotta stay crunched together in cubicles down on the main floor? I don't like it."

"Sucks," the other voice agreed. "But we wouldn't have gotten offices anyway, Drew. The detectives—"

"I've been on the force twenty years. I'd have gotten an office."

The pause on the other end of the radio said it all. Mr. Twenty Years would have stayed right in his cubicle in any case. Ranger, who was recording the conversation, snickered.

"Well, I say these guys have the right idea," the second officer said, changing the subject. He sounded younger. Less experienced. "IOs always scared me. With what they can do. If these guys need some of our space to stop them, I'm willing to give it."

New occupants in a police station in Arlington—a stone's throw from D.C.—with labs and certain ideas about independent operatives? Intriguing. Dolly leaned in, staring at the scanner as though she could see the EAEA through the speaker.

"Nah," the first guy said. "The EAEA scares me. You let 'em register one group, they'll start registering everyone. You'll see."

Dolly shut off the radio. She had no interest in hearing what these idiots thought about independent operatives, or enhanced humans. She could break them in half with a wave of her hand.

She didn't care what the world thought, and neither would Sever.

Sever would slice them all apart. And once Dolly reclaimed the Knife, she'd deal with him, too. She might even be able to use it to wield its maker's powers.

She'd be a hero again.

Ranger was grinning, while Carlisle worried his lip between his teeth. "Don't tell me," he said. "I already know the answer. We're going to raid a police station."

It was almost blessedly easy when you could make portals. She couldn't bring them directly into the lab—not without having been there, so not without potentially destroying the power-erasing serum they were hoping to retrieve—but it was simple enough to get the three of them onto the police station's roof.

The portal zipped shut behind them, and Dolly headed for the door, a distant soundtrack of sirens playing in her ears. The air was thick and sweet smelling, the freshness of spring marching headlong into summer. Above, stars winked through a patchy haze of clouds.

When she turned to beckon her colleagues inside, Ranger had a squirrel perched on his shoulder.

"Can you at least try to be scary?" Dolly said.

He shrugged. "Squirrels can be scary."

If Diana were here... but no. Dolly was stuck with who she was stuck with. Dolly would retrieve the Trap soon enough. And the others.

Dolly got out her pick and started working on the lock, but the door swung open, nearly hitting her in the face. She sprang back, ready to make a portal, but a line of figures was already streaming out onto the roof. Some of them wore those ridiculous EAEA armbands, while others were simply clad in police gear.

One of their assailants knocked Ranger to the ground, while another nudged Carlisle toward the corner of the roof, separating the trio.

For an instant, Dolly considered leaving them here. She could do it. Open a portal. Step right through.

What would Sever say?

"To me," Dolly shouted, but Carlisle was fighting off three people. He couldn't take a step, let alone get to her.

The squirrel leapt off of Ranger's shoulder, screaming with an unearthly noise as it dug its claws into his ambusher's face. Apparently squirrels really could be dangerous.

The attacked officer fired his weapon—by accident? On purpose?—and Ranger staggered back, clutching his stomach as blood seeped through the fabric of his shirt. His heels caught the raised lip at the edge of the roof, and he started to fall.

Dolly flinched toward him, but another agent barred her way, a blur of black and red and gun-metal char blocking her from getting to Ranger.

Her fingers were hot, the solution begging for release. She slashed the air before her, digging a portal into the ether and right through her attacker.

The man didn't even have time to scream as his body split in half, blood rushing out to the beat of his confused heart. The copper horror of it lodged in the back of her throat, but she pushed past it and into the portal.

She emerged behind Ranger, her feet to the side of the building, gravity pulling her into a tumble toward the street. She caught his arm and portaled them both across the roof to where Carlisle was overwhelmed, unconcerned about the way the portal ripped through a second agent's body.

Fatigue thrummed through her head, but she managed a

third rip in space, barely. A chorus of horrified screams, and they were gone, falling through the portal to a clear Texas sky.

And to Sever, who stood not ten feet from where they'd made the safety circle for the portal. Rage contorted his face into a wide-eyed monstrosity, and for a moment Dolly could see the demon who'd destroyed entire worlds.

For a moment, she thought he would destroy her next.

But he knelt by Ranger, who was writhing in pain in the dirt. Examined his wound.

And narrowed his eyes at the place where the portal had disappeared.

Only then did Dolly turn to see that one of the agents had followed them through, and was currently attempting to stagger to his feet.

Sever stood, his movements as fluid as ever as he approached the shuddering EAEA agent. The man's armband had come loose, and it was hanging half off of his arm. He reached for a case at his belt, hands shaking, but Sever got to him before he could secure it.

"You injured my associate," Sever said. "Perhaps fatally."

At Dolly's feet, Ranger sobbed.

The EAEA agent opened his mouth. Closed it again. In an impressive gathering of courage, he drew himself up straight and pointed at Sever. He stood half a head taller than the alien god, but somehow he seemed to know he was outmatched. "You," the agent said, then swallowed. "You're under arrest for—"

Sever placed a hand on the man's neck. For a moment, Dolly thought he was taking the agent's pulse.

The man convulsed, his back cracking into a rigid arch as he collapsed to the ground. Blisters exploded from his skin like tiny volcanoes, spilling fat raindrops of his blood into the dirt, where bubbles frothed to the surface of each puddle. At first,

Dolly thought Sever must have injected some sort of a chemical, that the man's blood was reacting to the air. But heat emanated from the agent's body, so hot that she took a step back, and when Dolly looked again, it was obvious enough, though she didn't see how it could be possible. The man's blood was boiling.

The agent had gone still, his visible skin a mass of bloody blisters. Carlisle was emptying his stomach into a patch of grass.

Dolly had seen worse.

She glanced at the fallen agent again. Well. Not *much* worse.

Sever swept over to Ranger and stooped to draw the animal wrangler into his arms. Ranger had gone limp, but his chest still rose with shallow breaths.

"I will do what I can for him," Sever said, and Dolly wondered if his powers included healing. And if they didn't, what Sever could possibly hope to do.

She fell into step beside him. "I'm sorry. They were waiting for us. We failed you."

Sever glanced in her direction. "No. I failed you. This world has fallen much farther than I believed. If we want to correct it, we'll need to attack the problem at its source."

Dolly followed Sever into the farmhouse, afraid to ask for clarification. Afraid to respond at all. She thought of the man's blood, boiling to stains of red in the dirt, and swallowed hard. She'd controlled Will's powers for years, and though she'd never used them quite so... creatively... she'd certainly couldn't pretend she hadn't used fire to torture.

But this man—this *god*—could do it without tapping anyone else's power. He could reach through space, the way the Knife could. Bend it to his will. If his stories were to be believed, he could burn entire planets to ash.

Dolly had manipulated plenty of people in her time. Still, it felt like she was treading along a crumbling mountain pass.

For now, she'd do what he wished. Gain his confidence. Then, she'd convince him to storm HQ.

Once she had the Pearl Knife, her powers would surely be equal to Sever's. Once she had the Knife, she would bring this god to his knees.

HE MIGHT BE BRUISED, and he might be embarrassed, but there was no denying the truth: Travis Bertram had come up in the world.

New office, new assistant, new title. And now, a movie star on the phone. Oh, he knew Jeff Hayes had been spouting some kind of pro-enhanced-human nonsense in the news. Giving speeches, holding fundraisers, something or other. But now that they were face to face—over a video call, of course—Travis couldn't help feeling like the whole thing might have been an act. A publicity ploy.

In real life—video totally counted when you were actually speaking to a person—Jeff Hayes didn't seem driven enough to cause any real trouble. The man was calling from his pool deck, which wouldn't have seemed all that strange if he'd happened to be wearing a shirt.

"You really need to come out here," the movie star was saying. "I've had D.C. sushi, Trav. It's not OK."

Jeff Hayes excelled at small talk. He'd been drawling out similar advice for the past ten minutes. Travis made a concerted effort to look at the camera, rather than the screen, where the other man's abs were distressingly central. "That would be—"

"And does D.C. even have a single decent club? Talk about no nightlife. And then if you do go out, half the time you're probably running into people you've just tried to lobby and pretending you don't see them sucking on whatever it is they're... well, sucking. You know what I mean?"

Travis actually *did* know. "Mr. Hayes, you've—"

"Mr. Hayes is my cat. Call me Jeff."

Travis wasn't sure if he was supposed to laugh.

Jeff took a sip of something pink out of a daiquiri glass. If Travis hadn't been absolutely, one hundred percent certain that this was Jeff Hayes, he'd have thought it was someone *playing* Jeff Hayes. But Travis couldn't risk pissing this guy off. He'd find screenshots of his own face posted across the internet tomorrow. Or—if the sucking comment was meant to be a threat, which Travis hadn't actually considered before—much worse.

"Look, Trav," Jeff said, "I'm super busy. So I'll cut to the chase before my next appointment."

Jeff took another sip. Travis *still* wasn't sure if he was supposed to laugh. When it doubt, he found it was almost always better not to.

"I'm really fascinated by the work you're doing right now," Jeff said. "I'm not sure we see eye to eye on this, but I'd love to have dinner. Pick your brain."

The buzzer on Travis's desk rang, and he jumped. Jeff smiled, but didn't laugh at him. Travis hit the button. "Not now, Vic."

"But Mr. Bertram, it's—"

"Not now." Travis pulled the power cord out of the intercom and turned back to the camera.

"Shouldn't you take that?" Jeff asked. "Sounded important."

Travis straightened his tie. "You know how assistants are. The sky is always falling."

Jeff laughed. "Tell me about it. Well, if you're too busy we could always reschedule."

Reschedule? They hadn't *schedule* scheduled. "No," Travis said. "Not too busy."

The door opened, and Travis's rail-thin assistant slipped in the door, his hands flailing. He looked like a frantic mime. Travis frowned at Vic, shaking his head.

"I'm confused," Jeff said. "You want to meet, or you don't want to meet?"

Travis stared at the camera, ignoring Vic's ridiculous dance. "I want to meet. Yes, of course. Whenever it's convenient, Mr.—Jeff."

"Mr. Jeff is my dog." The man didn't crack a smile. He didn't even blink. "Tomorrow, six thirty. PM, kid. I don't do breakfast. The Park sound good? Mediterranean? I like the trees. I'll send a car. Ciao. And tell your assistant to chill out."

Jeff waved to someone off camera, and a disembodied hand ended the call.

Travis adjusted his tie. Coming up in the world. Jeff Hayes, who paid people to end video calls for him so he wouldn't have to sit up, would send a car.

"Mr. *Bertram*." Vic's voice was annoyingly close to a whine. Travis looked up, considering whether he'd be reprimanded for firing the guy so soon after hiring him. Probably. "The thieves tried to rob the EAEA."

Travis rolled his eyes. "Like I said they would." Vic either had a terrible memory, or he hadn't believed Travis's original prediction. If that were the case, he'd need to hire someone new immediately. He didn't need a genius sitting in his assistant's chair, but he certainly needed help that could follow his instructions without question.

Whoever these people were, they seemed to think they could swipe a CLEAR scientist out of nowhere without attracting his attention. See, this was the problem with enhanced humans. The sense of entitlement that came with the power to go in anywhere and blur the cameras to get what they wanted. It was infuriating.

But Travis wasn't an idiot. The scientists had checked, and nothing at CLEAR had gone missing. Whatever these people wanted, they hadn't found it.

So it made sense they'd try the EAEA next. There were only so many places left in the country for this sort of thing. If Travis had his way, the numbers would keep right on shrinking.

"Yeah," Vic said. When Travis frowned at him, he shook his head. "I mean, yeah, sir."

"So who was it?"

"Got pictures this time. It was some woman I don't recognize—no one seems to—and two former LIO members. The animal whisperer and the weather worker. The woman, she might have been one of the ones who used to wear a mask."

Former LIO members. Interesting. Coral had put on a good show of acting against them a few months ago, but it was possible they'd joined forces again. Or that the whole thing had been a ruse.

Travis opened his web browser and searched the location of the Park restaurant. He'd need a new suit, not this half-fitted monstrosity, if he was going to have dinner with Jeff Hayes. "So?" he prompted, still focused on the screen. It didn't pay for a mere assistant to think he merited Travis's full attention. That was just common sense. "What happened?"

"The EAEA injured one of them."

Travis could feel the 'but' behind the words. He waited.

Vic lipped his lips. "But they got away."

There it was.

Travis landed on a tailor shop that opened at seven AM. Surely they could do a rush job for him. "They'll try again," he said. "And when they do, we'll be ready."

ELOISE BALANCED her tablet on her knees, trying to keep track of the various moving parts that were involved in today's deception while Ire drove their SUV exactly five miles above the speed limit. In the back seat, Phil was wearing headphones and staring out the window, bobbing his head slightly to the music.

The formerly Gleeful EAEA agent who could track their location was still cooling his heels under Philadelphia. But Eloise liked to hedge her bets. So just in case the EAEA could still somehow track her—and Ire—then she figured they might as well give them something to see.

The tingling feeling hadn't disappeared from her fingertips. Days now, and the sensation remained, like cold sparks tickling her skin. She flexed her hands, rubbing her thumb along the pads of her fingers. It didn't help.

A green light flared on Eloise's screen, and conversation trickled out of the bug that the EAEA had planted in Jeff's car. On Travis's command, of course. Mary had suggested it to him through his assistant's email, and Travis had called 'Vic' a paranoid idiot before doing exactly as he'd suggested.

If Travis talked to Vic like that through email, Eloise couldn't imagine how he spoke to the poor guy in person.

"...make a second dinner reservation while I'm in there," Jeff was saying to the driver. She could just imagine him, leaning back in his seat, sunglasses tipped over his eyes, persona locked into gear. "I don't expect this Travis guy to be much fun."

"And that interferes with your ability to eat?" the driver said.

"Very funny. Just do it. Find somewhere good. Actually, D.C. wouldn't know good if it made an oversized campaign donation. Find somewhere half decent."

Eloise pressed her hands into fists and released them, still working on the strange feeling. Maybe there was a healer among the community in Philadelphia, someone who wouldn't mind taking a look at this after they'd been rescued tonight.

Jeff was still yammering on, dialing up the celebrity character. He'd turned out to be so much more helpful than she'd ever thought he would be. "The man loves a performance," she said.

Ire cast her a sidelong glance, as if he was surprised that she'd spoken. "Are your hands OK?"

Eloise looked down at her fingers. "They're fine."

"You keep fidgeting them."

Eloise half expected power to pour out of her body at any moment. It was bad enough when the Knife was out of her control. What would it feel like when its powers took over her body, too?

If. *If* its powers took over her body. Which couldn't happen as long as she kept a hold on things.

She drew in a deep breath, let it out slowly. "What did it feel like," she asked, "when you got your abilities?"

"It felt like watching all my friends die," he said.

Eloise's cheeks warmed. She knew it had been bad, that he'd gained his abilities through a chemical weapons malfunction back when he'd been a Marine. The accident had killed everyone else on his team. "I'm sorry. That wasn't... I didn't mean to pry."

Ire glanced at her again, then back to the road. "Not your usual M.O."

She sighed. "No. It's not. I've just... got a lot on my mind, I guess."

He kept his eyes ahead, the streetlights skimming by above their heads as dusk descended. "It hurt," he said. "The abilities. Agnes says—said—it was my cells mutating rapidly, which was exactly what the chemicals were meant to do."

"The military wanted to turn its enemies into super soldiers?"

"Sure. Think about it, I mean, the rest of the platoon didn't make it. Took me years to realize that was the real point. Kill fifty soldiers in one blast, then deal with a few ballooned muscles if you have to."

Eloise's stomach turned. "Do they really use it?"

"Not this specifically." He sniffed, rubbed the back of his hand against his nose. "Turns out you're right. Some general asked what would happen if the whole platoon of enemies had mutation-friendly cells. So that was the end of it."

Eloise looked at her hands. Her own maybe-powers weren't painful, really, just... strange.

"I was basically paralyzed for a week," Ire said. "That probably gave them hope of their weapon doing what they wanted."

Eloise cringed. Not a pretty thought. Weaponizing enhanced abilities was just as bad as criminalizing them. Couldn't there be some kind of happy medium here?

"Then one morning, I woke up and bam." He lifted one arm off the wheel. "No more gym bills."

On the tablet, Jeff was babbling about real estate in Paris or follow-up interviews with reporters who'd spun his story wrong. It was hard to say how much of what he said was a ruse, and how much was taken from his real life.

Real being a sliding term, when it came to Hollywood.

"So," Ire said, "are you getting powers? Like Dolly?"

Of course he'd know what was happening. Read between the lines. She supposed she wasn't nearly as secretive as she tried to be.

Eloise half expected the Knife to respond in her thoughts. But it was too far away, and moving farther. "No," she said. "Yes? Maybe. I don't know."

"Maybe it'd be good," Ire said. "Maybe it would free you from the Knife."

She wished she could believe that. She wished she knew what to say. Thankfully, Jeff was getting close to the restaurant, and it was time for the main event. Time to shift focus.

She'd worry about tingling fingers and possible powers later.

"Find the next rest stop," she said. "Let's get back to Philadelphia."

Stealth had been so much easier back in the day, when Mary had navigated two separate famous identities instead of one mega famous identity. Yes, wigs had been necessary. And hats, a lot of the time. But she hadn't usually needed to add glasses, or makeup.

Disguises were a major hassle these days.

But keeping tabs on Jeff's conversation was essential to the plan, so Mary endured the annoyance of fake lenses in bulky frames and a wig with auburn curls that tickled her neck.

"I can't believe all you need is a baseball cap," she grumbled to Nathan after the waiter had seated them beside a potted fern that was nearly as tall as she was. The restaurant had really committed to the park theme; they'd planted trees throughout the cavernous space, filling in around them with raised flower beds. Vines hugged the lattice-lined walls, crawling out above their heads, the glass ceiling above enhancing the outside feel.

"You're the one who said my face isn't that famous." Nathan glanced up. "By the by, why are we always hanging out in spaces with glass ceilings?"

"Relax. The EAEA isn't going to come through the ceiling." At least, she didn't think they would. She glanced around, but no armbanded agents stalked between the potted plants. They might be in disguise, too.

If everything was going according to plan, they'd be around here somewhere. And they'd be here in force.

"Let's hope they come at all," Nathan said, echoing her thoughts. "Chloe didn't seem all that excited to abandon her post in Philadelphia."

Mary couldn't tell how he was feeling about his sister's current engagement with the U.S. government. Not good, obviously, but did he still think he could save Chloe somehow? He'd clearly discarded the desire for her validation—she'd never deserved to bestow that, anyway—but it wasn't always so easy to set family aside. No matter how problematic they were.

The waiter returned to take their drink orders just as Jeff sauntered into the place with an entourage of four Armani-clad security guards, who split to two separate tables within hitting distance of the one they'd staked out for his conversation with Travis. Center stage. Jeff's specialty.

The movie star looked as golden as ever, slim waisted and broad shouldered, well aware that he sported the prettiest face in Hollywood. He sat down at the table after throwing a smile and a wave to the other diners, many of whom were staring openly at him. Probably used to seeing senators and cabinet members, this close to D.C. Not Hollywood icons.

When Mary had first met Jeff, every move he'd taken had been a self-serving one, from accompanying her to a party to trying to win a seat on the board of her foundation. She wasn't entirely clear on what had changed—aside from her barging into his home on a regular basis to hide from anyone and everyone—but he'd somehow become one of LIO's allies.

And it wasn't just because he liked her, either. Mary wasn't even sure he *did* like her.

She had to admit she was looking forward to seeing him

talk with Travis Bertram, who was just making his entrance now. The bureaucrat had upgraded his wardrobe since the last time Mary had seen him, when he'd tried to barge into HQ for an 'inspection'—though admittedly, he'd been wearing an overcoat then. But his shoes were polished to an almost blinding shine, and the fit of the sport coat was much better than the overcoat had been.

She couldn't help it. She noticed these things.

Jeff got up to shake Travis's hand, their greetings reaching Mary's earpiece by way of the wire Jeff wore under his collar.

"You seriously never dated that guy?" Nathan asked. "I'm not jealous, I swear. It's just that going by looks alone, I might date him. And I'm not even attracted to men."

"Plus, you kind of hate him." Mary kept her eyes on the door. "But no. I didn't date him. I was kind of hung up on someone else at the time."

Nathan just tipped her that half smile of his. In her ear, Pete grumbled something about not being able to hear what was happening. The guy was still on edge with her after she'd accused the team of spying, and she supposed he was within his rights to be angry. She'd have to figure out an apology later. Maybe Gail would have an idea. Unless Gail was pissed at her, too.

Greetings out of the way, Jeff and Travis settled at the table. Travis sat with his back ramrod straight, hands in his lap, while Jeff lounged. Mary didn't understand how anyone could *lounge* in these metal chairs—there was committing to a park theme, and there was overdoing it—but Jeff managed it. He draped his arm over an empty chair at a neighboring table, taking up the largest possible amount of space.

The man could look businesslike when he wanted to. She'd seen it. Today, he was clearly out to annoy.

She recognized the posture well enough. She'd certainly been on the receiving end.

"How'd you get started in your line of work, Trav?" Jeff asked. "Is it like politicians' school, or the Hague or something? I'm unclear on the process."

"I graduated from Yale law," Travis said. His back was stiff, his chin tilted up as though he wasn't sure Jeff was making fun of him.

"Ah, law. Of course. I love lawyers. They get me out of all kinds of trouble."

Travis narrowed his eyes. "Your lawyers get lots of people out of trouble. Where *is* Holland Gold these days, Mr. Hayes?"

"Who knows what kinds of caves lawyers hang upside down in when they're not wheedling me out of tight spots?" Jeff drummed his fingers on the table. "If you're referring to the incident in California, I assure you that Mr. Gold was as surprised as you were to find that those LIO operatives had escaped."

Travis gave him a tight smile. "I'm sure he was."

Nathan tapped Mary on the wrist to get her attention, glancing toward the door, where a trio of men in suits were moving into the room, eyes trained on their table.

"Ooh, almost good disguises." She leaned across the table to kiss him. "Pete? It's showtime."

"I gathered," Pete said. "Check your nine o'clock."

Mary glanced to the left, where everyone seated at the bar had abandoned their seats and fell into formation with the suits as they stalked toward the table. Even one of Jeff's security guards had stood up, joining his actual colleagues to block the other three from making a move.

Smooth. That was a good move, with the security guy. Mary would have applauded Travis, had he not made every choice exactly according to LIO's plan. It was almost too good.

Several of the other diners had stood to surround Jeff and Travis, leaving every other table empty. None of them wore armbands; none of them needed to.

Mary tried to feign surprise as the suits stopped at her table. The numbers were as good as she'd hoped they'd be. Maybe better; some of the waiters were watching too closely to be actual servers.

She could only hope there were more waiting in the wings. That the promise of catching a group of LIO operatives had been enough to draw the EAEA out of Philadelphia in significant numbers.

One of the suits motioned for her to stand with a condescending flick of his fingers, and she followed his instructions, raising her hands and affecting the most innocent look she could muster.

Instead of leading her away, the suits led her to Travis.

"It's like he's obeying a script," Pete said in her ear.

Yeah, well. Eloise understood the guy. Mary thought she did, too. He didn't like to be made a fool of, and he would certainly take any opportunity to publicly humiliate someone who tried.

Jeff, on the other hand, was humiliation proof. Or so he'd assured her.

The suits led her over to Jeff's table, Nathan right behind, and it really was as good as they'd hoped. Chloe was leaning beside the bar now, grinning like she'd just won the lottery. Her hair was eerily shiny, her freckles giving her a deceptively innocent look.

They'd brought everyone along for the ride.

This was going to be fun.

Travis stood. "You might expect everyone to bow to your whims, Mr. Hayes, but I'm not so easily misled."

Mary had to recall her celebrity persona to keep from smirking. It was like leading children to a candy store, honestly.

Jeff leaned back, propping his hands behind his head. "Whatever can you mean, Trav? I thought we were friends."

Travis touched his tie. "We most certainly are not. I had your car bugged. I heard everything."

Mary, who'd faked the message from Travis's assistant suggesting the bug, did her best to look alarmed. It'd been a while since she'd had to act at this level. It felt like stretching a little-used muscle.

"Oh, no," Jeff said, calmly. "You didn't."

If Travis noted Jeff's lack of distress, he didn't let on. The guy was practically vibrating. "I did. Your friends are under arrest. We'll find Eloise and the others. I know they're skulking here somewhere. We'll arrest them, and we'll arrest you, and we'll lock you away until the world says, 'huh, I wonder whatever happened to that guy who played the doctor in that one movie a million years ago.'"

Travis, Mary thought, was enjoying this a little too much.

Jeff made no move to stand. "You'll arrest *me*? Why, whatever for?" He held his hand out to Mary. "She doesn't have powers. Neither does her friend, beyond the power to annoy me. They don't need to register anywhere. Do they?"

Travis gave his head an angry shake. "They've aided and abetted—they're here to attack—"

"And you have proof?" Jeff asked. "Come on now, Trav, you're the lawyer. Explain it to me, won't you?"

"I don't need proof." Travis nodded to Chloe. "Arrest them."

Chloe moved, and the ceiling exploded.

For a moment, Mary thought Chloe had done it. And then everything was chaos, glass falling like rain as the EAEA scrambled into formation while trying to avoid the shards. Mary dove for Jeff, shoving him out of his chair and dragging him behind the bar as Nathan ducked in the other direction to shelter behind a table.

Huh. He'd been right about the ceiling.

"Part of the plan, darling?" Jeff asked.

Mary ripped off her wig, eyes glued on the ceiling. What was happening? Why would the EAEA shatter the ceiling when they had the place surrounded? "This isn't us."

Jeff ripped off his tie. "Yes, I suspected that was going too smoothly. Do try to keep me from getting killed, won't you?"

A trio of dark figures descended through the open ceiling and landed on the latticework above before dropping over the sides and into the restaurant. Chloe was shouting orders to her people, who fumbled for the serum packets at their belts. They probably thought it was El breaking through the ceiling.

It definitely wasn't.

"I'll do my best," Mary said. "Stay here."

"Wouldn't dream of doing otherwise."

Mary crawled to the end of the bar and peered around. Had Wave come to assist them? If so, it only proved why they ought to be working together instead of apart.

The newcomers were wearing all black. As she watched, one of them stretched out a hand, and a bird fluttered down from the latticework to land on his palm.

Ranger. It had to be.

Thunder rolled outside, though the day was perfectly clear. Carlisle.

Mary knew who the third figure was, even before the woman turned. She looked like a different person, the wrinkles smoothed out of her face, her back drawn straight. But no matter how her appearance had changed—no matter how many years the clock seemed to have reversed—she would always be the woman responsible for killing Mary's parents.

After months of hiding, Dolly Reyna had chosen this moment to reappear.

SURVEILLANCE HAD NEVER BEEN QUITE SO SATISFYING as when Eloise used it to watch half of the Philadelphia-based EAEA clear out of the city.

Jeff Hayes, it seemed, made for good bait. And if the EAEA had reached the mistaken conclusion that the rest of the league would be joining him in D.C., and not just Mary and Nathan, well, Travis would just have to add it to her growing list of offenses.

During her brief jaunt toward the capital with Ire, the underground community's new hiding spot had transformed into a training facility. They'd lost all their cookware, their sleeping bags, pretty much everything when they'd evacuated, but someone had scavenged for cardboard targets, and now half the hidden enhanced humans were practicing shaky abilities under Tally's direction—levitating the targets, throwing vines at them—while the other half practiced self-defense with Dad and Quin on the other end of the room.

Even with half the EAEA cleared out of Philadelphia, there'd still be plenty of agents on the street. But the people here were far from powerless—that was the foundation of the whole problem—and it was time for them to use their abilities to escape the city's checkpoints.

Now, as they prepared to leave, Eloise called on them to split into their assigned teams. When the EAEA activated their version of Dawn's tracking powers, they'd find everyone had scattered.

Eloise's fingertips burned, her mind tilting as if to reach for the Knife. She'd stretched their connection even further on the way to D.C., but now that she was back in Philly, the sense of it was stronger again. As if the stretch had just extended the blade's reach.

"Are you sure those fingers can't open us a portal?" Ire asked, stepping up beside her. He was leading one of the larger teams, a group of twenty. Dad was entertaining another bigger group, this one with several children, by turning his fingers into sparklers. The recruits—Quin, Tally, and Len—each led a team of fifteen.

And Eloise would lead a team, too.

"I can't," she said. "You didn't see what the Knife did, how I lost control. If I use powers it gave me... I can't."

The Pearl Knife could harm these people, far more than it helped them. And so could any enhanced abilities she'd leeched out of it without meaning to.

Pulling herself together, Eloise gave the command, and everyone in the community made for the tunnels—where the teams promptly scattered in different directions. Eloise guided her group forward as the others dispersed, fewer footsteps surrounding her as they ascended ladders and broke through bricked-up passageways.

Eloise's com buzzed with action as the other teams reported their locations, popping out of the tunnels in what the EAEA would hopefully soon experience as the world's largest whack-a-mole game. Tally had taken the jumpers, the flyers, and the very brave on a tour of the city's rooftops, while Dad—who shouldn't be trackable—set off fiery distractions on the other side of the city.

Eloise's team was taking on the old city.

When she reached her access point, she climbed quickly and shifted a manhole cover out of the way, pulling herself out onto the brick street in front of Independence Hall. Lights shone out of the bell tower like beacons as her group emerged behind her.

Up ahead and to the right, a pair of armbanded operatives bolted toward the group from beneath the triple archways. They must have been tracking her progress underground, using the Dawn-inspired serum. Just as she'd hoped they would.

And, as she'd hoped, there was only a pair. They were stretched thin, expecting the league to be in D.C. They must have been surprised to see her pop back up here. And her colleagues, too, making waves all over the city.

Eloise prodded her team into a run. "Remember," she said, "we're not hiding anymore. We just have to make it to the river."

Eloise dodged to the front of the group so she could lead the way to Penn's Landing. Stocky colonial buildings filled the blocks to her right, a flat grassy field to the left. It made her feel exposed, and she had to keep reminding herself that that was the idea.

Her group followed on her heels, some of them breathing hard, but keeping up nonetheless. Ethan was perched on his dad's back; the rest of the kids were older, getting by on foot. They surged into the intersection and hurried to the other side, hugging the walls of a gray-stoned restaurant, a small beauty salon, a basement bar with music blaring onto the sidewalk.

This part of the city was all bricks and columns and tree-studded parks to the right, statues of long-dead founding fathers and picturesque brick cobblestones that caught the edges of her group's feet. To the left, modern hotels rose up beside coffee shops, offices, banks.

Boots pounded behind them, along with shouted orders. Five blocks to the river. They just had to make it to the river.

"Landed," Quin's voice said into her com, breathless. Eloise imagined the others, fighting, running. How many of them would make it? How many would get taken? It felt like a certainty that someone would be captured.

The agents shouted behind her, close now, and Eloise fell to the side, waving her group toward the river as she dropped to take up the rear. It was a straight shot to the water, but they weren't the fastest group—hence the relatively easy route—and some of them were going to need to fight back.

Gina fell in beside Eloise as they urged the group on, and Grant must have passed Ethan to someone else, because he joined them, casting uncertain glances back. "They're gaining on us."

"They should have caught us," Gina said. "What are they waiting for?"

Another pair of agents appeared out of a side street, as if from nowhere. But the first pair's delay—waiting for backup, apparently—was going to cost them.

The pavement shifted to cobblestone here, the buildings dropping into short, brick-faced historicals on either side. Or they were all made to look like historical buildings; who could say? The street had gone bumpy and narrow, cars wedged into parking spots on either side.

It was perfect.

Eloise spun, Gina and Grant at her sides. And they didn't wait for her instructions. They dropped to the ground, throwing their palms against the street.

Plants trembled up out of the cobblestones, cracking into

the city with audible groans, and their pursuers faltered. As quickly as Eloise could blink, there was a forest crawling toward the buildings, out of the buildings, vines reaching across the narrow street to twine together.

"Landed," Ire said, followed quickly by a second confirmation from Len, the sticky-fingered recruit who preferred to stay at HQ. He was doing great. They all were. Just Tally and Dad left. And Eloise.

The vines were thickening; they'd block the street soon enough. But they weren't fast enough to stop the EAEA. The agents seemed to have realized what was happening, and they pushed forward, no doubt wishing their little serum kits held fire power right about now so they could incinerate the barrier.

Eloise attacked, rushing the nearest agent and forcing them to shuffle back and evade her punch. She could have, perhaps should have, asked another of her group to stay behind and fight. But she wanted to get them to safety as quickly as possible.

In the meantime, she'd just have to avoid getting arrested while her team fled to safety. She threw another punch at her attacker, catching him in the jaw and tripping up his partner with a roundhouse kick that took him out at the shins. She was vaguely aware that a third agent had vanished, no doubt to run around the block to try and head off her group. The fourth was trying to climb the vines.

In her ear, Tally was shouting as Dad's confirmation came in. Two groups left, but Tally's was in trouble. Eloise tried to block out the sound—she couldn't do anything to help. She could only fight one battle at a time.

Eloise shouted for Gina and Grant to go, and they ran, their greenery continuing to thicken into a wall that blocked the road. The climbing EAEA operative screamed as vines crawled over his wrists, locking him to the web even as the growth slowed in its makers' absence.

Eloise elbowed opponent number one in the neck as number two staggered to his feet and tried to circle her from behind. He reached for his serum kit, and Eloise lunged, but his partner caught her from behind, twisting her arm painfully. She wrenched out of his grip as the other guy toasted her with his bright green serum.

But the taunt cost him. A streak of light rushed past him, snapping the serum out of his hand. Before the vial could shatter against the cobblestones, the agent's head snapped back with an unseen punch.

Or at least, with a punch that was too fast to see. Because it was Steve Taylor who materialized before her as the agent collapsed. "Hey, El," he said. "You look like you could use an assist."

Nathan's past melted into his present as Dolly Reyna loomed over the restaurant, standing on the rim of the raised flower bed as if it were a stage. So like the figure who'd dropped into his school all those years ago. When he'd thought she was saving them all from Wave. And though the message was tangled now—the notion that LIO had framed Wave an intellectual certainty—the fear that washed over him was, for a moment, that of a twelve-year-old kid who just wanted to save his little sister.

A sister who was currently striding toward Dolly with all the confidence of someone who believed she stood on the right side. Across the way, Mary was peering out from behind the bar, watching the scene unfold. They'd split in opposite directions when Dolly landed, because of course they had. At least she was safe.

Chloe stopped in front of Dolly, and Nathan tried to blink away the image of kid Chloe, her red pigtails, her dolls. That girl was gone, replaced with hate and cruelty. But to Nathan, it was like watching a scene play out in double negative, history writing over the scene in front of him.

Dolly raised a hand, as if to cut Chloe down, and Nathan

lunged out of his hiding spot to tackle his sister out of the way as a fissure sizzled through the air, splitting a metal table in half and missing them by mere inches. He recognized the heat from that wonderful experience where Sever's robo-soldier had dangled him above a portal not all that long ago.

Dolly was using her portals as weapons. Great.

Chloe tried to scramble out of Nathan's grip, but he dragged her back under a table and held on tight.

"I'm not your sister anymore," Chloe said through clenched teeth. "Let me go."

"You're welcome," Nathan said. "So glad you're alive, Chlo."

Travis Bertram might have been the only person in the room who hadn't moved. He was still seated at his table in the center of the room, as though he still expected prompt delivery of his lobster.

Finally, Travis shook himself out of his open-jawed stupor to face the LIO retirees, frowning so hard that Nathan half thought the man might plant his hands on his hips and send them to their rooms.

"You," Travis said, panting ever so slightly, "are under arrest."

Huh. Not that far off, then.

Travis did have a lot of backup, though. He waved a hand, and the EAEA agents who'd been hesitating on the sidelines started to move in. A couple of them tipped back vials of serum.

Dolly was smiling. Serene, though the agents were closing in. How many portals could she make? How many people could she split into pieces? And what was she even doing here?

Birds swooped from the latticework above, some screeching as they dive-bombed the oncoming EAEA agents. Sparrows and crows alike, digging talons into shoulders and necks, leaving bloody trails across the faces of the EAEA operatives as they tried to take cover.

Rain dropped in suddenly, as though someone had overturned a bucket, and Nathan wiped streams of water out of his eyes, completely at a loss as to what he ought to do next. He honestly didn't know whether he should join the fight, or who he should even be fighting.

Mary was opting to remain hidden behind the bar, and that was good enough for him, as long as he could restrain Chloe long enough to keep her from dying.

She didn't deserve it. He knew that. But he couldn't let her go, either.

Chloe obviously wanted to get back to the fight, though. She fought his grip, trying to twist away, her bangs stuck flat and glistening against her forehead as she screamed instructions into a com unit.

But the EAEA either wasn't as well trained as they should be, or simply not used to... unusual combat situations. The league had mostly worked to avoid the EAEA, fighting only when they were forced. Yes, the agents fought well when they entered combat. But fighting LIO was one thing.

Fighting enemies who'd actually try to kill them? Definitely another.

Travis stood stock still in the midst of the chaos. The birds ignored him, and he seemed entirely unbothered by the rain as he reached into the inner pocket of his jacket.

Nathan had a split second to wonder whether Mary had noticed the kid was carrying—he certainly hadn't—before Travis pointed a standard police-issue Glock at Dolly and, with a look of intense concentration, pulled the trigger.

A wall of energy surged across the restaurant, splitting the place in two as bright yellow lightning bolts chased one another out from where the bullet must have hit. It reminded Nathan of one of Mary's forcefields, or the walls of the LIO prison, which shifted from clear to opaque.

The air sizzled with burnt electricity, acrid and cloying, and Travis's bullet clinked to the floor, useless.

The energy settled, the smell of smoldering metal and ozone thick in the air, and even Chloe stopped struggling as Dolly stood unharmed, untouched. The shield faded, but Nathan had no doubt it was still there. No doubt at all.

Travis was shaking, raindrops pouring down his cheeks, but he didn't lower the gun. His teeth were bared, and—it didn't seem possible—he seemed far more angry than he was afraid.

Nathan, for one, felt icy dread clenched in the pit of his stomach. He searched for Mary, but she'd disappeared. Back behind the bar, he hoped.

Travis's finger twitched, and Chloe tensed as though to cower away from another surge from Dolly's shield.

For a beat, no one moved. Except for the birds, still swooping and screeching.

And then Travis's body jerked. His arm twisted toward the ceiling with a resounding crack, bending at an unnatural angle, and he screamed as the gun dropped out of his fingers. It was as if an invisible hand had reached down to control him, like a horror movie where a ghost snapped the bones of the person it had possessed.

Nathan didn't have time to move. He didn't have time to think. Travis screamed again, and Mary darted out from behind the bar, moving toward him. Moving, Nathan was sure, to help him.

It was too late. Travis's neck snapped, the invisible hand crushing it into a right angle, and his scream ended in a wet gurgle before his body had hit the floor.

Still hiding next to Nathan, Chloe doubled over and vomited.

Nathan couldn't take his eyes off of Dolly and her two companions. They couldn't have done this. Could they? The Knife had given her the power to make portals on her own. It could do plenty of impossible things; fly, reach through space to cut people, communicate in people's thoughts.

But Nathan had never seen it create a shield. He'd never seen it break a man in half, or twist bones. Besides, Dolly seemed to be waiting for something.

A breath, and then another, his head reeling from the blood, the sickness, the still-dissipating smell of burning ozone. Nathan expected the something to drop through the ceiling. Someone.

Instead, he walked right through the door. A slight man with a dollop of curls and the kind of saunter than Nathan associated with kings. A step behind him, a familiar face: the elf-like man—being?—with the shoulder-length curls who'd communicated with Sloane. Who'd sent her friend to steal the Knife, and then killed him when he'd refused to hand it over.

The pieces snapped together, and Nathan's stomach nearly joined his sister's.

Sever had come to Earth. And LIO's retirees were working with him.

ELOISE LOOKED ABOUT AS happy to see Steve as he'd expected she would be. Which was to say, not very. Even though he'd just punched an EAEA agent before the guy could swallow an enhanced-abilities serum—which most definitely would have made her life more complicated right about now—she was frowning at Steve like he'd joined the other side or something.

Talk about misplaced rage.

The first EAEA agent shook himself out of his shock and came for her, but she repeated the elbow to the neck Steve had seen her land right before his arrival. The agent caught her and tried to push her back, but she used his momentum to drop him to the ground with little more than a twist of the wrist.

She was the most beautiful woman he'd ever seen in his life.

"Great," Eloise said, "Mary doesn't think I can handle myself."

Steve held out a hand. "Nah. Mary thinks you're under-staffed, and I'm fast."

Eloise didn't take his hand. Instead, she turned for the plant-wall behind her—he was going to need an explanation on that—and started to climb. "I know you're fast," she said. "You ran away quickly enough."

Steve looked pointedly at the EAEA agent, who was sinking deeper into the tangle of greenery by the minute. But El was climbing without a problem, so Steve followed, keeping pace with her. "You're going to pretend you didn't push me out the door?"

She shimmied over the top of the barrier with the grace of a gymnast, then grabbed a loose vine and used it to swing to the ground. She dropped the vine and looked up at him, her expression just a little too neutral to be believed. "So you're here to stay, then?"

Leave it to El to answer a question with a question. Steve paused at the top of the barrier, lush greenery just casually strung up between a salon and a bar. In the middle of historical Philadelphia.

He didn't know the answer to her question, didn't know how to begin to sort through what it meant, so he stalled, allowing his gaze to drift out toward the river.

Eloise's group had nearly cleared the highway overpass, the last stretch of road before the river—and escape. Buses dotted the route alongside a wide stretch of red-bricked sidewalk, which was no doubt there for the benefit of river-bound tourists heading for the ferry.

Her people were closing in on their goal. One couple lagged a block behind, but they were catching up. They were going to make it.

A van screamed around the corner and onto the overpass, careening toward the sidewalk. But the buses shielded the walkway, so that the van could only drag along beside them, the screech of metal nearly unbearable even at this distance.

It was almost like the van moved by instinct, trying to reach its mark without registering there were obstacles in its path. Steve couldn't see who was driving the thing. If anyone.

Eloise spun in the direction of the sound, but Steve was already moving. The jungle-wall crystalized, every detail freezing as time danced to his demands. He leapt down from the wall, sweeping El along with him, and the world spun its slow march as they outpaced the van to its destination.

Because now, with the route to Penn's Landing inching toward its destiny at a crawl, Steve caught sight of a second van careening its way up the ramp toward the bridge. It was speeding the wrong way, headed straight for the first.

Steve shifted course, blowing past the bus-swiping van—driverless, as he'd suspected, and he knew too little about its mechanisms to stop the inevitable—to meet the escapees from the front.

The world jolted into its usual time, and Steve let go of Eloise to throw his arms to the sides, barring the escapees' path. "Get back," he said. "Behind the buses!"

The group obeyed, turning around to head back for the bridge. Steve swiveled to face the river—there had to be *something* more he could do—but this time Eloise swept him to the ground as the vans crashed behind them, the second coming fast enough to knock the first into the blue fencing that surrounded the ferry boarding area. The vehicles stopped just short of a patch of trees, smoke belching out of both crumpled hoods.

For a second, all he could do was breathe. El had her hand on his back, her body half wrapped around his.

"Wow," Steve said. "They really didn't want you to get to the river."

Eloise got to her feet quickly and offered him a hand as she beckoned her group forward. She didn't even look shaken, though Steve thought he knew her better than that. "They're stretched thin. But Tally's group is in trouble."

She pointed to her ear, indicating her com. Whatever she was hearing, it wasn't good.

"Where are they?" Steve asked.

Eloise drew her phone out of her pocket and activated the map, pointing to the 30th Street Station. Almost a straight shot from here, if he dipped north first and added a jaunt around City Hall.

Steve took off, the city fading to the periphery of his awareness as he pulsed through time and space. He understood the theory of relativity about as well as the average Ph.D-lacking Joe, but his cells lived it. They played with time and space like concert pianists, moving along the keys of the universe with dexterity that felt like part muscle memory, part intensive study.

And part pure luck.

Steve mostly just went along for the ride, allowing Philadelphia's music to wash around him as he rocketed through its streets.

When he stopped, the world crystalized around him into utter madness.

The EAEA had cornered Tally's people outside of Philadelphia's 30th Street Station, the building's stately columns forcing a head-turning contrast to the chaos of the battle taking place on its doorstep. Armbanded agents had the group surrounded, and several people lay with their backs to the columns, hands tied behind their backs.

As Steve arrived, Tally was leaping to the top of one of the central columns to hang off of the Corinthian embellishments. An EAEA agent followed, ascending as if someone had sewn springs into the bottoms of his heels and trying to pin Tally down before she could jump away.

Great. Just great.

Steve blurred into motion, hoping he could move fast enough to evade the EAEA's notice. He snapped the zip-ties on a young man's wrists, and the kid opened his eyes a slit. "Took my powers," he said. "I'm sorry."

Anger burned hot in Steve's chest. At the EAEA, at the entire country, for forcing them into this situation, for their hatred and their fear.

"Hang on, man," he said. "I'm getting you out of here."

He whipped away with the kid, depositing him in an alcove by City Hall before ripping back through space to the station. He was only one person, but he was fast.

He knelt by a second enhanced human, this one a middle-aged woman. She was unconscious.

Fighting rising rage, Steve snapped her zip ties.

And then something knocked him back into regular time, shredding his shirt across the pavement as the super-speeding EAEA agent knocked him across the steps. He narrowly missed smashing his head on a column, rolling instead.

He'd fought an EAEA super-speeder last March, with El and Ire and Will.

He really hated these guys.

Tally was screaming in the background as the speeder attacked, fists flying too fast for Steve to make out any details about their source. He needed to get back to the group, to the people—EAEA agents were loading them into a van, dumping unconscious bodies and struggling conscious ones alike onto the floor—but it was all he could do to defend, to keep from getting slammed into unconsciousness himself.

His attacker swung and Steve ducked, using the agent's momentum to flip them to the ground. Tally dropped from the column, throwing punches in midair and stumbling her landing. Her opponent used the split-second advantage to plunge a syringe into her neck.

Steve lunged for her, but his own foe staggered to his feet, ready to attack again, and Tally called for Steve to run, even as the sedative took hold and her eyes fluttered shut.

He didn't want to run. He couldn't run, couldn't leave these people.

But there was another person to save, the young man he'd left vulnerable at City Hall. If he stayed here, he'd only get stuffed into the van with everyone else.

Steve dodged his attacker and abandoned the station, running in circles and stopping to hide in a doorway until he knew for certain that no one had followed him. With his heart as heavy as lead in his chest, he returned to City Hall and retrieved the still-sleeping young man.

He'd saved one, and left at least five to the mercy of the EAEA. Who knew where these people would take them?

TRAVIS'S BODY had barely hit the floor, and the EAEA was swiveling to face the newcomer, hands trembling on weapons they'd been using for a spare few months. Some of them hesitated, casting anxious looks back toward Dolly, clearly aware that they'd found themselves in a two-fronted battle.

It hardly mattered. Sever lifted a hand, dropping the first wave of agents like a fist through sand. Loud, bone-cracking, bloodstained sand.

Cold rain fell in torrents, washing rivers of blood across the restaurant floor as birds spiraled above like a tornado ready to attack, blue jays and starlings and robins crowded together into a muddy assembly of sharp talons and beating wings.

Mary's hair stuck to the back of her neck, cold and dripping. It was a strange thing to notice, a useless thing—Jeff's hand was on her arm, Nathan frozen across the room with Chloe half-senseless at his side—as Sever faced down the next wave of EAEA agents. He was completely dry, unaffected by the rain, the eye of a frenzied hurricane.

He looked like a man—not a god, not an alien—with dark hair, gentle spiderwebs of lines crisscrossing in the corners of his eyes, standing there with his eyebrows raised. Waiting. The man they'd been warned about, here at last, with Dolly Reyna somehow at his side.

The woman who'd killed her parents, who'd corrupted the league and sent Wave into hiding. Who'd used Mary for her money, controlled Eloise, and held Will hostage. Dolly wasn't looking at Mary, and though Mary stood out in the open now, she thought perhaps Dolly hadn't noticed her.

A trio of EAEA agents blurred toward Sever, as if suddenly remembering that they had access to super speed. Sever batted them away like flies, hardly moving more than he had when the un-serumed group had attacked. They fell, squirming, as the next group hesitated. Their numbers were dropping fast, their leadership dead at the enemy's feet.

"Mary," Jeff said, hardly audible amid the rustling and the screaming. "We need to go."

Go. Yes, they needed to go. Mary's eyes drifted back toward Dolly, but her attention caught on Nathan. She had to get him out of here, and Jeff. And, she supposed, any of the EAEA who would be willing to trust her. Assuming they lived through this.

Assuming they intended to escape at all. Because the remaining agents parted to make way as if responding to a silent command, making way for a single agent to stomp out of the kitchen, letting the double doors bang shut behind him. His muscles bulged under his armband, and Mary wondered whether the temporary nature of the serum made them swell and contract. And how much damage that might cause.

Or maybe the EAEA had embraced some permanent powers. It honestly wouldn't have surprised her very much.

Sever allowed the muscled agent to approach, a pleasant smile on his lips—if a destroyer of worlds could ever be said to look 'pleasant'—as he allowed the man to swing a punch at his face. He caught the fist in his palm, which didn't look like it should be possible, such a huge fist in such a small man's palm.

But when the agent pushed back, Sever's smile actually widened.

He didn't seem worried about making it across the room to the shield that, she assumed, still protected Dolly and the other retirees. He didn't look like he'd ever been worried about anything in his life.

Mary moved back behind the bar, scanning the space and trying to assess their exit routes.

"Please tell me you've got a toy that can get us out of here," Jeff said. "Like a ladder in your purse. Or a hologram."

Mary shook herself. They needed a solution. How was it that Jeff was the one with the clear head right now? "How is a hologram going to get us out of here?"

"You're the one who makes the advanced tech. I just work here."

"Do you?"

He rolled up his sleeves. "Trust me, it shocks me more than it does you."

The super-strong EAEA agent was still holding his own against Sever, though surely the alien god whatever-he-was could have snapped the man's neck in a moment. Mary didn't need to understand Sever's motivation; she only needed to get her people out of here, and Sever was distracted. Enjoying himself, or so it appeared.

"They put the bar here for a reason," Jeff said. For a second, Mary didn't understand what he meant—he couldn't possibly be considering a drink right now—but then he nodded to the taps. "Where are the kegs?"

Mary glanced down. While the rest of the floor in the restaurant was hardwood, she and Jeff were standing on metal.

She frowned, picturing getting trapped underground. "What if there's not a way out?"

"Then I suppose I'm fired." He pointed to the window. "But there's a delivery entrance in the sidewalk."

Sever had fully engaged the strongman now, though he still seemed to be lightly sparring while the other man glistened with sweat. Mary caught Nathan's eye and tilted her head toward the taps, beckoning him to join them. But the floor was littered with bodies and toppled tables, and the distance—though it couldn't have been more than thirty feet—might as well have been a cavern.

Still, Nathan began to circle around the back of the scraggly remains of the EAEA, dragging Chloe with him and keeping an eye on Sever's back. The alien-god continued pushing his fight through the center of the room, stepping easily over Travis's fallen body as he made his way toward Dolly. None of the other people in the restaurant, it seemed, had been actual diners; Mary didn't see a single civilian in the place. Even the waitstaff seemed to have evaporated.

Travis Bertram had really committed to this one. A sick feeling twisted through her stomach, and she kept her eyes away from Travis's ruined form, focusing instead on Nathan's progress across the back of the room.

Having made his way to the front, Sever clenched a fist with the air of a child who'd finished playing with a toy. The temporary strongman dropped to his knees, clawing at his throat as his face turned red, his mouth gaping.

Mary itched to help him, to do something, but she was no match for Sever.

This was not how this was supposed to go.

Jeff dropped to open the trap door, lifting it slowly and setting it silently against the concrete. Mary watched Nathan, willing him to hurry. He was close now, skirting along the window, just yards from where she stood. He was going to make it.

But Sever's attention was drifting back toward the door he'd entered through, his eyes landing on Nathan and Chloe. The strongman was still alive at his feet, his mouth opening and closing as he desperately tried to draw breath, but Sever seemed to have forgotten him already as he stepped forward.

"Stop," he said.

When Nathan didn't, Sever waved a hand. The remaining handful of EAEA agents—so few of them now—stepped aside, confusion blurring their eyes as their legs carried them out of the alien-god's path. What kind of monster cracked spines and snapped necks when he could control his opponent's movements? Why not just freeze them in place until he'd gotten what he wanted?

Cold dread curled through her body, and she swallowed hard to keep from being sick. Everything Sloane had said was true. This was not an enemy they could match. Not on their own.

Mary didn't know if Sever recognized Nathan from the fights with his robo-soldiers, or if he recognized Chloe. Perhaps he simply meant to exert control over everyone here. Prevent anyone from escaping.

As if responding to the thought, Nathan froze mid-run, his limbs obeying Sever's command just as the EAEA agents had done. Chloe lay half-draped across his arm, and Mary couldn't tell whether Sever had frozen her, too, or if she was simply insensible with shock.

She wouldn't wait to see. Nathan was in reach, two arms' lengths from the other end of the bar, and she'd be damned if she was going to lose him. Motioning for Jeff to go, she stepped out from behind the bar and faced Sever head on.

Behind Sever, Dolly gasped. Like someone had shut off a faucet, the rain stopped. Mary couldn't help feeling a tinge of shock at the idea that they cared at all. They couldn't possibly be afraid of her, not with such power on their side; was it possible they were afraid *for* her?

As for Sever, Mary wasn't sure what reaction she expected from him. Anger. Laughter. Unbreakable pressure against her windpipe.

Instead, the alien-god dropped his hands. She met his gaze, somehow holding his attention, even as Nathan collapsed in her peripheral vision, even as he began to crawl toward the bar, still dragging his undeserving sister.

Sever's eyes were black, his pupils like points of fire ringed by emerald green. Mary stared at him, and he stared back, lips parted as if in shock. He might be a god, but something akin to blood had to be pumping through something akin to veins, because his already pallid skin dropped another shade.

"Adina," he said, his voice deep and craggy, like scraping boulders. "My... my beloved. How is it possible?"

Mary felt herself clenching her jaw, the muscle ticking frantically, but there was no way to release it. Her teeth might crack, and still she wouldn't be able to let go. She gave her head a shake, unable to understand what Sever was saying. She didn't know anyone named Adina.

Sever's expression was locked onto hers, a literal storm playing across his irises as the orange spots crackled with jagged scars of lightning. He recognized her, clearly—as his beloved? Really?—or he thought he did. But Mary had to fight the urge to turn and look behind her, for some person he surely was addressing over her head.

Mary honestly didn't know how she was supposed to react. He couldn't possibly think she was some immortal alien goddess. The idea was ludicrous. But this guy was looking at her with open wonder. He certainly believed he knew her.

And she didn't need the answer now. Nathan stumbled the last three steps and disappeared behind the bar at her back.

Mary moved to follow, and Sever raised a hand as if to stop her in the same way he'd stopped Nathan and the others. She tensed, ready to fight, ready to do anything if it meant Nathan's escape.

But nothing happened. For a second, Mary thought Sever had lost his nerve, that whoever he thought she was, he couldn't stand to control her. When Sever turned his palm over, staring at it in wide-eyed disbelief, she realized that his attempt to control her had failed.

Mary didn't know why, and she didn't care. She dove behind the bar and swung herself into the basement, pulling the metal door shut and practically falling down the ladder, the scent of hops not enough to replace the metallic tang of blood from above. Nathan was running for the open delivery entrance, where Jeff was waiting with the doors open. Mary nearly wanted to laugh in giddy shock at the fact that he'd been the one to save them.

On the heels of the others, she fled to the street, leapt into the driver's seat of their waiting van, and sped toward HQ.

WHILE HER GROUP celebrated inside the ferry, ecstatic at their escape, Eloise stood outside by the back rail of the ship, sifting through reports on the price they'd paid for that success. Steve leaned beside her, elbows on the rail, watching the Delaware River part calmly before them as they made their way north. He didn't say a word as she spoke with Pete and Nathan, Pete's voice shaky, Nathan's ragged. He merely stood beside her, and she couldn't bring herself to be sorry he was there.

Tally and five other innocent enhanced humans had been hauled off, to god knew where. Travis Bertram was dead, the EAEA cut to pieces. And while she couldn't be sorry that they'd been stopped, she would never have wished for it to happen this way. She suspected that was more compassion than Travis would have shown her, but she couldn't help it. She wouldn't try. She could only hope that there would be a way to liberate Tally, somehow.

Sever was among them at last. He'd appeared like the fulfillment of some dark prophecy, with Eloise's mother at his side, and the other retirees who'd evaded capture. Mary and Nathan had barely escaped with their lives, along with Chloe and Jeff.

And Eloise didn't dare use the Knife. Though she drew ever nearer to it, the blade remained silent, beaming no thoughts or feelings into her head. She might have thought it had been cut off from her again, except for the growing background thrum, like a heartbeat. It was there. Waiting.

When Nathan signed off—they were still in the van, headed for HQ—Eloise dropped her face into her hands, trying to rub away the shock. Someone had put on music inside the ferry, and people were dancing, their shouts and singing echoing out into the night.

"I can ask them to stop," Steve said.

Eloise shook her head. "They should have their party. They don't need to know any of this."

Not unless they absolutely had to. She wished she could hope they never would, but she had no way of knowing Sever's agenda. No way of guessing how to stop him. And certainly they'd notice that some of their friends had failed to make it out of Philadelphia. They'd learn the truth eventually.

"It's heavy," Steve said. "A burden like that."

"It's called leadership."

Steve tipped his head up, turning his gaze toward the stars. Aside from a thin haze of clouds, the sky was clear. The further they got from Philadelphia's lights, the more stars began to peek through. "It's funny," he said, "how fear of enhanced abilities becomes... pervasive."

Eloise gripped the rail, trying to ground herself in the cool metal, in the bumpy feeling of the paint. "How so?"

"Well, Travis and his followers, they didn't understand enhanced abilities. They both outlawed it and ran headlong into it, not totally understanding what it meant."

"What, because they used the powers themselves?"

"Sure. Used them, changed them. Outlawed them, in practice if not in name."

Eloise watched the lights on the banks, their reflections distorted in the dark water and blending with the silhouetted trees. "I'm not sure what you mean."

Though she kept her own gaze averted, she knew he was watching her. He'd always *seen* her, somehow, always known what she wasn't saying. Even when she hadn't wanted him to.

"Didn't see you use the Knife back there," he said.

Eloise narrowly stopped herself from reaching for a hilt that wasn't there.

"We don't understand the Knife much more than Travis understood enhanced abilities," Steve said softly. "Caution, that's one thing. But honestly, El, I think you're more afraid of yourself than you are of it."

Now Eloise did look at him. He was staring at her as intently as she'd thought, and the open expression on his face nearly sucked the air from her lungs. "The Knife took over someone's powers without me," she said. "It hurt someone."

"The Knife took action." Steve held up a hand, as though to stop her from launching into the tirade he knew she was about to throw at him. "I'm not saying it's not scary as hell. But maybe it acted for the right reasons. Maybe we need to understand it, instead of pushing it away."

Eloise didn't know how Steve knew that, but she supposed Mary had to have filled it in. And she complained that the recruits were gossipy.

"Its powers rubbed off on Dolly, and look what she's doing now."

Wreaking havoc. Siding with a genocidal alien maniac. The usual, really.

Steve rubbed his chin, thoughtful. "Exactly. Your mom's queen of the awful choices, no lie. But I'm thinking you're afraid you might become her."

Eloise swallowed her tirade. Unfortunately, that only made room for the tears. But she swallowed those, too, dropping her elbows to the rail to mimic Steve's posture. She'd missed his warmth, his candidness. She wanted to lean her head on his shoulder, to cry, to breathe him in for a while.

But she also wasn't sure if she could let him stay. Or if he'd even want to.

"I am afraid," she said, then stopped. Licked her lips. Those words were not words she said. Ever. She let her arm touch his, elbow to shoulder, let his heat ground her. "I'm afraid the Knife made her."

He looped his arm under his elbow, lacing their fingers together, his touch sending goosebumps trailing along her skin. She thought of their kiss on the plane, of how hard it had been to push him away, of how easy it would be to tug him closer now. "The Knife," he said softly, "tried to *stop* her."

In the distance, the Knife's rhythm quickened, perhaps in agreement. Or in hope. It *had* tamped down the powers that Dolly had gained by using the blade over the years, making her sick to stop her from using them. That was part of what frightened Eloise about it, this enigmatic artifact from beyond the stars.

What would it do to her, if it disagreed with her methods? The Knife didn't argue; it merely lapsed back into its rhythm of steady silence.

Steve was still looking at her. She thought of asking him again if he planned to stay. She thought of requesting it, of finding some way to articulate how much she wanted him around. She could run LIO without him; it was just that, when it came down to it, she didn't *want* to.

But she couldn't quite find the words, either. She let herself drop her head onto his shoulder, willing Mary to drive as fast as she could, willing Sever to stay distracted, somehow, while they formed a plan, and willing her tears to stay away just a little bit longer.

Sever did not ask Dolly to return them to Texas. Instead, he stayed in the restaurant, ignoring the sirens that sang in the distance as he waved the remaining EAEA agents to their knees just to cut them down like grass in a field. She could feel his shields extending outward to surround the restaurant, as though something about them resonated in her own cells.

Sever exhaled, and every body in the room ignited, burning to piles of ash in a matter of moments. Carlisle staggered to the corner to vomit, while Ranger merely settled his birds to roost. They perched in the latticework, on the bar tops, on chairs and tree branches and lanterns, peering around as though wondering how they'd come to be here.

When Sever had swept the bodies into a current of ash, he turned to Dolly, his eyes alight with anger. "You led me astray."

Dolly let her jaw drop. She'd stormed the restaurant for him, watched him cut down these people without so much as a hint of remorse. She was not the one vomiting in the corner. "*I* led you astray? How?"

It was Morik who replied. "The powers on this planet are like those of children," he said, his tone dripping with disdain. "Nothing they do can rival our lord's."

Dolly ignored the long-haired advisor. He was no one. She kept her eyes on Sever. "That was never my intention. I didn't... How could I know your strength? I've never seen powers like yours. I could not imagine it."

Sever glanced at Carlisle, who was wiping his mouth with the back of his hand. For all his queasiness, Carlisle's abilities went far beyond any they'd seen from the EAEA today.

"And those people," Dolly added, pointing to the last wisps of disintegrating ash, "were not like the league. Their powers were new. Fabricated in a lab and largely untested."

Police cars careened onto the street, and Sever flicked a finger, sending his shield jutting outward. It smashed into the cars, pushing them into simultaneous rolls, the sirens twisting and burning in her ears.

"Perhaps you're right," Sever said, but he looked at her sideways, as though he wasn't completely assuaged. Well, the man was no fool. She knew that already.

Dolly turned her back to the street and the suite of smoking police cars. "So, what happened? With... with Mary? You didn't kill her."

Dolly didn't want to feel conflicted about that. Like her parents before her, Mary O'Sullivan had caused headache after headache. She'd uncovered Dolly's deceptions and was responsible for her current banishment.

And yet... and yet, Dolly had still raised the girl. She could be excused for a moment of sentimentality.

Sever looked down at his hand, just as he'd done when facing Mary. "She is... *was*... my beloved," he said. "The woman I told you about. I forged the Blade of Starlight for her, and she betrayed me."

Dolly had watched Mary grow up, had tracked her Wave-guided existence from the moment of her birth. Mary was not centuries old. She couldn't be Sever's long-lost beloved.

As though sensing her confusion, Sever withdrew a small silver disk from his pocket and compressed a button on its side, then handed it to Dolly. "My Adina," he said, his voice rough with grief.

The disc showed her as a hologram, one that almost looked real enough to touch. The golden hair, though styled long, and the green eyes. The shape of her cheekbones, the cut of her chin. This woman looked exactly like Mary.

"If you need more proof," Sever said, "I could not control her as I did the others. It must be due to the Blade's influence."

Morik scoffed, as if any demand for proof from his master could be no more than a ridiculous insult. The birds shuffled on their perches as Ranger gasped over Dolly's shoulder, eyes locked on the hologram. "It's her," he breathed. "It has to be."

It couldn't be. There was no scenario in which Mary could be the lover who'd betrayed Sever and disappeared.

And yet... and yet, her mother's name had been Celestine. *Of the sky.* Dolly knew no more of Mary's ancestry than that. She'd never needed to. But perhaps there was more to learn.

And certainly, there was more to use. She'd been trying to get Sever to confront LIO from the start. She wanted her allies, locked within the depths of HQ. And she wanted the Pearl Knife.

Dolly handed the hologram back to Sever, who slipped it back into his pocket. Outside, the shield shuddered as more police arrived, some extracting their colleagues from the crashes while the rest attempted to break through the barrier.

"I imagine you'd like to find her," Dolly said. "And I know exactly where to look."

"Yes," Sever said, his expression distant. "Yes, I would. But first I need to finish what I started here. We must return to Arlington."

NATHAN KNEW BETTER than to ask Mary if she wanted him to take over the driving. She bore down on the gas like she could use it to interrogate the highway, fingers wrapped around the wheel, eyes bright with unshed tears. Nathan reached out to touch her shoulder, and she flinched.

Chloe sat beside Jeff Hayes in the row behind them, staring out the window. Her lips moved, but no sound came out, as though she were silently uttering a mantra. Shock, most definitely, and who could blame her? Nathan's shoes were speckled with blood and feathers, his knees similarly stained where he'd dropped to the ground. His clothes were still damp from the rain.

Jeff had already been in the back when Nathan had reached the car—always expecting the chauffeur, as far as Nathan could see—and Nathan hadn't exactly wanted to insist. He wasn't sure he wanted his sister here at all, but between leaving her in the restaurant to die by Sever's hand and stuffing her into their getaway car, he'd chosen the latter.

Besides, he'd wanted to stay beside Mary. She was so tense, he thought she might crack. He didn't know how to help.

As he considered it, her lips trembled, and she pressed

them together as though willing her shock to stay contained. "Why," she said, then stopped. Breathed. Bore down on the gas. "Why does he think I'm his girlfriend?"

There was no need to say Sever's name, clearly. Even thinking it felt like a summons.

Jeff leaned in between the seats. "Ex-girlfriend, I suspect."

Mary glared at the road, but Nathan glanced at Jeff. "What makes you say ex?"

Jeff shrugged. "Either that or he thought she was dead. Maybe both. Though if Mary doesn't ease up on the pedal, it may have been pure prophecy."

The look on Sever's face had been pure confusion. Dismay. Shock. Well, there was plenty of that going around.

Nathan wasn't sure gods *had* ex-girlfriends. From what he knew about Greek myths, the powerful didn't take too kindly to rejection.

Not that he believed Sever was really a god. He thought of the way his own limbs had seized up, his brain still frantic to get moving. Not to mention the cross-room bone breaking, a trick Nathan had thankfully never seen before. No arguing with the fact that Sever was extremely powerful. But what was the difference between a powerful monster and an actual god? Godlike, maybe. God complex? Certainly. But what made a god... a god?

Sever tore things down well enough. But what did he create?

Nathan squeezed Mary's shoulder. "Jeff has a point," he said. "If nothing else, we'll be delayed if we get pulled over."

Mary flung her glare at him, still red hot. "Can you two remember you hate each other and get into a fight?"

Jeff, still leaning forward, gave her a sympathetic grimace. "Sorry, doll, I have to be in the mood."

"Watch it," Nathan said. "I can still punch you."

Mary let out a breath. "That's better."

In the back, Chloe's silent mantra rose to a whisper. "They're dead," she said. "They're dead. They're dead."

Jeff sat back, dropping his head against the seat. "Yes, darling. Let it out."

As if his words sparked some kind of realization, Chloe sat up straight. Nathan twisted to look at her, and she stared back, eyes blazing. Thirty seconds ago, he wouldn't have been able to say for certain that she even knew where she was.

Judging by the way her eyes narrowed, her lips folded into a grimace, she did now.

"Let me out of the car," she said.

"No problem," Mary said. "Next rest stop, you're out."

Nathan wasn't sure how to respond to that, but luckily Jeff said, "Is that the best idea?"

Mary banged on the wheel with the heel of her hand. "I don't want her at HQ. She hasn't technically committed any crimes, unless you count following orders from the U.S. president, so we can't really throw her in jail. I say let her out."

"She could reconvene the EAEA," Jeff said.

Mary let out a laugh, hoarse and humorless. "What EAEA? They're gone. They're dead. Sever killed them all."

"Not all," Nathan said. "They still have a headquarters."

They'd taken an entire team in Philadelphia—minus one, a guy Steve had whisked out of danger at the last minute—but Nathan hadn't told Mary the news from Eloise's side of the mission.

She had enough to process at the moment.

"Is it wise," Jeff chimed in, "to give your sister ideas?"

"Albany," Chloe said. "That sign says Albany. Let me out."

When no one responded, Chloe slammed her fists on the back of Mary's chair, making them all jump. Nathan would not have risked that. Not at the best of times, and certainly not today, when Mary's fuse was ragged and spent. But Chloe kept pounding. "Let me out of the car. *Now.*"

"We're on the highway, doll," Jeff said. "Going ninety-five in a sixty-five, not that it's relevant, but all the same—"

Chloe flicked her seatbelt off and fumbled for the door handle. Nathan twisted, trying to reach her, but she writhed away.

"Stop her," he said to Jeff.

Jeff threw up his hands. "*I'm* not a vigilante. You stop her."

But there wasn't time to do anything. The door banged open, and then she was gone, tumbling out into the narrow shoulder between the north and south lanes.

Jeff cursed, and Mary hit the brakes, pulling as close to the left-hand guardrail as space allowed. Nathan leapt out of the van, headlights flashing in his eyes as traffic sped by. He dashed back, trying to find the spot where Chloe had jumped.

He might not consider her family anymore, but that didn't mean he wanted her dead.

Chloe wasn't there. Not on the shoulder, or the median. Nathan shielded his eyes against the periodic flashes of headlights threading their way along the highway even now, at this late hour. A truck went rushing by in the middle lane, and when it was gone, Nathan made out a silhouette disappearing into the trees on the other side of the road.

She stood impossibly tall after such a fall, not limping, not struggling. Just gliding effortlessly into the trees. A beat, a blink, and then she was gone.

As soon as there was a gap in traffic, he ran for the woods, ignoring Mary and Jeff's startled cries behind him.

"Did she take a serum?" Mary asked, running up beside him as he traced his way back along the road until he reached the spot where she'd disappeared into the trees.

Nathan pushed the branches aside and headed into the trees. "She couldn't have. I disarmed her."

Mary didn't try to stop him. Instead, she clicked a flashlight out of her tool belt and directed the beam at the ground until it landed on a pair of narrow footprints. "Maybe she took one during the fight."

"She didn't. She might have taken one before she came into the restaurant, but that would have been hours ago. They're temporary."

"Did not seem that way to me," Jeff said. The actor only sounded a little out of breath, and Nathan stifled a spike of displeasure at the fact that he'd followed them out here. What help could he possibly be?

Of course, he had found a literal escape hatch out of the restaurant earlier. But Nathan wasn't entirely willing to admit Jeff could actually be useful.

It didn't matter. Let him come. Nathan needed to find his sister.

He wasn't sure if he needed to find her so he could help her, or to prevent her from hurting more people. Probably both, if he was being honest, though the latter was far more likely. Especially if she had actual enhanced abilities.

How long had she had them? And how could she continue this crusade when she shared abilities with the people she was persecuting?

"Do you think she registered?" Jeff asked.

Nathan doubted it. Chloe's footsteps disappeared into a thick section of brush, but it didn't matter. Through the trees, a huge gray wall loomed beside the river. It was surrounded by a barbed wire fence, with floodlights posted at the corners. Nathan could make out the silhouettes of guards pacing on the ground, guns cradled in their arms as they moved.

Nathan stumbled, and Mary caught his elbow, keeping him on his feet.

"There's not supposed to be a prison here," Jeff said.

Nathan turned to ask him how he knew, but the movie star had his phone out and was running a search. Mary rolled her eyes and grabbed the device out of his hand, lobbing it across the strip of woods and into the river.

"They'll be looking for you," she said.

"There's no one left to look," Jeff complained, but he didn't seem so sure.

The prison—or whatever this building was—certainly made it seem like there might be someone left. Quite a few someones.

A shadow darted through the brush to the right, and Nathan was following before he'd thought it through. Mary grabbed his sleeve, pulling him back. "Let's just see what she does."

Right. They needed to find out what this place was about.

Chloe's figure was clear enough in the lights that beamed from the prison walls. She walked up to the gates like she owned the place, and after a short conversation with the guard —one Nathan couldn't hear—the doors opened for her.

Mary was tapping her index finger on her lip. "Dawn Kimble's enhanced neighbor went missing after he listed his powers. Any chance he could've wound up here?"

If Chloe was going inside, there had to be a connection. "The EAEA also dragged Tally and her team off tonight," Nathan said.

Mary whipped her head to look at him. "They *what*?"

He cringed. "Everyone else got out of Philadelphia, but Tally's team was captured. I'd have told you, but it didn't seem like it was going to be immediately relevant."

She could hardly blame him for that.

Mary frowned at the building, as if trying to see inside it.

Quin's x-ray vision would be very useful right about now. "Could they be here?" she asked. "How long does it take to drive from Philly to... Where did Chloe say we were? Albany?"

"I'd tell you," Jeff said, "but someone threw my phone away."

The sound of helicopter blades cut through the rush of highway noise behind them, and moments later, the chopper descended onto the roof of the building.

Slick. And honestly, not all that secret, to anyone who was paying attention.

"Nathan," Mary said, "call HQ and ask them to get a plane down to Albany. I think we're about to have more passengers."

Jeff sighed. "I'm guessing that means we're not going to say 'oh well' so we can go straight to your secret base and its secret stash of beds."

Mary was already moving. "Nope. Come on, let's sweep the perimeter. This place has to have some vulnerabilities. And we're going to find them."

No fortress was impenetrable, as far as Mary was concerned. Even super-secret, government-run fortresses that appeared to have been here much longer than the three months that President Caldwell's executive order had been in play.

Mary stalked through the woods, weaving away from the facility's walls and the glaring lights of the guard stands. A block of concrete stood in the woods by the river, and she circled around to examine it.

The opening was maybe as tall as she was or a bit higher, clearly there to allow for maintenance. A grate covered the opening, but when she ran her fingers along the spots where the bars met the concrete, the connection felt weak. A faint vibration echoed through the bars, as if they were feeling something she couldn't hear, and when she tested the bar's strength, it felt like it was ready to cave.

Bizarre. And familiar, too. It reminded her of the Knife's vibrations, in a way. She couldn't feel those, obviously, but she'd studied them from a distance when she'd set up the portal jammers in HQ.

They were using something like that here, too. She could feel it.

"What are you going to do?" Jeff asked. "Get out your grapple and rappel up the walls? Melt the fence down with your fancy tools?"

Mary glanced at Nathan, who shrugged. She gave the bar a tug, and it came loose in her hand. "Actually, I thought I'd just walk in."

Jeff sat back on his heels. "Please tell me this isn't a sewer."

Mary pulled another bar loose, and Nathan reached up to free a third. The iron felt almost pliant in her hands. What could do that?

"OK," she said, "it's not a sewer."

Jeff wrinkled his nose. "You're lying."

"Pick a door, Jeff. Comfortable lies or pure truth."

Jeff sighed. "It's the sewer."

As if he couldn't already tell that from the smell. Mary directed her flashlight down the tunnel, then edged between the remaining bars. "Come on. Let's find our people."

If she was guessing right, they'd find a lot more people as well. She hoped El had sent that plane out. And a bus to get them to it.

Water sloshed up to Mary's ankles as they walked, cold water already seeping through her socks. She refused to think of it as anything but water, though she truly wished she'd worn Coral's boots to the restaurant. It felt like a million miles away and a million hours ago instead of just a few. She didn't want to think about it—or what Sever had said about her—so she focused on the moment instead.

Unfortunately, the moment included a fat rat skittering along the edge of the water and the uneasy sound of water dripping from the ceiling of the tunnel. It was still better than thinking about Sever.

Behind her, Jeff was muttering. Not quite under his breath, and in a voice that, if he wasn't careful, Mary might interpret as an imitation of her own. "'Make a date with a politician,' she said. 'Help us set a trap, Jeff. You'll be helping so many people.'"

"You *are* helping people," Nathan said.

The tunnel branched in two directions, and Mary turned left. Back toward the prison. Hopefully this would lead them inside, like a reverse *Shawshank* situation.

Jeff snorted. "So far, I've merely lured a young bureaucrat to his untimely death and allowed your sister to leap from a moving vehicle. The only person I'm helping is my shoe guy, who will be very excited when I call to reorder this pair. They're Italian leather."

Nathan paused. "You have a shoe guy?"

Voices echoed down into the tunnel, the walls breaking them into unintelligible murmurs, and Mary held up a hand to silence the men. She followed the sounds of the voices until she reached a maintenance hatch—she was really getting tired of navigating tunnels—and when she climbed a short ladder to shift it aside, the murmurs crystallized into words.

"...at all times," a voice was saying. "Cell doors open, you step to the back and show your hands. When the science heads ask for you, you go without question or you get sedated. If you follow the rules, there's a forty-five-minute period of outside rec every day."

Someone was giving instructions. Or could it be an orientation, for newcomers from Philadelphia perhaps?

Mary climbed up into the facility and shone the light around as Nathan and Jeff followed. It was a maintenance closet, with a churning machine in the middle—a water heater, maybe?—and a mop and bucket propped up in the corner.

Mary inched the door open and peered out. It was a bathroom, naturally, with grimy tile floors and a row of yellow-painted stalls. The voice she'd heard from underground had sounded stern, but the woman whose face accompanied it looked tired. And maybe a little worried. She kept licking her lips and re-straightening her posture, as though trying to seem confident.

She'd probably heard about D.C.

The guard woman's back was to Mary, so she slipped out a little further. Tally stood against the far wall wearing a navy-blue jumpsuit, her hair a tomato-red flare amid the beigey gray drabness of this place. Mary recognized her companions from the hideout in Philadelphia: a middle-aged woman who could hover several feet off the ground, and a pair of women who'd been married a week before the president signed his order.

Mary would have expected her anger to have burned out by now, but nope. There it was, a spark of fury that pounded through her ears at the sight of innocent people being tossed into a place like this without so much as a hint of due process.

"No cameras," Nathan whispered, and Mary glanced at the ceiling. There were no telltale black orbs, or obvious surveillance equipment, but she wasn't willing to assume there were no smaller devices hidden in the room.

At a certain point, though, she had to take a risk. She held up a hand to tell the men to stay put—to which Jeff mouthed 'no problem'—before slipping out of the maintenance closet and into one of the bathroom stalls. Feeling more than a little silly, she shook the door until the guard's voice stopped rattling instructions at Tally and the others to come over and inspect.

As soon as she got close, Mary slammed the door into the guard's face. The woman clapped a hand to her nose, blood streaming. Mary grabbed her by the collar before she could stagger back and hauled her into the stall, hitting her in the neck with a sedative before she could make a sound.

Not completely clean, maybe, but not bad either.

"Smooth," Jeff said. "Now what?"

Mary half expected more guards to come pouring in the doors, or alarms to sound far off down the halls. When they didn't, she left the guard slumped against the stall and made her way over to Tally's group. The women were still standing against the wall, many of them looking dazed, eyes wide, lips parted.

When Tally saw them, she actually jumped—to a normal height—and threw her arms around Mary.

"You might not want to do that," Mary said. "We came through the sewer."

"I don't care if you came through the... OK, there's not much worse than the sewer, but it doesn't matter." Tally released her, beaming. "How is this possible?"

"Luck," Nathan said.

"*Bad* luck," Jeff clarified.

Mary scanned the group, but no one seemed to be sporting injuries worse than bumps and scrapes. "Your powers?"

Tally grimaced. "There's something blocking them. Not a serum. It's like... it's like the air feels thick. Heavy. It's holding me to the ground."

Mary thought of the weak spots in the iron bars. "They're using a jammer," she said.

Tally blinked at her, then shrugged. The rest of the women just stared blankly.

"It's a frequency," Mary said. "Like the one I use to block Dolly's portals." She tapped a finger to her lower lip, thinking. "I'd have to see it. But the main idea is that animals can sense Earth's magnetic field. They use it to navigate. You can jam their connection and confuse them by creating a low-frequency magnetic field. Like around power lines."

Tally frowned. "That's what you did at HQ?"

"No, and it's a good thing I didn't, since it looks like it would have blocked everyone's enhanced abilities. I honed in on the Knife's frequency. Targeted the field more specifically."

Blank stares all around. Nathan raised his eyebrows, tilting her a small smile—maybe that science book he'd been reading really *was* helping him to keep up with her—but otherwise they all looked like they were going to hemorrhage from the effort of trying to understand what she'd said. Jeff was leaning with his shoulder against the wall, eyelids half shut as if he might drop off to sleep at any second.

"Never mind," Mary said. "If we shut the power down, everyone in here will be able to use their abilities again. And then we can get the hell out."

And run into Chloe in the process. She wasn't sure if that would make them lucky, or the opposite.

"Sounds good to me," Tally said. "But how do we get there? There are definitely cameras in the hall."

"Oh, that's easy." Jeff was still leaning against the wall. "You put on the guard's uniform and lead us like we're prisoners."

"You've seen too many films," Nathan said.

It might work, though. At least for a brief while, long enough for them to get deeper into the facility.

One of Tally's charges leaned in to whisper to another, her expression more dazed than ever. "Is that Jeff Hayes?"

But they were going to need more help. This place was massive, and Mary had no way to guess where the frequency might be playing. In the middle of the building, to get the most range? In the basement with the breakers? On the roof?

She needed help. As she slipped back into the stall to borrow the guard's uniform—OK, she really had no intention of returning it—Mary turned on the com unit in her ear. "Pete, are you listening?"

"I can't talk right now, I'm busy planning to betray you."

Mary discarded her shoes—she wasn't sad to lose them, anyway, since they were waterlogged and ruined—with a sigh and pulled on the guard's boots. They were tight, but they'd work. "I'm sorry I thought there was a spy on the team. You know I appreciate everything you do for us."

"I know that? I don't know that. I haven't slept more than four hours in the last two days because I'm in here making sure everyone does their job correctly. Because if they don't, you get killed out there."

Mary tied double knots in the guard's bootlaces, working quickly. "Can you yell at me later? I'm kind of in a jam."

"That's exactly what I'm talking about." Pete huffed out a breath. "You know I'll help. But you also owe me."

"Big time," Mary said. "A million cups of a coffee. A raise. A trip to Disney World. Whatever you want."

"Fine." She could hear him typing in the background, the murmur of voices in the surveillance room. What time was it, even? Late, for sure. "What do you need?"

Mary let out a breath, relieved. She shouldn't be, though; he wouldn't have refused to help. She knew that. "How fast can you pull up some super-secret blueprints?"

▭

Whoever had designed this place, they'd gone with Option A when they'd installed their enhanced abilities jammer: centralized location.

That made life a little easier. For once.

They didn't encounter any guards on the route from the prison orientation bathroom, even when Mary led the group into the stairwell and up one flight. Either they were going the expected direction—unlikely—or the EAEA drama in Philly and D.C. was sucking everyone's attention away from the facility.

Mary wasn't about to complain about that. She led the group on a twisting route through the halls until they reached a pair of glass doors with a crimson red 'hazard' notice that made her pause.

"That's your place," Pete said.

"You're *sure* you're not trying to kill me?"

"I know I didn't just hear you accuse me of anything."

"Definitely not."

The doors parted. "Good," Pete said. "Because I'm your key out of here."

Mary tried to picture him scanning blueprints while taking over the facility's systems at the same time—he was probably directing the person who'd taken over the systems, but still—and decided it was too much multitasking even for her.

She really would have to buy the guy a trip to Disney World.

Mary led her group inside the doors, where a second set of doors chuffed open as soon as the ones behind them had shut. "Are we sure about this hazard thing?" she asked.

"The room has a weird layout, but I can't find anything about what's in there," Pete said.

"Not just radio frequencies and power stations?"

He paused. "I don't think so."

Well, there was no time like the present for making discoveries. Mary stepped through the doors, beckoning her group to follow.

The room that stretched before her was bathed in blue light, giving the place a kind of underwater feeling. It didn't look like a machine room at all, or a control center. The room felt vast and cool, with no humming machinery or smell of exhaust. If anything, it smelled earthy and fresh, with the edge of something that reminded her of frost. Strange.

As her eyes adjusted to the low light, she could make out a line of glass cases along the wall to her left. A sour taste rose in her mouth, and an ache in the back of her throat throbbed with the desire to turn around and flee before she could see what was in those cases.

But Tally had already broken away from the group to approach them.

"Don't touch anything," Mary said. She shouldn't stray from the mission, from her purpose here, but she found herself following, anyway. Some part of her mind hummed frantically in the background, begging her to turn and run.

She didn't.

Tally stopped in front of the case. "It's a person."

Mary wouldn't have recognized the shadowed form as a human being, but she'd known—hadn't she?—before crossing the room that it was what she was likely to find here. The body lay completely still, their skin so pale it was almost looked blue, though that might have been the light. Someone had shaved the person's head, and their eyes were closed.

"'Specimen 455,'" Tally read, pointing to a sticker on the upper corner of the case. "'Telekinesis. Object manipulation.'"

The bitter taste in Mary's mouth escalated, and she swallowed the urge to spit it onto the floor. "What is the EAEA *doing?*"

Was it the EAEA? Or was it... something else?

Someone touched her shoulder, and she jumped. Nathan gave her an apologetic grimace, tilting his chin toward the door. "We need to move."

Mary nodded. There wasn't anything she could do for this person, not until she turned off the frequency that was jamming abilities. She couldn't even tell if the person was alive, and she didn't dare count the rest of the cases that were lined up along the walls. Dozens of them.

Mary thought of Dawn Kimble's neighbor, with his healing powers. The one who'd disappeared after adding his name to the enhanced-human registry. Could this frequency have kept Dawn from tracking him into this awful place? Or somewhere like it?

Tally was still staring at the case, and Mary touched her arm. "Keep a watch on the door, and alert us of anything strange. We need to access the control room."

Tally nodded, but she didn't look at Mary. She only had eyes for the case, and Specimen 455.

"Don't touch anything," Mary said, keeping her voice as gentle as she possibly could. Which she was afraid wasn't very gentle at all. But Tally merely nodded again, her red-streaked ponytail bobbing.

Mary followed Pete's stream of instructions to the other end of the room, trying to avoid glancing at the walls and the cases. They'd deal with it. They'd have to.

But not right now. Nathan followed her to a hefty looking metal door set into a wall of mirrors that Mary would have wagered her fortune were two-way. The door was covered in more hazard notices and bolts of painted-on lightning, and a thick iron lock securing it shut.

As they reached it, the bolt slid open with a loud clang, and Mary pulled the door open. "Pete, have I mentioned I love you?"

"Not nearly often enough."

The control room was much smaller than the one they'd just exited, and Mary would have won her bet since a pair of windows looked out at the specimen room. For lack of a better word, though it made her cringe. Wide banks of consoles glittered with blinking lights.

Nathan ran his hand lightly over the controls. "Which one do we shut off?"

There wasn't time to explore. They needed to get Tally's group out of here, and locate any other enhanced humans who might be locked up. Even with the distraction of the EAEA's implosion tonight, and Sever's appearance, the rest of the people running this place would eventually notice something was off.

Mary joined Nathan at the controls. "All of them."

She glanced around for the power source. As she did, she caught sight of Tally through the window. The recruit was reaching for the latch on Specimen 455's case. Before Mary could shout for her to stop, she'd unlocked it and flung back the top.

Alarms blared from the ceiling, and Mary dove beneath the console to pull the power lever, plunging the room into darkness. She hoped to god the thing had been controlling the frequency, but there was no time to check her work.

Mary ran out of the control room, Nathan on her heels. Red lights strobed out of the ceiling, and Mary could feel Pete saying something in her ear, but she couldn't make out his words beyond the screaming of the alarms.

She grabbed Tally and pulled her away from the case, but Nathan stopped to reach inside, feeling for a pulse. He caught her eye, shaking his head, and Tally actually looked like she might cry.

The automatic doors shuffled open, and black-clad guards poured into the space, guns hefted to their shoulders. Mary didn't know if those things would shoot bullets, serum, or something else, but she wasn't about to wait to find out.

She rushed the first set of guards from the side, dislodging the weapon from his hands and ramming the butt into his face. Alarms rang in her ears as he staggered back, teeth bared, but

Mary didn't give him time to renew his attack. Keeping a firm hold on the gun, she slammed the back-end into his chest, and he lost his balance, falling backward and taking down one of his companions with him.

Behind him, Tally swept through the line of guards feet-first, her leaping powers clearly returned. She knocked them down like bowling pins, while the members of her group scrambled to kick weapons aside.

Mary resisted the urge to throw the gun as far as she could. She didn't like firearms, didn't like the heft of the metal in her hands, but they needed to resolve this quickly, so she pointed it at the now-disarmed guards. "Into the control room, friends," she said. "Quick like bunnies."

Once they were inside, she fired off a single shot into the machinery—which pained her, truly, but she couldn't have these guys ripping her friends' powers away—and backed out of the room so Pete could slide the bolt into place, locking the guards inside.

As soon as they were secure, she dropped the gun. She'd rather use her fists, honestly.

They reached the hall, and the alarms cut off abruptly. Before Mary could ask if it was Pete's doing, his voice echoed through the speakers in the ceiling, directing everyone to evacuate. A handful of glassy-eyed prisoners in gray jumpsuits joined Mary and the others. One man flickered in and out of sight as if testing his invisibility, while another walked with visible shields raised around his body as though expecting an attack.

Lightning fizzled out of fingertips, sandaled feet rose off the floor, and all Mary could think was that she hadn't been able to save them all.

Eloise and the team had come through with the plane, and Nathan headed up the logistics—with a surprising amount of help from Jeff, actually—by walking the group to a short stretch of road near the river, where the plane waited. Mary nearly thought that El would be getting an angry call from Travis about that, before she remembered.

Once the plane took off—a short flight, from here to Niagara—Mary found a seat next to Tally.

The recruit was looking at her hands, flicking her thumbnails back and forth to make an annoying clicking noise. But Mary ignored that. It was nerves, or anxiety, or just trauma after a hell of an operation.

Traumatized or not, they needed to have a chat.

"Remember how I told you not to touch anything back there?" Mary asked.

Tally cringed and kept flicking her nails. "Yeah."

"You have got to stop doing shit like that."

"I know."

Mary opened her mouth, then closed it again. She'd expected more of a fight, more accusations, or at least defensiveness. "You do?"

Tally sniffed, and Mary wondered what she was supposed to do if the other woman started to cry. "Yeah. I almost blew the whole thing."

Accurate. Mary leaned back in her chair, fatigue thrumming at her eyelids. "I need to be able to trust you."

"I know. I'm sorry."

Mary let the murmuring voices on the plane wash over her. The plane would descend soon, in Canada. They'd deliver all these people to safety.

How many more were there? Enhanced humans? Facilities?

"Mary?"

Mary cracked an eye open and looked at Tally. "Yeah?"

"Can we be friends now?"

Mary closed her eyes. If she and El could sort out their differences, there was no reason not to give Tally a chance. "Don't worry," she said. "We already are."

It wasn't until they'd left the plane and headed back to HQ, the lights of Niagara beckoning her home, that Mary realized: they'd never found Chloe.

IT WAS EXCEEDINGLY SATISFYING to watch Sever crush the Enhanced Abilities Enforcement Association's headquarters into dust. A step through a portal from the D.C. restaurant to the blocky police precinct in Arlington, a blink of Sever's eerie, orange-spotted eyes, and the building was nothing but a dusty wreck.

As for the people inside of it, Dolly didn't see anyone emerge. And she wasn't sorry.

Sever stood in the middle of the street, seemingly unaware of the traffic halting on the streets, the shouts, the percussive shock waves pounding beneath their feet as tons of ground-up concrete collapsed into a foundation-sized sinkhole. His expression was distant, his crow's feet deepening as he stared at the EAEA's former home, and Dolly wondered if he was thinking about Adina.

She couldn't be Mary. She truly *couldn't* be.

"Now the league?" Dolly asked.

Sever brushed his hands together, as if he'd dirtied them in truth, and turned to look at her. He felt, suddenly, much taller than he actually was. He seemed to loom over her. "Every movement needs its headquarters, and every savior needs a bed to sleep in," he said.

Was the godlike monster who could slice down whole platoons asking for a *nap?* Dolly blinked at him, uncertain, but Carlisle said, "There's a Holiday Inn around the corner."

Sever nodded, then patted Dolly's arm as if he could read her thoughts, her questions. His eyes did look pinched, his skin a shade paler than it had been. She suspected that, tired or not, this man could wipe the league away with his thumb, if he wished to.

"Even my powers need recharging, upon occasion," he said. "Come."

THE TRAINING ROOM was dim and quiet when Steve eased the door open, everyone else at HQ apparently either resting after the big rescue or planning their next move. OK, so that last one only applied to Eloise, but he had to guess that was what she was up to. The woman's mind never stopped working.

Even after the ferry ride up the Delaware and the bus ride that followed, Steve felt too hyped up to rest. When he stopped moving, his mind spun with crashing cars and billowing smoke, and the soft weight of Eloise's head against his shoulder.

Everyone had made it to Niagara, even Tally and her group. Everyone and then some, actually, and they were all safe. But still, his mind wouldn't stop churning.

He padded across the training room to the punching bags that hung in a row near the back wall. They were reinforced to withstand all manner of abuse from extra-strong attackers, but Steve had seen them knocked down a time or twenty in his day.

As a kid, Steve had spent all his non-league time wishing he could be back at HQ, with the kickass training room and so many people who had enhanced abilities. Like he did. Dad had wanted Steve's life to be normal, never understanding that it wasn't possible. Not when he'd been forced to hide his abilities from his friends. Which had made it pretty damn hard to keep them.

Dad had pretty much only given in to his constant begging during the summers, and when there was no one else to watch his super-speedy son. When that happened, Steve had been able to fling his secret-Steve identity aside and embrace everything he was capable of.

Those precious months at LIO, pulling off hijinks with El and Mary? The best memories of his life. He'd been allowed to shadow Dad and Will, and the other retirees who, even if they'd turned out to be pretty much evil incarnate, had seemed like the coolest people in the world at the time.

Except Diana. She'd always been terrifying.

This place, with its smells of rubber and lemon cleaning solution, with its wall of mirrors and stacks of targets in the corner? This place felt like home.

Steve threw a punch at the bag at normal speed, the chains clanging as the bag moved. He'd worked out this way plenty of times during cadet training for the police, and high school gym class. No one had ever been allowed to know who he truly was.

Across the gym-sized space, the doors slid open with a soft shuffle, and Ire stalked into the room. Steve tensed, hiding it with another hit to the bag—he and Ire didn't exactly see eye to eye—but Ire just nodded to him and took up a position at the end of the line to punch his own bag.

Steve's phone chimed in his pocket, and he slipped it out. *Unknown number.* He thought he could guess who that might be, though he couldn't help a twinge of surprise that Wave hadn't found a way to make their symbol come up or something like that. He ignored the call and went back to punching, allowing a trickle of his speed to bleed into the process.

His phone rang again, and again he silenced the call, this

time setting the device on 'do not disturb' before shoving it back into his pocket.

"Someone wants to know you're all right," Ire said.

Steve grunted. "Someone wants to know what happened tonight."

Ire just gave him a sidelong glance and pounded his bag hard enough to rattle the triple supports in the ceiling. And Steve thought *he* was the one who disliked cryptic comments. "Wave approached me when I was in Berlin," he said. "They want to recruit me."

He wasn't sure why he wanted to tell Ire about Fran's visit. They certainly weren't friends. It wasn't that Wave's offer was a secret, exactly, but that he still hadn't quite decided what he wanted to do. What he *should* do.

Maybe it was just that Ire was neutral. If anything, he'd probably tell Steve to go.

Ire braced his feet on the mat and gave his bag a few rhythmic punches. The percussions echoed into the mostly empty space, a canvas muted *pah pah pah* that might as well have been the soundtrack of Steve's childhood.

"You're not really choosing between Wave and LIO," Ire said, still facing the bag.

Steve felt the irrational desire to start hitting his own bag again. Instead, he leaned against the back mirror. "Oh?"

"No."

Steve waited for Ire to go on. The strongman hit the punching bag hard enough to send a cloud of dust flying out of it. Hard enough, probably, to split a normal canvas down the middle.

When Ire didn't continue, Steve crossed his arms. "And you say that because?"

Ire still didn't look at him. "Agnes chose Wave. I chose LIO. For us, there was never any question. You don't like secrecy?

There's going to be secrecy in both. If anything, Wave has to hide more than we do. You go in expecting otherwise, it's like you're asking for military security clearance just so you can push to declassify everything."

"It's not the same—"

"It is the same." Ire's words landed along with his fist. Steve could see how the guy made a good teacher. "You can't escape the secrecy. It's part of what we do. You saw what happened when Jenna blew our cover and we had to start working even a little more openly."

Disaster. Sure. But it wasn't so much because of the blown-open secrets, was it? More than she'd opened a pandora's box of other problems. "What are you saying?" Steve asked.

Ire brushed his hands together and turned to face Steve. His red hair was sticking up in all directions, and he stood bare-footed on the mat, at least a head taller than Steve. "I'm saying that your choice is between superhero and normal life. Those people in Philly? We saved them so that they can have *normal* lives. You've got that option, too."

"We saved them because the government is making people disappear."

Ire rolled his eyes. "But where are they disappearing *to*, Taylor? What's happening in those facilities? Maybe the government is experimenting. Running tests. Maybe they want super soldiers or weapons. Or yes, maybe they're making them disappear for good because they're just that terrified of someone who's not like them. I don't care what they're doing, because those people deserve a good life. And to them, that means a normal life. As everyday heroes who sell flowers and teach children and drive food delivery trucks."

Steve had never heard Ire say so much at one time. Admittedly, he hadn't spent a great deal of time with the man until recently, but it was still a bit shocking to hear such a speech out of him.

And apparently, Ire wasn't done. He approached the mirror, and Steve narrowly stopped himself from flinching as Ire placed a hand on his shoulder. A friendly hand. "You want to walk away? Walk away. But don't pretend this is a choice between LIO and Wave."

Steve struggled to keep his expression neutral as Ire let go of his shoulder with a curt nod. Steve was the one who'd dealt with enhanced abilities his entire life—the strongman had gained his what, a decade ago?—yet Ire seemed to understand this life much more deeply than he did.

Suddenly, Steve felt ashamed that he didn't know more about Ire, where he'd come from. Or his real name, for that matter. Steve might have spent his childhood wishing he could display his talents for all to see, but Ire must have spent his adulthood trying to reconcile his place in the world.

Ire, with his extraordinary height and his sleeve-busting muscles, didn't have the luxury of hiding away. He didn't seem to want it, though maybe he'd simply made his peace.

Steve nodded back, grateful for this place. The retirees might have betrayed them all with their true natures, but Eloise was making LIO better. So were Ire and Mary and Nathan, and everyone on the team.

"Come on," Ire said, "punching bags don't fight back. Let's spar."

Steve followed, the room coming into focus in a new light. Maybe LIO could be his home, after all.

MARY DIDN'T WANT to spend another second thinking about those gray-walled facilities buried in the woods less than a hundred miles south of HQ, or how many other places just like it could be scattered across the country. How many enhanced humans, registered or not, had been dragged to places like that? How many were suffering, all alone, and hoping the league would come save them?

It was too much. It was too much to bear.

Unfortunately, the only other thought that could possibly occupy her mind at the moment had to do with why the hell some intergalactic wannabe god with genocidal tendencies had pegged her as his beloved.

They'd arrived back at HQ in the dead of night, battered and exhausted. She'd showered in the hottest water she could manage, as if she could scour the whole day from her mind.

Unfortunately, it wasn't the kind of scene that magically evaporated just because she was back at HQ. It would take a hundred showers to purge the scent of blood, and she couldn't think of any solution for the soundtrack that played on repeat in her head, the last gurgle of life leaving those agents' bodies.

Rest was unthinkable. Bed? Not even a possibility. Her

muscles itched for movement, for action, like she'd implode if she tried to sit still. She didn't think Nathan would appreciate her wearing a hole in the floor of their room while he tried to sleep, so she was wandering the halls aimlessly instead. Her boots clipped along the floor as she tried to look like she knew where she wanted to go, even though there was probably no one else awake to see her.

She wanted to forget about Sever, preferably forever. She was no alien goddess, or whatever the guy thought. She remembered her childhood on Earth, vividly. There weren't blank spots or questions about her parentage. So she looked like some lady from outer space. It didn't matter.

What *did* matter were the enhanced humans who still needed her help. The EAEA might be broken, or they might just be scattered. Even if they did disappear for good, the president's executive order still stood.

Mary had no doubt there were more pockets of enhanced humans hiding out in secret, like they'd been in Philly. They might be in even worse situations. More people packed together, no way to get food. Afraid for their lives.

She was going to find them. And she was going to root out every last government facility. If she could, she'd burn them to the ground.

With a goal finally in mind, Mary headed for El's office, hoping Pete had left their research out where she could find it.

When she rounded the corner, though, she found that Nathan had beaten her to it. He stood in the corridor, hand poised as if ready to knock on the door. He smiled when he saw Mary, but he was pale, his shoulders tense. He looked almost haunted, though he might have been thinking of Chloe's dramatic departure from their car.

Mary joined him at the door, resting a hand on his cheek. His skin felt warm, and he leaned into her touch. "I thought

I'd collapse into bed," he said. "But my brain had other plans."

"My thoughts won't stop racing, either."

Eloise opened the door before they could knock, dark circles bruised in half-rings under her eyes. Her mission might have succeeded tonight, but she looked exhausted. "I suppose no one can sleep tonight," she said, motioning for them to come in. "I can't stop worrying about the people from Philadelphia, and the poor people you found tonight. Whether they have what they need."

They were set up in hotels for the night, where surely they'd be able to get anything. Everything. Comfortable beds, room service. But no one could protect them from the news of what the operation had cost. Sever had murdered dozens of people in the middle of D.C. The restaurant looked like a bomb had gone off there, cars toppled, glass obliterated. It was impossible to avoid.

"Quin and Elle are keeping an eye on them," Nathan said, following her inside. "And Len, right?"

Eloise headed to the wet bar she kept blissfully stocked in the corner, clinking ice cubes into glasses as she talked. "Exactly the details I keep running through my mind. But sadly, the worries refuse to acknowledge sense."

She poured Mary a healthy splash of gin, topped with tonic. Whiskey for Nathan, and for herself. Nathan accepted his drink and dropped onto the couch in the back of the room, while Eloise perched on the edge of her desk, her glass already apparently forgotten as she stared off into space.

Mary's muscles still wanted her to pace. She stayed on her feet, but made herself stand still as she sipped her drink. Savoring the bite of the gin, she looked at the map that still beamed from the wall-sized screen behind El's desk, the multicolored pins as mysterious as ever. They simply refused to sharpen into any kind of pattern.

The room had changed, somewhat, since the days of Dolly's rule. No more shag carpets, for one thing. El had finally started to add her own touches to the place: a photo collection of city skylines dotted the wall above Nathan's head, and Mary wondered when she'd had time to buy it.

El's knives sat on display in their case, short and long, straight and sickle-shaped. The Pearl Knife's spot was still empty, though, and the blade wasn't at El's waist, either. Not surprising, after everything that'd happened, but Mary couldn't help wondering where she'd stashed it.

Nathan had shut his eyes, but the tension in his shoulders said he was still awake. Her own eyes were dry, aching to close, but it was hard enough to stand in one spot. If she tried to sit or lie down, she'd implode. She took another sip, trying to find something to say.

Thankfully, another knock sounded, and Steve poked his head in. "A party? My invite must've gotten lost."

"We saw the light," Ire said from behind him.

"Might as well join us," Eloise said. "Though it's not much of a celebration."

Steve and Ire both looked wide awake, though, foreheads bright with a sheen of sweat. Mary hoped it was because they'd been exercising or sparring, rather than trying to kick each other's asses. They looked friendly enough as they took up the seats in front of El's desk.

"Have we figured anything out yet?" Steve asked. At first, Mary thought he meant the map, and the location of more enhanced humans. But he was looking straight at her. "Like how Mary could be this Sever guy's long-lost love?"

Heat surged into her face, and she gripped her glass. "I'm not."

She willed him to drop the subject, but Eloise was looking at him, thoughtful. "We know he made the Knife, and that it ended up on Earth somehow. It's strange, isn't it, that Sever would mistake one of us for someone he knows?" She frowned, swirling her drink gently. Mary willed her to stop talking. Unfortunately, she didn't. "They're both so strongly connected to him. Mary. The Knife. And no one in his galaxy seemed to know Earth even existed until Sloane found this place."

Someone had to have known. How else could the Knife have gotten here? Mary ground her teeth until she thought they might crack. She didn't want to talk about this now. Or ever. She didn't want to know why he thought what he thought.

Maybe his universe was an alternate one. Maybe she just had some doppelgänger. Either way, this had nothing to do with her.

"I'm not connected to him," Mary said.

"His powers didn't work on her," Nathan said. He sat up, looked at his hand as if surprised to find a drink there, and took a swallow.

Mary glared at him, but he just shrugged. "They *didn't.* Does the Knife work on you?"

Mary flinched. "It definitely does."

Eloise's flinch actually matched hers. "I had some trouble with the 'cut something through space' feature when I first inherited the Knife."

"I still have the proof." Mary held up the back of her hand, where a pinprick-sized scar on the back of her wrist would forever be a way to tease her sister for her lack of control. Not that she used it. Often. "I've also tried to touch the Knife. No dice."

No scars, either. But a very strong memory of a very strong sting. She'd as soon stick her finger in a socket as try that again.

Eloise twisted on the edge of the desk, now, turning so she

could examine the map. She had a bright-eyed expression that could only mean she wasn't going to let the subject drop. Great. "Nathan, didn't you study LIO operations when you were researching the Wave prisoners?"

"I did."

"Was there anything notable in Philadelphia?"

The door opened again, and Tally's appearance proved that not a single soul in HQ was actually capable of resting at the moment. When she saw them, her face blushed as red as the current color of her hair. "I'm sorry," she said. "I thought Rajni would be working in here. We're supposed to swap shifts with Quin and Elle soon."

Seemed like Tally should get a pass on guard duty tonight. Especially if she hadn't slept.

Eloise beckoned her in as Nathan got to his feet, eyes trained on the map. So he wasn't going to let this drop, either. Mary wasn't sure where El was going with this, only that the conversation seemed to be veering away from her own situation. And that was a good thing.

"Philadelphia," Nathan said. "Yeah, actually. Big Wave raid. I'd have to check the date, but they were using the old subway tunnels as safe houses."

"Handy, those," Steve put in.

Eloise hopped off the desk, rounding on Tally. "How did you get your powers?"

Tally's eyes widened, and Mary couldn't help thinking of a mouse wandering into a test lab at just the wrong time.

Then, weirdly, Tally turned to Mary. "Look, we were just starting to get along," she said. "I'd rather not answer."

Mary frowned. She hardly wanted to be the center of this conversation, but now she was curious. She tipped back the rest of her drink. "It can't be worse than Sever thinking I'm his woman."

Tally licked her lips. "OK. I grew up in South Dakota. Tiny town called Warner. My sisters and I, we'd spend pretty much every free day outside, riding our bikes and whatever. One day there was thunder in a clear sky, and a tower of smoke in the distance, so we came home..."

At this, she turned to face Mary. Looked her directly in the eye. Mary's stomach hardened, like a ball of ice had just formed inside. She didn't know what Tally was going to say. She didn't.

"We came home, and our mom was crying." Tally spoke softly. "She told us about your plane crash, Mary. That it had happened close by. That your parents were dead, and you might be, too. We loved Celestine... we loved you mother's movies. Used to sing her songs. I was so upset, I dashed outside." She swallowed hard, wincing. As if she couldn't stand connecting her powers to that day. "And then I leapt straight up to the roof to cry. Grass to gutter in a split second."

Coincidence. It had to be. Tally's powers couldn't possibly have anything to do with Mary's crash.

Didn't matter. Mary could smell the smoke Tally had mentioned, acrid and burning in her nostrils, choking her.

Months ago, Goldi had forced Mary to relive the experience with her illusions. Well, the joke was on her, because the scene was even more vivid in Mary's mind. She wavered on her feet, trying to blink away the visions of clouds rushing by the window, the ground ascending too fast. Her mother's arms around her, the wrench of Dad trying to pull the protective shell Mange had designed around them. The searing pain of metal lancing across her hand. Sinking through her palm.

"What about your family?" Eloise asked. Her voice was quiet, too, but the distant part of Mary that still existed in the room heard the businesslike tone behind it. The quest for answers. "Did they get powers, too?"

"No. Just me. Though I did hear rumors later about another

kid in Warner who could lift stuff with his mind. I kept mine a secret, though, so who knows?"

A hand slipped into Mary's, and she remembered to breathe as Nathan covered her scar with his warmth, leaning in so his arm was flush with hers. Solid. Comforting. Here. The room spiraled back into focus, and she breathed, tears collecting at the corners of her eyes.

Safe. Visions still lurked behind every blink, but she was at HQ, and she was safe.

Eloise was scanning the map. "Niagara for Rajni. Philadelphia. St. Louis—that was another big Wave raid, the one where Dolly captured Dr. Gordon. South Dakota." She pressed her lips together. "And Chloe... Nathan, you two were saved as kids. Yes?"

Nathan squeezed Mary's hand, the pressure grounding her in this space, in this time. "If 'saved' means Dolly holding our school hostage, pretending someone else was doing it, and then 'rescuing' us, then yes."

Eloise looked at the map again, then at the case where the Pearl Knife's spot stood vacant. "It's the Knife," she said. "It doesn't just control and remove powers. It grants them."

Mary gasped, her heartbeat kicking up three notches. Her thoughts blurred, and she blinked to bring the map back into focus. How could it be? Without any of them knowing?

El was staring at the Knife's empty shelf, as if she could will the Knife to show up and explain itself. Or maybe it *was* explaining itself, inside her thoughts.

"Could it have protected Mary today?" Steve's voice. Or maybe Ire's. It was all running together now, sounds blending, the room melting like drenched watercolors. Panic locked around her throat, and it took everything she had to continue drawing breaths.

"It must have." Definitely Eloise. "We need to figure out how."

But Mary had heard enough. Heart still pounding, breath shallow in her chest, she detached her hand from Nathan's and ran for the door.

THE DOOR SLAMMED SHUT behind Mary, and for a brief instant, the room was silent.

In the back of her mind, Eloise felt the Knife's attention spin into focus. It hummed, a gentle resonance, and for the first time in a long while, she didn't shove it aside. She'd taken it out of its drawer earlier, set it on the coffee table in her room, but she'd left it there when she'd come up here for a drink. She had half a mind to call it to her side now. She'd certainly done it before.

At the thought, the Pearl Knife quivered, ready for action. But Eloise willed it to stay where it was. She wasn't ready to face it. Not yet.

The Pearl Knife created powers. Of course it did. Obviously there had to be another variable, something that gave Tally enhanced abilities and bypassed her sisters. Same with Chloe and Nathan. In a city like Philadelphia, the numbers had been greater—but the percentage, Eloise suspected, still relatively tiny.

Agnes would need to know about this. She'd know what to look for. Rogue genes? Blood type? Nail polish color? Eloise didn't even know where to begin.

Eloise would reach out to her again. She had to get the scientist on her side.

Tally cleared her throat, and Eloise shook herself out of her plans and into the present. "I better go find Rajni."

She hesitated, though, as if waiting for a dismissal. Eloise nodded. "Thank you for telling us your story."

The woman practically ran out of the room. Eloise couldn't blame her, though Mary was the one who usually glared daggers at her.

Nathan said something about going to find Mary, looking somewhat dazed himself—his sister had apparently been hiding enhanced abilities for years, all while railing against them—as he exited the office. Ire followed, not bothering to make any excuses. Sometimes, Eloise thought he was the most normal person out of all of them. At least, he seemed to draw the least amount of drama.

Perhaps he just managed to keep his drama private. Though if that were the case, Eloise could use a lesson or two.

Steve, unsurprisingly, stayed where he was, leaning back in the chair across from her desk. When she realized she'd been assuming he'd stay behind, she wasn't sure whether to smile or grimace. He'd only been back in her life for a few hours, and already she was thinking of him as a fixture.

The Knife buzzed, perhaps objecting to her trust in Steve. She could trust them both, couldn't she?

Eloise returned to her desk, leaning on the edge and facing Steve with her back to the screen. "I can't help feeling like I may have misjudged the Knife. This whole time... it's not like it chose Dolly as a partner. And it doesn't seem as if it chose to grant her powers, either. What if it couldn't untangle itself from her any more than she could from it?"

A vision flashed into her mind, heat and fear and sheer force of will, her father's hand on the hilt, the Knife quivering with the effort of restraining its defensive measure so he could carry it to Eloise's room. With Dad's help, the Knife had withdrawn its tendrils from Dolly's mind to reach into Eloise's.

The amount of energy it had taken... she couldn't even comprehend it. Fear pulsed through her gut—was this her fate, to be so deeply entwined with the Knife? Forever?—but this time, she breathed into it. Let it settle.

You still used my powers without me. She sent the words through her thoughts as gently as she could, but firmly, too. *That's still a problem.*

It knew. She could tell that it knew, and that something was happening to it. Some resonance.

Steve stayed where he was, and Eloise let her eyes flutter shut. The Knife was sending her information, and she opened herself to the experience. She could feel the blade working to tell its story, the jarring grind of its vibrations as it tried to communicate in words.

It came through as sound, as tremors, as flashes of light. But it was as clear to Eloise as it could have been. Dolly's powers, pure moonlight dotting her cells. The Knife, reaching back toward her. Taking control. It was all pain, dissonance, divided energy. And... and scars. The Knife was exposing its wounds to her.

Trying to regain her trust.

Eloise opened her eyes to find Steve on the edge of the chair, leaning forward to look up at her in concern. Eloise swallowed. "It says... I think it's telling me that it was injured when it wrenched itself away from Dolly. Or... changed, maybe. It spent years stopping her powers from manifesting on their own."

In her mind, the Knife wept. Eloise regretted the distance between them. Physical, emotional, everything.

Steve got up, shifting his weight uneasily. "I don't want to overstay my welcome, El. But I'm here if you need me."

Eloise reached out for his hands, pulling him toward her a step. "Stay. Please, stay."

"You know I will."

Eloise looked at their hands, fingers woven together. "You probably want me to make a league-wide announcement. Inform everything immediately. Test the team for latent abilities. Call a press conference."

She would do those things. Well, maybe not the press conference. But the rest of it. When she could. The Knife was still weeping, in its way, its sorrow trailing through her fatigue. Rather than dampening her hope, though, it seemed to play in harmony with it.

Steve lifted her hand and pressed his lips to her knuckles. His was breath warm against her skin, and Eloise shivered. "No, I don't," he said. "Actually, this might be a bad time to ask, but I was wondering if you might let me join the league. You know, officially."

He dropped her hand, and he was so close, mere inches away, and she could barely collect her thoughts enough to answer. "Welcome aboard, then," she said, throat dry, and then he was kissing her, one hand on the small of her back, her legs hemming him in as he braced her against the desk. He tasted like mint, the smell of spiced coconut spinning her into a daze. She let herself draw him closer, let her fingers trail along the waistline of his jeans.

For the first time in a long time, Eloise let herself relax, let herself feel. She let herself lean into the moment, to savor this man's arms around her, and the feeling that, whatever was coming, they'd be facing it together.

NATHAN TOOK his time heading for the garage, where he was fairly certain Mary would have gone after storming out of Eloise's office. But if he knew her at all—and he thought he did —she'd also need a few minutes to herself, some time to process what she'd heard.

There was a lot to process.

She was connected to the Knife, somehow. And to the man who'd forged it, an alien who'd ripped through dozens of people without a single sign of remorse. Mere hours ago. Right before they'd liberated an armored facility.

And now the Knife could give people powers? If Mary was connected to it, why didn't she have any?

Nathan paced slowly through the halls, muscles sore from the fight and head beginning to blur with fatigue. Still, he wasn't sure sleep would descend anytime soon. Not with the screams of those EAEA agents in his memory, nor the gasoline-tinged smell of that facility in his nostrils.

He glanced into the training room as he passed, though he was fairly certain she'd be neck-deep in some kind of machinery or invention by now. The way her muscles had been coiled in Eloise's office, like she'd been practically ready to snap, he figured he'd find her doing something physical, and that could mean the training room.

She wasn't there. But Jeff Hayes was.

The film star was wandering somewhat aimlessly through the room. He brushed a hand along a target, inspected a punching bag, lifted a couple of free weights out of their rack in the corner.

On a whim, Nathan opened the door. Mary would need a few more minutes to cool off, anyway. "Looking for a yoga video?"

Jeff waved a hand over his head without bothering to turn in Nathan's direction. "Do not knock yoga, Mr. Bond. It's exercise for the mind as well as the body."

"And you're supposed to be the evidence of that?"

Jeff splayed his fingers over his heart. "You wound me. I thought we were friends now. We escaped a horrific experience together. Actually, I'm losing track of how many of those there've been now."

Nathan supposed that, if he were being honest, Jeff tended to display more positive qualities than negative ones. The guy was full of himself, yes, and he shifted between masks like the most secretive independent operative. Nathan didn't know which version of Jeff to believe.

But he'd helped Mary. He'd sent his lawyer to help Eloise.

"Why have you been fighting the EAEA since President Caldwell signed that order?" Nathan asked.

Jeff nudged a pile of mats with his toe. "Because it's wrong, Pearce. Because Holland filled me in about that terrifying hidden prison and that Travis Bertram asshole." He pressed his fingers to his forehead. "Sorry. RIP Travis, I guess. I didn't want the guy dead, for god's sake. But what they're doing is wrong."

Jeff stopped fidgeting with the mats and faced Nathan head

on. "I've got a name. A platform, as my publicist so annoyingly calls it. I figured I might as well do something good."

The guy was a good actor, sure. Among the best, if the Academy Awards could be believed. But Nathan's instincts said Jeff was telling the truth.

And here Nathan had assumed Jeff was doing it all for some good publicity or something. Nathan knew the film star had struggled to find work after his association with the league.

Maybe the prejudice against enhanced abilities was more widely spread than they thought.

Jeff dropped onto the floor and crossed his legs, leaning back against the stack of mats. "So, that was your sister who jumped out of the car back there, was it?"

Nathan tucked his fingertips into his pockets. Had Chloe really had powers all these years? Permanent, Ire-level powers? He sifted through memories, trying to imagine when she might have given it away, but he'd never even suspected. If there'd been clues, he'd missed them.

Of course, his own childhood had basically ended at thirteen, in the most distracting way possible. He supposed he could be forgiven for an ounce of self-involvement.

"Yeah," Nathan said. "That was my sister. Is."

Where was she? Who was she with? They'd followed her out to the hidden facility, but they'd lost track of her there. He didn't want to waste sympathy on a woman who'd played such a major role in their current circumstances, in the suffering of so many enhanced humans. But like Jeff, he didn't want to see her dead, either.

Jeff closed his eyes, like he might fall asleep right here surrounded by the scent of rubber and the whirring of air conditioning vents. "Huh. Don't see the resemblance."

Nathan left Jeff to nap against the mats and went back out to find Mary. If she wasn't in the garage, he'd check for her downstairs in the engineering lab. Their suite was probably a last resort. She was more likely to have gone out to the casino, if it was even open at this hour, than to bed.

Sure enough, he entered the garage to the sound of clanging metal and strings of curses. She couldn't have beaten him here by more than a few minutes, even with his dawdling, but she was splayed out under one of the larger vehicles in the far corner, surrounded by mysterious blocks of metal and coils of wire. They all looked important to the operations of various machines, but Nathan could not have said what any of them did.

Nathan sat down next to her legs with his back to the side of the vehicle—he supposed it was some kind of an extra-long van, with shiny black siding and only a couple of dents—and rested his hands on his knees. At first, he wasn't sure whether Mary knew he was there. But then she started to talk, her voice muffled.

"It's been too long since I made something new around here," she said. "I need to tear this thing apart. It's past time we had something that flies."

Nathan glanced over his shoulder. He couldn't claim any mechanic abilities or engineering prowess—the fact that he could jump-start a car was enough to make him proud—but he didn't think this hulk of a van would take too well to an addition of wings. He knew better than to argue, though, so he just rested his head against the vehicle and waited.

Unlike the rest of HQ, where every inch was plated in titanium, the ceiling here was made of rock. It smelled like the inside of a cave, too, earthy and sharp with mineral undercurrents. He could hear the falls rushing beyond the wall, even through Mary's clattering, which jarred through the metal at his back.

Finally, she eased out from under the car, threw her

wrench at the wall—where it chipped the stone before crashing to the floor—and settled down beside him. "I can't be this person," she said. "This... Adina."

He didn't want to think so, either. Truly. "No. But there's a connection."

"And even if I wanted to find it, I'd have to what? Sift through family trees? Heft documents out of storage? Try to find some family secrets, as if there aren't enough of those already?" She matched his posture, dropping her head back against the car. "I can't do it. I know it's been forever, and I should be over it, but just standing in that room with Tally talking about the crash... I can't do it."

Nathan edged closer to her. "First of all, you do not need to be 'over' the traumatic death of your parents. Which almost killed you, too."

She shuddered, her body shivering against his. Not for the first time, he cursed the people who'd done this to her. Some of them were in prison beneath their feet. The rest? They'd find justice, too. He'd make sure of it.

"Secondly," he continued, keeping his voice soft, "contrary to popular believe, I can actually read. I'm good at research, and I can summarize what I find. I'll help you. We'll figure it out together."

Mary let her head rest on his shoulder. "Maybe Wave knows something. My parents did support them."

Maybe. And Nathan had the means to reach out to them without causing a major... diplomatic issue, he supposed. At least, he thought Dr. Gordon would still be willing to talk to him.

When Mary had left the league last fall, Nathan had half expected her to find her way to Wave. Given her parents' history with them, it would have made sense. But she was never the predictable one, and she'd gone off on her own instead.

If she'd gone to Wave, he wondered if LIO ever would have won her back.

Nathan twisted a strand of Mary's hair around his finger, letting his hand brush her cheek. "You know what we need?"

She tipped her head to look at him. "If you propose to me right now, I'll punch you."

"I was going to say 'a vacation.' But noted."

Mary closed her eyes and leaned into his neck, tucking her body into his as if they'd been designed to fit together. "Vacation. Yes. Somewhere warm."

She deserved crystal-blue water and toes in the sand, or sweet-smelling jungles with ruins to explore. He could give her rest, and gourmet meals, and nights spent dancing until the sun rose.

He wasn't sure when, or how many problems they'd have to solve before they could sail away unimpeded, but he was going to make it happen.

THE DAWN'S first light bathed Niagara Falls in a blanket of blue as Dolly stepped through the portal with Sever at her side, Ranger, Carlisle, and the ever-present Morik a step behind. Her arms prickled with the chill of early morning, and it was easy to remember how long it took spring to fully awaken up here. There were times when the wait had felt excruciating. At least, back when she'd had the Knife by her side and the ability to wander where she wished.

She'd have it again. In minutes, it would be at her side. And this time, she'd never let it go.

The portal deposited them on the patio beside the visitor's center, which looked out over the exact point where the water tipped over the horseshoe falls and into the gorge, sending plumes of spray puffing back into the air.

"Remarkable," Sever said, a note of true reverence in his tone even as he raised his voice to be heard over the pounding falls. She recalled, for the first time, the way he'd described his destroyed court as a place for art and beauty. A strange sort of kingdom for a man of such violence.

Dolly thought of asking if he was glad he hadn't incinerated the Earth without question, then decided she might be better not to put thoughts like that into his head.

They were already there, true. But there was no need to encourage that kind of thinking.

The Pearl Knife was here, practically within her grasp. Oh, she couldn't feel it anymore, but she knew it was nearby. She'd portaled outside the falls to get a sense of whether it would anticipate her presence and try to hold her back. She didn't feel sick, or unwell. Perhaps it didn't know she was here.

"I'll try to portal to the prison level, if you agree." Dolly nodded to Sever, as if in deference. "We can liberate my colleagues."

As soon as she had the Knife, she was certain she'd be able to use Sever as she saw fit. She wondered what it would feel like to control his abilities, to freeze even un-enhanced humans in their tracks, to boil a person's blood. Not that she intended to do much blood boiling—the memory remained somewhat off-putting—but still, the power would be overwhelming. And she'd be unstoppable.

A ranger darted out from behind the visitor's center behind them, dressed in blue-gray and holding onto his wide-brimmed hat as he ran. He opened his mouth, clearly planning to stand in their way, but Sever flicked his wrist in the man's direction, stopping him in his tracks. "The prison level will be fine."

The frozen man's eyes moved wildly, but Dolly didn't think he could even blink. Yes, that power would be very handy indeed.

Dolly raised her hand, digging into the resonance she now recognized as easily as she did the Knife. But when she tried to drag the portal open, the air... resisted. She tried again, but the air fought back, like waves forming a wall of jittering molecules. She stopped, pressing her hands to her temples as if she could stop the feeling of nails dragged along a chalkboard.

Sever frowned at her, though she thought it might be in concern rather than displeasure. "What's wrong?"

"They're blocking me," Dolly said, breathing hard. Why was she breathing hard? "Or the Knife is. I can't tell."

Sever sighed, looking back over the falls, eyebrows lifting in an almost wistful expression. "A shame. I so hate to ruin beautiful things."

For a beat, Dolly didn't understand. He hadn't moved—hadn't flicked wrist or fingers or raised his hands above his waist —and she couldn't see what he could possibly *mean* by that. He just stood there, the wind whispering through his curls, that wistful expression locked on his face.

Beneath her feet, the ground rumbled.

If her attempt to open a portal had felt like a screech, this felt like thunder, but only until the crack resounded through the falls, as if lightning were striking from within. The water before her rushed toward the same drop-off point she had known all her life, that her mother and her mother's mother had known all *their* lives—until, suddenly, it rushed elsewhere.

From the center of the horseshoe, the falls opened, rock screaming as it broke like an eggshell. The water receded, leaping to fill a new gaping fissure as the horseshoe falls broke into a new shape, a jagged handle that extended back along the river and split the falls in half.

Dolly tried to think of the power she'd command, once she held the Knife. But her mouth was dry, her thoughts a jumble, and all she could think of was the destruction.

Eloise. Her daughter's name coasted through her mind, and Dolly shoved it savagely away. She would save her daughter, if she could. But first, the Knife.

Sever held out a hand to her, and Dolly took it. "Let us try this again," he said.

THE GARAGE CEILING BURST OPEN, gray-blue sky glinting above for a millisecond before water leapt into the new rupture, bringing with it the wrenching thunder of tearing rock.

Mary jumped to her feet, the water already lapping at her ankles. Nathan pulled her back toward the corner as boulders crumbled into the gap, free falling with the water and cracking into pieces when they hit the floor.

The spray coated her eyes, making it hard to see. She tried to wipe it away, but her hands were wet, too. As far as she could tell, though, the ceiling had split—through several meters of limestone—so that a wall of water now blocked their side of the garage from the exit.

The water crashed to the floor in a mad rush, seeking corners to fill as momentum pushed it toward its usual drop-off point. Mary clung to Nathan's hand as the water surged back toward the wall, lifting the vehicles off their wheels.

"The smart car," she shouted, cold water streaming down her face, sticking her curls to her skin. "It's a submarine."

She wasn't sure how the silver smart car would take a drop from the falls, but they might be able to get it out the usual way, and at least it could operate in water. At least it would give them a chance. Maybe they could maneuver it past the pounding wall of water that blocked them from the door. The car was only a few meters away—reachable, surely—though the water was tossing it around more easily than some of the heavier vehicles.

Mary let go of Nathan's hand so they could swim, but the pressure of the falls made the current a formidable enemy. Choppy waves pounded all around them, white bubbles churning on every side, and it took all the focus she could muster to keep kicking. To keep moving.

As they swam—or tried to—a wave caught the van she'd been working on and catapulted it toward the back wall, catching Mary against its rear doors as it swung wildly through the current. If it dragged her under, she might hit her head and drown. If it bashed her against the wall—well, same story. Or worse.

She floundered, her head dipping beneath the surface for a second as she tried to force her body out of the van's path. But the vehicle was moving too fast, picking up speed as the current threw it toward the wall.

She surfaced to hear Nathan shouting, but she couldn't make out what he was saying. She grabbed for the door handle, for anything that would give her purchase—maybe let her climb to the roof of the van—but her hand slipped, her wrist wrenching awkwardly.

With the wall nearly at her back, Mary had no more choices. She took a breath and dove, slipping beneath the van moments before the waves smashed it against the stone. The vehicle spun away, and she struggled toward the far corner, forcing her lungs to hold out long enough for her to swim out of its orbit.

Pure luck, that she'd lived without bashing her head on a wheel. Pure luck.

She pulled herself out of the water with a gasp, grateful to whichever historical league operative had decided to leave the walls rough instead of coating them in metal. Handholds were nice to have.

Everyone else in HQ might be facing tougher odds. The gash in the ceiling went past the garage, opening a small gap in the top of the wall that the water hadn't found yet, but it was too high to see through. Too far to climb, too, especially with the water making it slippery.

Nathan had followed the wall back to the corner, and he braced himself against the rock as he made his way to her side.

"If I had my grapple, I might be able to get us out of here," Mary said. Her wrist was smarting, and her whole body was trembling in the cold water, but she could definitely operate a grapple. Get them to higher ground, or something.

The water had settled somewhat after its initial onslaught, now rushing headlong toward its original drop point. It was just... broken now. And something about the shape of the cavern left a pond beneath their feet, the surface choppy and bathed in white bubbles.

As she watched, the current caught her silver smart car and carried it swiftly beneath the new falls, where it disappeared. Presumably into the gorge.

Nathan shook the water out of his eyes, blinking rapidly. "You don't keep a pocket grapple on you at all times?"

She twisted her hair out of her face, tying it into a rough knot. "Trust me, I'm changing that policy immediately."

If they survived this. Mary hit the com in her ear, calling for Eloise, for anyone, but only static replied. The com was working—she did not create tech that couldn't be drowned once or twice—but who knew whether anyone was alive? The crack in the ceiling clearly extended beyond the garage. Behind the rock at their backs was a corridor, and then the training rooms before the offices. How far did it go? Could the cracks have spidered outward to hit the living quarters?

She itched to go find her friends, to help them. But she was trapped. Trapped behind the falls, and everyone else might be dead.

Nathan was scanning the area, hand gripping the rock. Mary edged her hand closer to his. "Sever, right?" she said.

Nathan dropped his gaze to hers, his eyes shining gray. "I don't know. But if anyone can break Niagara Falls..."

Yeah. It was the guy who could snap bones with a thought. Bones, rock. What was the difference, really?

Even if they did survive this, how could they ever beat him? What did he even want here? The Pearl Knife, certainly; he'd sent Sloane and her friends to retrieve it. But why break HQ to get it? And why now?

Mary's com buzzed with static again. And then, a voice. "Anyone out there?"

Mary let out a breath. "Jeff. Nathan and I are here. Trapped in the garage."

The com crackled. "I've always heard I should experience Niagara Falls," Jeff said, "but I have a feeling this wasn't what people had in mind."

Nathan's com must have been working, too, because he rolled his eyes. Though Mary thought she saw the hint of a smile, too.

"Can you evacuate?" Mary asked.

"Affirmative, captain. Gail's already on it. We have access to the casino entrance."

Gail. Of course she was on it. "Good. Help her get the team out of here."

Mary wasn't exactly up to date on her protocols, but she was pretty sure that 'evacuate non operatives' ranked pretty high on Eloise's priority list. And Gail practically breathed protocol. Mary supposed she could see the benefit in that.

"Roger that," Jeff said. "The Inferno's with us, too. We'll try to send some help your way."

Mary didn't know what help Jeff Hayes could possibly send, but she appreciated the sentiment anyway. If Will was with them, he'd be able to get them all out safely.

A chunk of rock broke off the ledge above, crashing to the center of the former garage. "What's going to kill us first?" Her teeth were chattering, her arms numb. Which was good for her injured wrist, but bad, she suspected, for sustaining life in the long term. "The rocks or the cold?"

Nathan edged closer to drape an arm around her shoulders. "Neither. Because we're getting out of here."

As if in response to his statement, the falling water parted. It was like someone had drawn a curtain, splitting the water in half. On both sides. With the new gap, Mary could see that the crack was wide enough to allow for double waterfalls, a new step on the staircase to the Niagara gorge.

Rajni stood by the doors with her arms extended to either side, her braid flung back over her shoulder, face scrunched in an expression of intense concentration as she held the falls at bay. The water receded, and Mary's feet hit the floor.

She didn't stop to wonder. She ran.

Tally appeared at Rajni's side, leaping over the gap in the floor to grab Mary and sweep her back to the door. "She can't hold it for long," Tally said, as if in apology.

Mary might be cranky sometimes, but she was not going to be cranky about being rescued.

Tally deposited Mary beside Rajni and leapt again, returning with Nathan a moment later. The four of them dove for the doors, and Rajni collapsed against the wall in the corridor, awake but breathing hard as the water crashed back to the stone.

"That does it," Mary said, when her heartbeat calmed enough to let her speak. "I'm promoting you two to full operatives.

"Funny," Tally said, "because I was just composing my resignation."

She smiled, as if to show she was kidding, though Mary had her doubts. HQ under attack? It was unprecedented. Judging by the inch of water pooling at her feet, and the distant groans of metal, they weren't safe yet. In fact, she had a feeling the fight was only just beginning.

Mary pointed to the recruit's cluster of pastel horse pins. Tally had followed her advice and secured them to a strip of Velcro. There was hope for her, after all. "I'll buy you a new Fruit Loop pin if you stay."

Tally tilted her head, as if considering it. "Deal."

"I don't think there's a My Little Pony named Fruit Loop," Nathan said.

Mary shrugged and offered Rajni a hand, helping her to stand. "Ire would know. Come on. We'd better find Eloise."

ELOISE'S OFFICE WALLS SHUDDERED, shedding her photographs, the frames shattering against the floor. Bottles shimmied off the bar and smashed, diffusing the room with odors of whiskey and gin.

She clung to the desk, Steve's arms still around her as the lights blinked, the furniture stuttering across the floor.

Something behind her snapped, and she turned her head in time to see a crack snaking up the screen behind her, creating a schism through the U.S. map that still shone there. The screen tipped, and the world lurched as Steve whisked her out the door and into the hall to a soundtrack of breaking glass and screaming metal.

"Convenient, that," she said, but her mind was on the Pearl Knife. On keeping it safe. Because this wasn't some natural disaster. It couldn't be. No, this was an assault.

They were coming for the Knife.

The blade sang its agreement, sending news of a resonance it could feel in the air, in whatever power had been unleashed.

Eloise grabbed Steve's hand, pulling him along the hall. "We need to get to the Knife."

Water trickled down from the ceiling, rivulets finding their way through layers of stone that ought to have been impenetrable. The lights dimmed and sparked back to life, the infrastructure strong enough to keep them on. For now.

How long that would last, she couldn't say. And once they were plunged into darkness? What would they do then?

Images flipped in her mind, making it feel like she stood in two places as the Knife superimposed a vision of Eloise's room, of walls crumbling around the spot where it sat on her coffee table. Waiting for her return. *We're coming*, Eloise thought. *Hold on.*

Ire rounded a corner in front of them, eyes wild, whirling around to match their direction as they raced forward. "I can't reach Mary and Nathan," he said. "The halls are caving in. I think they're in the garage."

The garage. The closest spot to the falls, except for Dolly's old living quarters. Eloise swallowed. Mary could take care of herself. She'd have to.

Ahead, the titanium-plated ceiling dented inward, as if to reinforce Ire's words. Ire shouted, shoving Eloise and Steve back and shielding them with his body as the metal gave out, filling the corridor with busted limestone.

Eloise coughed as dust invaded her nose and mouth, thick as smoke. She swallowed thickly, trying to clear it away before rising slowly to her feet. "Everyone OK?" she asked when she could speak again.

OK being a relative term. Boulders filled the corridor in front of them, blocking any hope of passage.

The men nodded, both wide-eyed. Miraculously, the light still sputtered above. She should give whoever'd designed the electrical system a medal.

Ire brushed a layer of dust out of his hair. "I can clear that, but it'll take a bit."

"What," Steve said, breathing hard, "you can't bust through it?"

Interestingly, he said it without the vitriol he usually reserved for Ire. It sounded more like... a joke?

Under different circumstances, Eloise might have been intrigued.

"I can, if I want to risk the structural integrity of the whole place," Ire said. "I could bring down a crucial support."

Steve glanced at the ceiling, where severed wires showered sparks down on parts of the new rock pile. "I think structural integrity might be a thing of the past."

Eloise had to agree. Still, she didn't want to bring untold tons of rock down on their heads. Blinking dust out of her eyes, she hit her com. "Mary?"

A second of static. Then, "We're alive. For now."

Eloise let out a breath. Alive. Thank god. "We're trapped," she said.

"On our way."

Eloise shook her head, teeth sinking into her bottom lip as her thoughts raced to form a plan. Dolly had been with Sever at the restaurant. Eloise didn't know why, or how, but she could make a few guesses about what her mother would do next.

She and Sever might both want the Knife. But Dolly would have another priority, too.

"No," Eloise said. "We're fine."

"Relative term, El," Mary said.

Eloise forced herself to stay calm. Or at least, to sound it. "If Mom... If Dolly's involved in this, she'll start with either the prison or the Knife. I'll handle the Knife. I need you to secure Diana and the others. We'll meet you down there."

Eloise could have sworn she heard Nathan utter a curse in the background. She couldn't blame him. She'd have liked to tell them to evacuate rather than diving deeper into danger. But at the very least, they couldn't leave the retirees to die down there if Dolly somehow wasn't involved.

"On our way," Mary said. "Stay safe, El."

Eloise swallowed. She wasn't sure there was much hope of that. "You, too."

She left Mary to her mission, turning to the men. "We need to secure the Knife."

"How?" Steve asked. "We're kind of surrounded here."

Eloise's fingertips tingled, but she pressed them into fists. Now wasn't the time to call on untested powers, if that was even the source of the feeling. She closed her eyes, focusing on the Knife's presence. It wasn't so far to her room. She'd called the Knife to her in the past, sent it flying through HQ on its own, and that was before she'd known it could make portals.

The Knife sent her an image, and this time it was unlike any she'd ever received from it. This time, it was as though she were seeing the world from the blade's perspective as it hovered, prepared to cut a door through space to get to her.

The walls shuddered, and Eloise bit back a scream as the ceiling caved in on her room, burying her bed in rock. The Knife twitched, and then all it could send was darkness and pain as HQ collapsed around it.

Eloise staggered, a sob lodged in her throat. The Knife sent a weak pulse back, like a heartbeat. It was there. Alive, if that word even applied. It was the closest term she had.

It was alive, but it wouldn't be coming for them. Powerful as it was, it couldn't disintegrate boulders. They needed some other way to get to it.

The tingling sensation in her fingertips escalated, like tiny beads of electricity running along her skin. In her mind, the Knife's answer rang like a church bell, resonating throughout her body.

Steve's fingers dug into her shoulder, and she opened her

eyes. Ire was on his knees, shifting rock, but it would take far too long to create a path.

"The Knife is buried," she said. "We're trapped."

DOLLY DIDN'T KNOW if the Pearl Knife had been jamming her ability to create a portal, or if LIO had installed some kind of device to stop her. She could picture Mary concocting something like that, though the girl would have had to coax the Pearl Knife to let her study the way it made portals. Unless she'd found another way.

Whatever the blockage was, Dolly no longer felt it churning against her.

She had to suppress the knot of pain in her stomach that quivered at the sight of what Sever had done to LIO HQ, and the thought of what must be happening underground. The rock vibrated beneath her feet, and she could picture the chain reaction well enough, the water pouring in, the limestone crumbling.

Dolly had built this place, but it had forsaken her. There should be nothing tragic about watching it fall.

In any case, there was no cause for delay now. Dolly plunged a fingertip into the air, unlocking the ether as though with the turning of a key. The portal zipped open, offering her passage to a silver-tinted cellblock, and she stepped onto the prison level with Sever at her side.

Or perhaps, more accurately, she stood at his. Not for long, now. Not for long.

Here, the lights flickered frenetically, dust shaking out of the corners as the walls rumbled with distant trouble, but the level seemed otherwise undisturbed. The cells were intact, the prisoners shouting for release. She doubted anyone at HQ cared enough to release the people who'd done them so much harm. In their eyes, anyway.

"The control panel is on the wall by the door," Dolly said. "I'm sure I don't have access."

The place smelled like ozone and fear, an undercurrent of something chemical and dangerous. She couldn't quite place it.

Sever smiled at her. It was the look an indulgent parent might give to a well-behaved child. "No need."

He made a fist, and the cells cracked open. Not with the violence of the upper floors, but with a gentle tap. Like a sculptor carving the final details into his masterpiece.

Monster's hulking figure emerged first, his scales shining blue in the shivering light. Even with his abilities suppressed, he was a giant of a man, a force to be reckoned with. Mange's serum couldn't restrain physical alterations.

When he saw her, he grinned, displaying two rows of pointed teeth.

Then the narrow corridor was full of movement as the rest of the retirees climbed through the gaps in their cells, Goldi stepping daintily over a short ledge of stone, the twins moving together like magnets to clasp each other's hands, Rocker touching the wall as though testing his camouflaging powers. Still suppressed. But not for long.

And, emerging from the cell closest to where Dolly stood, the Trap. Diana Morton, industrial-strength gloves chained to her wrists to stem the poison that the serum couldn't stop from leaking out of her fingertips. Her black hair was tied back in a knot at her neck. "Good to see you, boss," she said.

Sever snapped his fingers, and the chains at her wrists fell away. Diana raised her eyebrows and stripped the gloves off her hands. "I see you brought a friend."

Oh, he was more than a friend. He'd be the key to securing the life they'd once had.

The retirees in the hall parted, somewhat reluctantly, and Dolly frowned as Jenna Carpenter worked her way to the front of the crowd. Even with her petite stature, everyone moved aside for her. Everyone let her pass.

The girl's eyes were wide and wild, her shirt rumpled, her fingertips singed black. As if she'd been trying to push past the drug to work her powers. She ignored Dolly, walking straight up to Sever. He wasn't a tall man, but Jenna had to tip her head back to look him in the eye.

"I can throw fire, and I hate these people," she said. "I'll help you do... whatever."

Dolly wasn't sure whether Jenna meant the retirees, or Eloise and the league, or... well, everyone.

The latter, she decided. She narrowed her eyes, edging half a step closer to Sever, but Jenna didn't react. Jenna didn't seem to see her at all.

Sever stared back at the girl, a dangerous glint in his eyes. "Beautiful," he said. "Dolly, if you will. It's time to make our grand escape."

THE STAIRWELL to the prison was blissfully clear, even as thin rivulets of water streamed down the walls. It might be bunker-like down here, but the respite wouldn't last forever. The pressure from above would eventually crack these walls, too. Mary barreled down the stairs, skipping every other step and trusting Nathan, Tally, and Rajni to stay with her.

When she reached the landing, she scanned the door open with shaking hands and shoved her way inside.

Dolly was already there, surrounded by the prisoners as she traced a line of silver into the air.

There was no time to think. Mary threw herself into the group, knocking Dolly to the floor and leaving a jagged gash of melted silver hovering in the middle of the room.

Chaos erupted behind her as Nathan and the others crashed into the room, but Mary held Dolly down against the concrete floor, focusing on keeping her wrists pinned down. If the woman opened a portal, they'd be done. Blue light flickered out of Dolly's fingertips, as if she wanted to try it. But all she could do was sneer in Mary's face.

"What's wrong, Mary?" Dolly asked. "Aren't you going to hit me?"

Mary rolled her eyes. "You know I wouldn't."

Dolly only smiled. "Yes, doll. I do. So very ethical. When it serves you to be, that is."

Mary ignored the jab, trying to glance back over her shoulder without giving Dolly an opening to attack. Goldi was diving into the nearest cell to hide, while Nathan had taken on the twins. Even without their mutual mind-reading powers—Mary assumed the serum should still be working, at least for a few hours—they fought with precision that clearly took all of Nathan's concentration to combat.

Meanwhile, Tally and Rajni were fighting Monster, Ranger, and Carlisle, a combination that might have been more difficult had Carlisle been flinching less. Mostly they were fighting Monster while Ranger and Carlisle distracted them from cornering him.

Mary didn't see Rocker anywhere. Was it possible that his abilities could have returned already? He could be sneaking up on them from behind.

The recruits needed Mary's help. She had no idea how long it had been since the retirees' last serum dose. If they regained their powers, this fight would get much uglier.

But it was Sever who unnerved her the most. He'd stepped back against the far wall, his face wreathed in shadow and Jenna Carpenter at his side. Mary couldn't see his eyes, but she imagined his attention locked on her, like it had been in D.C. Why wasn't he freezing them all in their places? At any moment, he could shatter everyone's bones.

Everyone except Mary.

"Well, Mary, you're the genius." Dolly wasn't even struggling, wasn't even trying to break free. "What's next?"

Mary ripped her attention from the fight to meet Dolly's stare. What she wouldn't give for a pair of handcuffs right now.

Or a pack of zip ties. Would Mange's serum even work on Dolly, with her Knife-granted abilities?

Maybe a tranquilizer.

She opened her mouth to respond, and a pair of hands locked onto her upper arms, burning through the fabric of her shirt as they yanked her off Dolly and onto the floor. Acid poison leaked through to singe her skin, pouring acrid fumes into her nose as she struggled against Diana's poisonous grip.

No power-suppressing serum in existence worked on the Trap.

Mary rolled, sending Diana into a tumble as she leapt to her feet. But Diana must have kept up some conditioning while living in that cell of hers, because she was already up, rushing toward Mary, fingers spread wide before her.

Shoulders stinging, Mary met Diana halfway, grabbing her by one wrist and twisting her arm behind her back. It was a hold that brought grown men to their knees, but unfortunately it left Diana's second hand open, and she flailed against Mary's grip, trying to reach skin.

Mary gritted her teeth against the memory of standing helpless before this woman. She still had scars on her abdomen from the day Diana had tortured her.

She caught Diana's other wrist, but the motion left her wide open. She tried to rectify it, tried to bring both of Diana's hands back behind her while trying to avoid getting stung.

Diana smashed her head into Mary's, filling her mouth with blood, but Mary didn't let go. "I'm not an amateur," Mary said, her lip already swelling.

"Neither am I." Diana flexed her hands, and Mary had no way to stop the flood of poison that trickled out of the Trap's fingers and onto her palms. She tried to maintain her grip, but the pain loosened her fingers, sending her hands into spasms until Diana broke free.

"Gravity," Diana said, spinning to face her. "So helpful."

Mary dragged her palms on her pants, trying to dislodge the poison that burned across her skin. They were still at the edge of the battle, Nathan fighting one twin now, Monster's hulking form lashing out at the two recruits. Shouts and scuffling footsteps echoed through the space, cutting through the sound of Mary's own breathing in her ears. Dolly had edged her way into a corner, probably ready to carve a portal to safety at any moment.

Well, too bad. Mary wasn't going to let that happen.

Diana was running for her again, but in the corner of her awareness, Mary felt Sever move. The chaos parted for him like water, though no one froze. No one did anything. It was like he was cutting through space, like it was bending around him to suit his whims. She blinked, trying to shake away the sensation.

"Stop." Sever hadn't raised his voice, hadn't shouted, yet the word reverberated through the room. Some of the fighting paused, though not everyone ceased moving at his command.

Diana did. Not in the creepy frozen-statue way of the EAEA agents in the restaurant, but of her own volition. At least, so Mary thought. The Trap offered Sever a shallow bow. "Trust me," she said, "this one's all yours."

Interesting. The Trap had always particularly enjoyed tormenting Mary, a tendency that had only increased when Mary had decided to punish her—and her friends—for their role in her parents' deaths.

It was hard to imagine Diana giving away her right to torture Mary. To anyone.

But then, Sever wasn't just anyone. He approached her now, hands at his sides, his long, midnight blue robes a clear indication that he never saw the need to get his hands dirty in actual combat. Why bother, when you could snap your fingers and force the world—worlds—dance to your whims? Might as well wear the longest, tangliest cloak available.

Mary made herself meet his gaze. His face was pale and mostly unlined, his nose long and narrow, his eyes black and green, with those eerie sparks of light blazing in the center. She thought there was a gray tinge to his complexion that hadn't been there before, a hint of spiderwebbed bruises under his eyes. But that could have been wishful thinking.

He tipped his chin up as he looked at her, as scuffles between the old and new LIO members flashed behind him. "How is it that you can be here?" His voice was low and musical now. He almost sounded haunted. "In the same facility that holds the Blade of Starlight. You hated it so."

Mary shook her head. "You've got it wrong. I'm sorry to break it to you, but I'm not your girlfriend."

Over his shoulder, Mary felt Tally break away from her fight to move in her direction. She tried to catch the recruit's eye, to warn her off, but Tally was sidling around to the side, and Mary couldn't see her face without looking away from Sever. Without betraying Tally's position.

Sever raised a hand toward his shoulder, and before Mary could guess his next move, Tally jumped. Mary threw a hand up, as though she could block the recruit from leaping across the space. "He won't hurt me," she said, though she wasn't at all sure.

And it was too late, anyway. Tally was already in midair, already knocking Mary out of the way, as if to block her from Sever's power. Mary's shoulder hit the concrete and something crunched, pain bursting through her right side, but she rolled onto her back in time to see Sever roll his eyes and whip his wrist in a circle.

Tally's neck cracked, and her body dropped to the concrete, where she lay unmoving. Rajni screamed, abandoning her fight to rush across the room, but there was nothing she could do. There was nothing anyone could do. With pain lancing through her upper body, Mary wasn't even sure she could stand.

She choked back a lump of tears, rage mixing with the screaming pain of her shoulder as Rajni dropped to her knees beside her friend, Sever looking on with his head tilted, blinking as though in curiosity even though the man—alien, god, whatever he was—had to have seen more death that Mary could even contemplate. He *definitely* looked grayer now, stretched to the limit of his monstrous abilities.

But it didn't matter. It was too late to save Tally. It might be too late to do anything but die.

STEVE HAD JOINED Ire in the mad rush to clear rocks from the hallway, but Eloise could see it was hopeless. There was no way out of here.

Her fingertips buzzed with electricity, and the Knife protested her hopelessness, though its voice grew fainter by the moment. It pushed a vision of searing white light into her mind, power leaping out of her very cells, and Eloise let herself answer with her own fear.

My mother has that power, she thought. *What if it corrupts me?*

The Knife shuddered in her mind, shedding sparks. It reminded her of her father, of the way his own fingertips could sparkle like the Fourth of July. The way he'd found joy in his powers, even as Dolly had used them against him. The way he'd found his way back to them in spite of her.

Eloise breathed. Right. So she'd channel Dad, rather than Dolly.

No. No, she'd always been inspired by her father, but this time she'd channel herself.

As Ire and Steve kept shifting rocks, Eloise closed her eyes. Tentatively, she touched a fingertip to the air at eye level, all her thoughts bent on the Knife. She didn't know how this worked, and now would not be a good time to accidentally open a door to Morocco or something.

She pushed her fingertip into the air, slowly, until the air pushed back. It was the only way she could think to describe it, a meeting of her flesh against a wall—only the wall was made of water, or perhaps something slightly thicker.

The Knife sent a picture of green jello into her mind, and Eloise actually smiled. *Was that a* joke?

The Knife didn't respond.

Eloise pressed her finger into the wall—it did feel like jello, sort of, though it was warm—and pulled her hand down.

Rocks tumbled out of the portal and into the hall, knocking her back before she could close the portal. She let it go, and it zipped shut, slicing a last rock into half as dust clouded up to choke her.

Steve rocketed to her side to help her to her feet. "You did it," he said. "Are you all right?"

Eloise breathed, coughed. The Knife glimmered, but despite the persistent feeling of hope, she could tell it was malfunctioning. Or... sick. Injured. Those felt like more appropriate terms. Its communication felt patchy and inconsistent, like it might blink away at any moment.

She wasn't sure how a bunch of rocks could hurt the Knife when it felt nearly indestructible. Maybe it was something about the power that had done this.

It didn't matter. The Knife was stuck and in pain, and she couldn't reach it.

"The whole room is buried," she said. "I can't get to it."

Steve licked his lips, thinking. "You're going to need to cut a passage to the exact spot where the Knife is buried."

"And how am I going to do that? I've never done this before."

"Sure you have. You just did. And if you don't, Dolly will."

He was right. Of course he was right. Eloise planted her feet hip-width apart. *I know you're hurt*, she thought toward the Knife, *but I need you to send me a thread to follow.*

Again, she closed her eyes and felt for the shimmering wall. This time, though, she listened for the Knife's song, for the rhythm that churned through her entire life. It underpinned everything she did, and she couldn't simply let go and trust it to work with her. She had to let it *in*.

Eloise exhaled, and the Knife's power flooded through her, like rays of sunlight through the rain, like prismatic rainbows spinning along the walls.

Eloise followed the path, dragging her fingertips slowly through the space and reaching through the fold to grasp the Knife's hilt. She pulled, and the rocks shifted around it, trying to reclaim their prize.

The Knife freed itself with a last, desperate surge of power, and Eloise yanked her hand out of the portal, slamming it shut before more rocks could pour in. The Knife quivered in her hand, and she cradled it to her chest, trying to send waves of comfort into it.

When she opened her eyes, Steve and Ire were staring at her. "Well," Ire said. "That worked."

Steve nodded. Those two, agreeing? This day had more than one miracle, clearly. "El," he said, "you know we're escaping. Right?"

Her breath burned in her throat. "We need to get to the prison and help Mary."

"Yeah," Steve said, "but after that. There's no defending this place. We need to run."

Eloise started to say that of course she knew it. But some part of her *had* been picturing a cleanup operation. Not intentionally, not openly. But this was her home. She'd grown up here, had made it her own.

"I don't know where we can go," she said. Travis might be gone, and the EAEA might be shattered. But as far as she knew, President Caldwell's executive order still stood.

Steve pulled a ragged business card out of his pocket and held it up. "I do."

Eloise opened a portal to the prison stairs, where she could be sure no one would be injured. And she stepped through into chaos.

Rajni was still screaming, hiccupping sobs interrupting her grief, as Nathan abandoned his fight with the remaining twin—he couldn't remember their names, and they blurred together, anyway—to move toward Mary. Her face had gone white with pain, her shoulder bent at an awkward angle.

He couldn't look toward Tally. He didn't dare. They'd lost a recruit. It was too much to bear, and if he let himself absorb it right now, he'd never get them out of here.

Nathan was still moving when Eloise barreled into the prison, flanked by Steve and Ire, the Pearl Knife clutched in her hand. Cracks of electric blue light fizzled along the blade, and Nathan had a feeling it wasn't demonstrating some power he'd never seen before. It looked like a good tap would shatter the thing, though he suspected it was a fair bit stronger than that.

Of course, he'd also thought HQ was a fair bit stronger than that. Sever might have the power to shatter the Knife. Who knew what he could do?

Ignoring the newcomers, Sever turned his attention back to Mary, and the intensity of his gaze told Nathan he was again trying to control her. Eloise was moving slowly toward Sever, as if she might unleash the Knife at his back, but Nathan had a feeling the alien was aware of everything around him.

Eyes still locked on Mary, Sever frowned, letting a sliver of irritation show. Whatever he was trying to do, it hadn't worked. He stared down at Mary, his fists clenched under the bell-like sleeves of his robes. "You need to come with me," he said.

Mary spat. "Doubtful."

Sever stared at her, focusing hard, but Mary struggled to her feet, holding his gaze. Holding his *attention*, so that Eloise could release the Knife, sending it sizzling toward his chest.

Dolly rocketed out of the corner, leaping to snatch the blade from the air. She cried out as threads of electricity bled into her hand, and she dropped the Knife. It lurched back into the air, weeping blue light as it streamed toward Sever.

But Nathan could see that the Knife was moving more slowly than it should, and Sever had ample time to throw up a shield before it could reach him. That shield had worked on the bullets in the restaurant, but the Knife merely paused and dug its tip into the energy, chipping away at Sever's defenses. A drop of sweat beaded at Sever's hairline, and for the first time, his face showed hints of strain, the corners of his eyes pinched with effort. Given time, Nathan thought the Knife might actually break through.

But time wasn't a luxury they had. Still maintaining his shield, orange light cracking as the Knife's blue dug at its foundations, Sever pointed to Mary. "I can't control her, but something will. What is it?"

Eloise's forehead was damp with sweat, her concentration pinned on the Knife. On getting to Sever. Nathan forced himself to focus on Eloise, to keep his eyes from drifting toward the woman he loved, even as everyone else stared at her.

It was Jenna Carpenter who sauntered into the center of

the room to look Nathan in the eye, tipping him a secret smile as she raised her index finger to point straight at him. "He can."

Pain ratcheted through Mary's body, her dislocated shoulder hanging, her collarbone digging into her lungs with every breath. Something was broken in there. Maybe several somethings. But she stayed on her feet, barely, fighting the blackness that clawed at the edges of her vision.

Jenna stood at center stage, a smirk on her lips and a crook in her eyebrow as she milked her spotlight moment, as she pointed an index finger in Nathan's face.

Sever must have grasped it, too, because he couldn't control Mary with his powers. But he could control Nathan.

Steve blurred toward Nathan, but Jenna anticipated him. She threw up a wall of fire, blasting Steve back against the door as Monster swept up behind her to wrench Nathan off his feet, carrying him across the room in two strides to deposit him on his knees before Sever. Like a criminal thrown before an executioner.

Mary stumbled toward them, the world lurching as she tried to stay on her feet, but the retirees surrounded Nathan, forming a wall in almost perfect coordination. He tried to struggle to his feet, but Rocker and the twins dragged him back down. Too many. There were too many of them, and they had all the advantages.

Above her head, HQ creaked and groaned, as if to remind her their time here was limited. It didn't matter. If they killed Nathan... her brain stopped there, unwilling to go on.

Diana stood at the head of the protective circle, eyebrows raised, fingers poised at shoulder level. Mary took another step toward them, agony clutching her heart—if she could only reach them, if she could only find a way to stall so the Knife could break through that shield—but the Trap let one hand drop to her side, and a dribble of poison sizzled onto the concrete half an inch from Nathan's foot. "Careful now," she said.

Nathan tried again to stand, and Monster kicked him in the stomach, doubling him over onto the floor.

Ire twitched as if he might attack, but Mary caught his eye, helplessness clogging her throat. "Don't. They'll kill him."

"Good," Sever said. She couldn't see Sever's expression, couldn't see anything but Nathan. "She understands. Go."

Go? Go *where*? The Knife pressed ever onward, but Dolly dragged a portal open, ushering Goldi through first. The illusionist had emerged from her hiding place, the coward, and she stepped through the doorway delicately, allowing Rocker to steady her. The twins followed with Ranger and Carlisle, and Sever nodded to send Monster and Diana through. Jenna wiggled her fingers at Mary before leaping through after them.

Sever bent, grabbing a fistful of Nathan's shirt and lifting him easily up off the floor, looking completely unworried as the Knife's tip wedged through the shield.

Sever turned to Mary, the orange spots flickering in his eyes. She made herself look away from him, made herself focus on Nathan. He was still fighting, grimacing in concentration, with his hands locked around Sever's wrists. Sever hadn't even bothered to freeze him.

She was too hurt to move, too hurt to think. If she could get past that shield, if Steve would wake up, if Eloise could make another portal—

"I'd meant to be kind to your world," Sever said, his voice soft. Almost contemplative. "But I will tear it apart, stone by stone, until I discover how you survived all this time."

Mary's cheeks were wet as Nathan met her eyes. He gave his head a shake, but she didn't know what it meant—let them take him? Let him die? How could she do either?—but then Sever was lifting him over the edge of the portal. Dolly followed without looking back.

They could be anywhere. Another world. Another galaxy. But Mary had a feeling they'd stay right here on Earth until Sever got exactly what he wanted.

The portal zipped shut, the shield collapsed, and the Knife clattered to the floor, twitching. HQ shuddered all around her, the walls groaning as water dribbled down the walls, but Mary didn't care. A monster beyond her imagining had wrenched away the man she loved. A monster she couldn't beat, that the Knife couldn't beat. He was too powerful for them.

Let the whole place collapse around her. Let it fall. The world would follow, soon enough. Mary was powerless to stop it.

And then Eloise was at her side, her face appearing through the blurred edges of pain and devastation. "We can't save him if we die," she said, taking hold of Mary's uninjured shoulder. "Let's get out of here."

AGNES DIDN'T KNOW why Fran had summoned her to the Yacht this time. She was making headway on the island, real progress, and she couldn't keep getting pulled away from her work. As Bradley Archer escorted her to the Committee's moving home base, muttering under his breath about his role as a glorified delivery boy, she rehearsed speeches in her head about the work they wanted her to do and the inability to make headway if they insisted on interrupting her.

But her protests died on her tongue as she entered the main hall of the ship.

They sat in a circle before the Committee, faces bruised and bloody, wearing Wave T-shirts and blankets slung over their shoulders. Mary's right shoulder was in a sling, her face contorted in pain as she stared silently into space. She was worrying a small disc between her fingers, and when Agnes squinted, she could just make out the tail of a cartoon horse. That... wasn't something she'd have expected Mary to be holding.

Eloise looked battered, resigned, the Knife's hilt peeking out of her belt. Ire was there, and Will. And, for reasons she couldn't begin to guess, Jeff Hayes. Steve Taylor, too—she remembered his presence in Vegas and on the airfield last March, as well as his sporadic visits to HQ before that. There were some younger people as well, operatives she didn't recognize. One of them, a young woman with a long black braid who looked to be of Indian descent, had silent tears tracking down her cheeks. Was the team here somewhere, too? Gail and Pete, and all the rest?

Agnes's gaze landed on Ire. Her closest friend, once. Her partner in the lab. "What happened?" she asked. It felt right, somehow, to ask him rather than looking to the Committee, even though she could practically feel Fran's eyes boring into her from the front of the room. She wasn't sure she could wrench her eyes away from her former teammates, even if she wanted to.

Ire cleared his throat. "Sever happened."

Agnes blinked. "Sever? The god the aliens told us about? He's real?"

What could he have possibly done to bring LIO to Wave's door, of all places? Fear thrummed through Agnes's stomach. They wouldn't be here if they had any other choice.

"He's real," Eloise confirmed, and Agnes wrenched her eyes from Ire—he was here, really here—to look at LIO's leader. Eloise's eyes were drawn, and Agnes couldn't help wondering when she'd last slept. She swallowed, glancing at Mary, and Agnes realized that Nathan wasn't among them. Where was he?

Eloise pressed her lips together. "I think we may want to revisit the idea of a truce."

<<<<>>>>

Thanks for reading!

Sign up for my VIP reader list at katesheeranswed.com to get *Power Struggle*, an exclusive LIO prequel novella!

Phew. All right. Well, if you've made it this far in the series, you're probably used to my cliffhangers. I do try to use them to get a head start on the next story rather than annoyingly interrupting the current plot, but in this case, it couldn't quite be avoided. I do apologize. Kind of. Sort of.

I have this thing for stories that build a beautiful, cool world and then tear it the heck down. I don't know why. Maybe for Mary, Eloise, and the members of the league, HQ represents a past they need to thoroughly break before they can move forward.

Anyway, I wanted to write a quick note about Philadelphia and its intricate network of tunnels, and the way I chose to depict that in *Nemesis*. As one of America's oldest cities, Philadelphia really does have a rather fascinating underground. The first Europeans in the area lived in caves near the river before they built homes. Canals used to run through the city and were later filled in favor of roadways. But some of those operations were complex, and little pockets of water still trickle around down there.

Strange wine cellars, pedestrian walkways, and old transportation tunnels still thread beneath the city.

Before you start spelunking under the Liberty Bell, however, I must alas remember that I am a fantasy writer. And I most certainly exaggerated the navigability of these tunnels. Like, a lot. In reality, our intrepid heroes would not have been able to tromp so reliably through Philly.

They wouldn't be able to teleport or throw fire, either, but I do like to point out when I've changed my real-Earth setting to a "kind of Earth" possibility.

As the pandemic prevented me from a research trip to Philadelphia (though I have been there in the past), I owe much to the book *Underground Philadelphia: From Caves and Canals to Tunnels and Transit* by Harry Kyriakodis and Joel Spivak.

I wonder if, during the course of writing their cool and rather niche history book, those two ever thought "I bet some fantasy author will come along and use our book to write about superheroes traipsing around these old tunnels in Philly."

What? It totally have happened.

Thanks for reading, friends. You mean the world to me :)

One
Frankie

Three years ago

Of the thirteen methods Frankie Hartiger had perfected for breaking into Sublevel D of Pathbound Enterprises Tower, scrambling the facial recognition panel on the Warren-700 security bot was usually the simplest.

Tonight, Frankie had been hunched in front of the malfunctioning heap of junk for so long that her legs were going numb. The new interworld transport operator's disembodied face hung suspended in midair before her, like a ghost returned to avenge a bad ID photo.

It was a hologram—a decoy Frankie had created to fool the dunce cap of a guard into opening the doors. She'd been doing this for months, using the trick to explore forbidden areas whenever she pleased. But this time, the bot wasn't budging.

When the real Liz Han dropped to a crouch beside her digital double, Frankie jumped. She hadn't even heard the doors open.

It was an awkward way to meet someone for the first time. Even by Frankie's standards.

The real Liz had a green yoga mat tucked under one arm and cursive tattoos on the backs of her hands: *If You* on the left, *Build It* on the right. She wore her black hair longer than it was in the picture, her ponytail tied low and flipped over her shoulder.

"Every time I sit for an ID photo, I sneeze," Liz said.

Frankie deactivated the digital Liz. The best course of action, she decided, would be to act like she was supposed to be here.

"I'm Frankie Hartiger," she said. "You secured a patent on citywide driverless car systems when you were nineteen."

At fourteen, Frankie figured she had time to beat that milestone.

"You're the daughter?"

A rhetorical question, obviously. Frankie hadn't made newsworthy contributions to the Hartiger Family Legacy—not yet—but she'd watched herself grow up on celebrity-zine covers. Family time, faked. The product of a talented photo collagist and a non-disclosure agreement as strong as soldered iron.

Fake or not, people liked to read about the first family of interworld travel. The *only* family of interworld travel. In the decades since her grandparents had succeeded in hopping between universes, no one else had come close to figuring out how they did it.

Frankie didn't even know.

Liz might.

"You've been directing commercial space flights since you were twenty-six," Frankie said.

"Don't tell me you know about the burger-flipping gig I had in high school, too."

Frankie did. She could have listed even more stats. Liz was thirty-three, Chinese American, five-foot-six. She'd also won eleven semi-professional digi-bowl championships, until she'd given up the sport seven years ago. Perhaps after recognizing the game as a mind-numbing waste of her significant mental capacities.

"I research every new high-ranking employee," Frankie said. "You actually deserve to work here."

"I'm not sure that's a compliment."

"It is. You patched the software on the security bots. Right? I'm the only other person who ever caught that glitch."

Liz allowed the bot to scan her face, then straightened as the glass doors slid open. "You aiming to be a commercial space director by twenty-six?"

"I'd rather build the rockets."

Liz started through the doors. "Come on."

It almost felt like a trick, like Liz might change her mind and slam the door in Frankie's face. But Frankie wasn't about to waste an authorized visit to the transport floor. She scooped up her trusty toolkit and followed.

Mom and Dad didn't spend enough time on Earth to bother with interior decorating. They'd stuck with the grounded-spaceship aesthetic that must have seemed appropriate when Frankie's grandparents had built the place. Metal walls, metal floors. Blinking blue lights ringed the raised control deck in the center of the room that operated all transport functions via touch screens and augmented-reality models.

Twisted together like an over-stylized puzzle at the far end of the room, the doors to the interworld transport dock gleamed.

Liz shoved the chairs to the perimeter of the elevated console and unrolled her yoga mat. "You watch *Mars Colony?*"

Disappointing. Liz seemed smarter than reality vids. "I

don't watch any shows, and before you ask, I only do virtual reality immersion for school assignments or history lessons."

The murder of Caesar was particularly good.

Liz sat on the mat and leaned against the railing that encircled the platform. With a few touches to the console, she pulled up a screen in augmented reality. The opening sequence began with its familiar blast of red particles—anyone who'd ever glanced at a billboard in New York City had seen that part—and the miniature cast members paced into view, waving and posing. What did they do for screen tests, check to see how good these people looked in spacesuits?

Frankie had a feeling this was not what her parents had had in mind when they'd hired a genius to run the interworld transport.

"Good, then you're not caught up." Liz patted the mat. "There's a guy this season who wants colonies on every planet in the solar system. He keeps saying he's going to Venus next. It's hilarious."

In real life, and with an occasional exception, human interaction was an unavoidable nuisance. The only reason most people talked to her at all was to get to her parents. As soon as someone learned that Frankie's parents basically ignored her, they'd drop her like an overheated drone.

Why would Frankie want to spend more of her time watching fools stumble around on TV?

"They shouldn't be sending those people to Mars," she said. "If he thinks Venus is habitable, he might leave the dome without his suit or something."

"The show is in its eighth season, and no one's died. The producers keep an eye on them."

"It's a waste of resources."

"It's science for the masses. Come on, sit."

Frankie sat. She wished she'd brought a sweater.

After the first episode, Frankie feared for the future of humanity.

After the fourth, she started to see Liz's point. A little bit. The show did use people-slash-characters to show how the colonies worked.

"My parents should do this with Suhainn," Frankie said.

She could suggest it to them. The idea might be good enough to earn her way back to their good graces—and maybe earn a ticket to Suhainn, too. They'd never brought her to any of their other worlds.

Before Liz could answer, the com unit buzzed to life with a shower of static. "Pathbound, do you copy?"

Mom. She never called before 2300 hours. Once, and exactly once, Dad had reported thirty-nine seconds late. He'd never been trusted to call on his own again. She knew, because that was reason number one for her trespassing down here. She liked to hear her parents' voices as they radioed in from other worlds.

Something was wrong.

Liz was already leaping for the table. "Copy, Cindy. Go ahead."

A burst of static. "We've got a situation. Retrieve the box for Sunset Protocol."

In all her years of spying, Frankie had never heard her parents ask for a protocol box. The word 'box' was something of a misnomer, since they were actually metal cylinders that lined the walls of the storage room—an excellent hiding spot for daughters who wanted to listen to their parents as they called in at 2300 hours every night. She'd hide, and she'd stare at the protocol names, from Asteroid to Zenith, imagining the kinds of disasters Mom and Dad might have planned for with the protocols. What failsafes they'd designed. She'd never quite been able to talk herself into disturbing one of them, in case its retrieval might give her away.

Liz hopped off the console and ran for the supply room. Maybe Mom and Dad were testing their new T.O. with a drill.

Or maybe Frankie should pick up the com and speak to her mother. Just in case.

When Liz stepped out of the supply room, her face was pale.

"What does it say?" Frankie whispered.

Liz shook her head, held a finger to her lips.

Thunder roared into the operations center, a sustained vibration that rattled up through Frankie's feet. She always pictured the tower trembling when the transport arrived, the city pausing its business to watch the floors shake. A scientifically improbable daydream, given how carefully the tower was designed.

Still. It reached into her bones.

The transport was back, and it was early. Sunset Protocol, step one? But Liz shook her head as she scanned the box's contents, the transport's arrival clearly as baffling to her as it was to Frankie.

Liz stuffed the box into her pocket and grabbed Frankie by the shoulders, shoving her across the room and into the supply closet. "Stay here."

Frankie didn't need the panic on Liz's face to convince her. She had no excuse for her presence here. She stayed, peering out while Liz sprinted to the console and opened the doors to the transport dock. The puzzle spun open with a dramatic twirl, revealing Frankie's mother and father. Behind them, the transport shuddered.

Whatever had gone wrong, it was not enough to upset the perfection of Mom's hair, a sleek waterfall that poured into a dark pool of curls. And Dad, so tall his sun-stained head nearly brushed the door frame.

"We agreed on Sunset," Mom said.

"Meteorite Protocol is more than sufficient," Dad replied. No trace of his usual humor, no hint of a smile. He wore his flip-flops, despite the many warnings Frankie had given him about the dangers of poor footwear.

Liz stood on the console, fingers whitening around the protocol box. She looked shocked, her lips parted, eyes wide.

For a second, Frankie didn't understand why. Yeah, her parents were arguing. A crack in their usually flawless performance, a slice of reality. Rare enough to warrant curiosity, but hardly worthy of the horrified look on the transport operator's face.

And then Frankie saw the shoe.

Behind her father, on the grated metal floor of the transport dock, was a brown shoe. And it was connected to a leg.

Frankie moved to the other side of the door and risked sticking her head past the frame.

A boy lay at her parents' feet, motionless, his skin paper white. As she watched, a spot of blood on his neck swelled to a bubble and burst, trailing across his throat like a slit.

No one checked on him. No one even looked at him— except maybe Liz—and he obviously needed help. Did her parents know he was bleeding?

Frankie abandoned her hiding place.

She made it all the way across the room before her parents noticed her and fell silent. She ignored their stares and bent over the boy, setting her toolkit on the floor to take his wrist between her fingers. His skin was cold, but his pulse rushed strong and even. She let out a breath.

"Did you know she was down here?"

Frankie tuned Mom out and replaced the boy's hand gently by his side. When she did, something tumbled out of his grasp.

It might have been her imagination, but she thought she felt him flinch when it skittered to the floor. It was a stone, flat and round, with a hole punched through the top. Frankie picked it up and turned it over in her hand, running her thumb along the smooth edges.

A stone from another world.

A *boy* from another world.

The stone had markings etched on one side, an intricate series of crisscrossing lines that reminded her of the Celtic knots her grandfather used to draw. The markings on the boy's stone might have been language or design. She couldn't tell.

Frankie tucked the stone into the boy's shirt pocket, so he'd have it when he woke.

He smelled like the sea.

Convinced for now of his safety, Frankie looked up to find her parents staring at her. "What's Sunset Protocol?" she said.

Mom peeled off her jacket. "All right. Meteorite. Take him up."

Dad scooped the still-unconscious boy into his arms and carried him off the transport dock.

"Who is that?" Frankie asked. "Is he from Suhainn? What happened?"

"What happened," Mom said, her voice clipped, "is that he nearly got himself killed. He's lucky we were there to save him."

Frankie tried to imagine what kind of scenario in supposedly safe Suhainn would have resulted in a need to bring the boy to Earth. Had he been acting as a spy? Betrayed the realm somehow? Committed a crime? Had he murdered someone?

As far as Frankie understood them—which admittedly wasn't very far at all—it wasn't exactly like her parents to intervene in a situation like that. Though what did she know, really? She was their daughter, and she had to break into restricted areas just to hear their voices. It was hardly surprising that a Suhainnan would secure more of their concern than she did.

As if anticipating the stream of questions about to burst out of Frankie's mouth, Mom raised a hand. "That's all you need to know about it, Francesca."

Mom shoved her jacket at Liz, and Frankie bristled on her behalf. Liz was the transport operator, not a laundry bot, though now was perhaps not the time to point that out. "You're fired," Mom said.

"Liz didn't know I was here," Frankie said quickly. "I swear. She even closed my usual entry points."

Mom still didn't look at Frankie, instead keeping her attention locked on Liz. "Fine. Francesca will provide you a list of her loopholes. You'll run security diagnostics on everything else."

As if that would keep Frankie out for long. Mom should know what she was capable of.

Liz nodded, and Frankie wondered why she'd accepted this job when she could be doing anything, anywhere. Pathbound might be prestigious, but working with her parents? Not worth it.

After eight months and eleven days spent off-world, Mom hooked slender thumbs through her belt loops and turned to face her daughter.

Funny how Frankie dreamed of Mom's attention, yet wanted to run when she finally obtained it.

"The Hartiger name is bestowed, Francesca," Mom said.

The refrain might as well have been tattooed on Frankie's heart, she'd heard it so many times. But there was nothing she could do to prevent her mother from finishing it.

Mom was already heading for the door. She cast the words

over her shoulder, an afterthought. Just like her daughter. "You earn your place in this family."

Frankie hugged her toolkit to her chest as Mom left her again.

Bypass the Stars is available now in print and ebook from your favorite retailer!

Kate Sheeran Swed loves hot chocolate, plastic dinosaurs, and airplane tickets. She has trekked along the Inca Trail to Macchu Picchu, hiked on the Mýrdalsjökull glacier in Iceland, and climbed the ruins of Masada to watch the sunrise over the Dead Sea. Kate currently lives in New York's capital region with her husband and two kids, and a pair of cats who were named after movie dogs (Benji and Beethoven). She holds an MFA in Fiction from Pacific University.

You can find more of Kate's work, and pick up a free novella, at katesheeranswed.com.

 facebook.com/katesheeranswed

 instagram.com/katesheeranswed

www.ingramcontent.com/pod-product-compliance
Lightning Source LLC
Chambersburg PA
CBHW031647100726
47898CB00006B/2007